DIGGING HOLES
IN
POPULAR CULTURE

Archaeology and Science Fiction

Edited by
Miles Russell

With a preface by
Douglas Adams

Bournemouth University
School of Conservation Sciences
Occasional Paper 7

Oxbow Books

Published by
Oxbow Books, Park End Place, Oxford OX1 1HN

© Oxbow Books 2002

A CIP record for this book is available from the British Library

ISBN 1 84217 063 5

Front cover: artist's concept of the Pioneer Venus Mulitiprobe entering the atmosphere of Venus on December 9, 1978 © NASA and the NSDCC

This book is available direct from
Oxbow Books, Park End Place, Oxford OX1 1HN
(Phone: 01865-241249; Fax: 01865-794449)

and

The David Brown Book Company
PO Box 511, Oakville, CT 06779, USA
(Phone: 860-945-9329; Fax: 860-945-9468)

and

via our website
www.oxbowbooks.com

Bournemouth University School of Conservation Sciences
Occasional Paper 7

Series Editor (Archaeology): Timothy Darvill

ISSN 1362 - 6094

Printed in Great Britain by
The Short Run Press
Exeter

For Douglas Adams
(1952 – 2001)

Mostly harmless, insanely great.
You will be missed.

Editor's note

Just as the final stages of this book were coming together, I received the terrible news that Douglas Adams had died. Douglas probably did more than any other to revive the genre that is Science Fiction through the phenomenon that is *The Hitchhiker's Guide to the Galaxy*. He was a great and enthusiastic communicator of ideas and, as a founder director of The Digital Village and co-builder of the online Guide to everything (www.h2g2.com), he remained the accessible public face of technology and the future.

I invited Douglas to attend the 1997 Theoretical Archaeological Group conference from which the present book is derived. His busy schedule prevented this, but he generously forwarded a paper for presentation. He was further happy to rewrite this paper as the preface to the current book. When we last communicated by email, he reiterated that he was very much looking forward to seeing the finished project. My biggest regret is that this is now no longer possible. Our thoughts are with his wife Jane and daughter Polly, and this book is respectfully dedicated to his memory.

CONTENTS

Preface

Douglas Adams

The thing that I have always liked about Science Fiction, or at least, my little corner of it, is that it gives you the opportunity of seeing familiar events from unfamiliar points of view and makes you think or realise different things about them. It illuminates the real world.

It's not just science fiction that does this, of course, most good fiction does something like this; it's just particularly clear (or should be) that that is what you are up to in science fiction. Aliens and robots and spaceships are just a bunch of fictional tools for doing it with. What is alarming is when people start to take these fictional tools literally. The seriousness with which people take *Star Trek* or *Star Wars* is worrying enough (I believe it was William Shatner who actually coined the phrase "Get a life!"), though mostly they know somewhere in the dark recesses of their brains that it's not real (the one that really worries me however is The *X Files*, which actively promotes credulity over rationality).

I had not previously thought about all this from the point of view of archaeologists especially, not being an archaeologist myself, but I think it applies across the board. Cartoon science means more to people than real science. It is no longer thought of as either an imaginative commentary on reality or a temporary refreshing escape from reality, but an effective substitute for it. It begins to worry me whenever I sit down to sketch out a new story that I may be contributing to a problem rather than doing anything, as I had hoped, more positive. So I now tend to find myself, in the current climate, taking an over-sharply sceptical view of things and coming on a bit like Richard Dawkins (whose thinking I greatly admire, but who sometimes attacks his targets too ferociously to win hearts and minds).

I read, with a sharply cocked eyebrow, some of the recent highly speculative books about the pyramids – all the Orion stuff – and the questions about how old they might really be. I found them to be frustrating. This was not just because the level of argument came across as tosh, (the answer to the rhetorical question "Can it be a coincidence that..?", is very often YES), but because it sounded as if there might genuinely be some stuff that should be analysed in a more rigorous way. However, it seems that the battle lines between the mavericks and the Egyptological establishment were much too deeply drawn to allow any actual information to pass either way.

I happened to run into an archaeologist who specialised in the middle east, and he confirmed what I had been wondering, which was that when you looked at it freshly, the assumptions on which an awful lot of Egyptology is based are actually no more or less conjectural than a lot of what the mavericks are saying, just an awful lot more entrenched. Hence the hostile defensiveness. It's just a pity that the alternative viewpoints are not better served by the level of argument with which they are presented, because if they were the establishment would have to put up a much better and more rigorous defence, which might in turn winnow out some of their own conjecture.

Years ago, I was very impressed (but unable to judge on anything more than a layman's respect for logic) by a book about Knossos by a German amateur archae-ologist/professional geologist called Wunderlich. In it he sought to completely re-evaluate the evidence starting from the standpoint of his own specialist knowledge. To cut a long, complex, but logically executed, argument to its conclusion, he suggested that Knossos was not a thriving metropolis as described by Evans, but a necropolis, and indeed the origin of Egyptian embalming techniques. What was interesting about the book was that Wunderlich came across not so much as a madbat attacking a supposedly dry and unimaginative establishment, but as quite the opposite. He seemed like a thoroughly logical rationalist exposing the degree to which Evans had subordinated the actual data to his own imaginative dreams of what Minoan Crete might have been. Of course, we know that Evans did this. What stood exposed, though, was that in the meantime we had merely adjusted Evans's view incrementally, and not stood back and done a thorough Poirot on the original evidence. I asked a friend of mine, an archaeology graduate (now occasional comedy writer) about the book, and she was very dismissive and said it was known to be nonsense. But when I pressed her about it, her argument only really amounted to the fact that it was not what she had been taught at Bristol, so I remained unpersuaded.

My favourite lost cause, though, is the Aquatic Ape Hypothesis, by which I am impressed. This is the notion that all of the palpable oddities about the human animal – our bipedalism, our hairlessness, our subcutaneous fat, our replacement of oil glands with salty sweat glands, the arrangement of our larynx and tongue, etc. – would be very neatly explained in one go if a small band of our ancestors had been trapped into making a living in an aquatic or semi-aquatic environment between 5 and 7 million years ago, specifically on the Danakil Alps on the east coast of Ethiopia (if you have not read "The Scars of Evolution" by Elaine Morgan, may I recommend it?). Whether or not it turns out to be a true account of what happened, I love it for the sheer elegance of its solution to a set of problems which, it seems to me, the archaeo-anthropological establishment has not properly addressed, but has merely buried under a sedimentary accretion of assumptions. It seemed highly curious to me that the two oddest features of human beings (bipedalism and hairlessness) rated scarcely a mention in the weighty and magisterial Cambridge Encyclopaedia of Human Evolution. The Aquatic Ape Hypothesis is an idea which, it seems to me, richly deserves to be properly tested. Dismissing it is too easy. Refuting it will be a much more rigorous task which, again, is better for all concerned.

Revolutionary changes to accepted models quite often come from outside the orthodoxy of any given discipline, but if a new idea is to prevail it has to be better supported in argument, logic and evidence than the old view, not worse. "Feel good" science is no science at all. Science fiction is a great territory in which to play with the kind of perspective shifts that lead to new discoveries and new realisations. But imagination tempered with logic and reason is much more powerful than imagination alone.

Introduction and acknowledgements

Miles Russell

"Who controls the past controls the future. Who controls the present controls the past"
(George Orwell 1949, 31)
"There is no past or future; only a multitude of possibilities"
(The Doctor)

As I sit at my desk and stare out of my window over the rooftops of Bournemouth, I have the somewhat worrying feeling that tomorrow will not quite be as it was predicted. Today is the 31st December AD 2000 and tomorrow, if you are familiar with the calendrical set-up of Britain at the start of the 3rd millennium, is New Years Day. New Year's Day 2001.

2001 represents a year which, due to the joint efforts of film director Stanley Kubrick and writer Arthur C. Clarke, has already been much (some would perhaps say over) hyped. Kubrick and Clarke's cinematic vision *2001: A space odyssey*, which emerged in 1968 a full year before humankind had set foot on the moon, has had a profound impact on the way in which the future has been perceived. In fact the year 2001 has itself become synonymous with the high tech future that we all knew would be awaiting us. Our ultimate destiny. It would be a future in which anything was possible: people would one day leave the planet; computers would have the power of life and death; there would be proof of life beyond our solar system.

Unfortunately, as most dwellers in the twenty first century are by now sick of hearing, 2001 does not look as if it will quite live up to the hype. True, society has new forms of communication and transport, medicines and diseases, philosophies and religions, but there are no great space stations circling the earth (and indeed what ones have been sent up seem to want to return home at a somewhat alarming speed). There are no regular flights to the stars. There are no sentient computers. There are, rather sadly in my opinion, no great black monoliths on the moon.

The *2001* cinematic image of these large alien monoliths, sitting happily on the earth, the moon and upon the moons of Jupiter, is one which had a considerable impact upon the young Miles Russell. Sat in the hushed cinema aisles (hushed, I now realise, because no-one had a clue as to what the film was all about), I was struck, not so much by the thought that humans were perhaps being guided by some great alien intelligence, but by the thought that archaeologists appeared to have a future. There on the moon, about half an hour into the movie, was a great big archaeological trench. The kind of trench that put all those cut by Heinrich Schliemann through the buried remains of Troy, to shame. At the centre of this excavation, freshly uncovered by the astro-archaeological community, was the alien artefact: the black monolith. Quietly observing, monitoring and waiting…

2001, science fiction and the whole mentality of the American/Soviet 'Space Race' had a profound effect on those growing up through the 1950s, 60s and early 70s. School playgrounds were filled with children making "beep-beep-beep" Sputnik noises, exterminating one another with sink plungers and taking "giant leaps for mankind". I remember that, aged 4, I was the proud owner of a poster of Edwin "Buz" Aldrin, taken from the Apollo 11 mission. Aldrin was standing proudly on the dusty surface of the moon in the full NASA regulation, moonwalk kit. A haunting image, Aldrin's basic frame was recognisably human, but disturbingly there was nothing remotely human about his head: no emotion, no features, not even a face. Totally encased within the large, goldfish-style helmet, all one could see was the legs of the Eagle landing craft and the distant figure of Neil Armstrong reflected in the large, glassy visor. I remember this particularly because next to this image I had a second poster: the ornate golden funerary mask of the boy pharaoh Tutankhamun. His features were recognisably human, but his penetrating, otherworldly stare was just as unsettling. I must have had some vivid nightmares.

Aldrin/Armstrong on the moon and Tutankhamun in his sarcophagus represent two of the most vivid (non-war related) icons of the 20th century. All of which brings me nicely to the point of this particular tome.

In December 1997, the annual Theoretical Archaeologists Conference (TAG for those in the know) was hosted by Bournemouth University. Some twenty seven sessions were held at this conference, covering subjects as diverse as applied meta-archaeology, the heritage of value, prehistoric technologies, theory and world archaeology, archaeology in Japan, behavioural and biological perspectives on the evolution of humanness, rock art, the archaeology of food, ancient DNA, and the nature of landscapes, monuments and Medieval society. One session in particular stood out from the list of usual suspects (probably because, in strictly alphabetical order of titles, it came last). This session was: "When Worlds Collide: Archaeology and Science Fiction".

The volume in front of you now expands upon and develops the themes covered in this somewhat unorthodox conference session. The session was originally designed to explore three specific, inter-linking themes: to understand how archaeologists are viewed by the public and within popular culture; to see whether ideas and concepts central to science fiction may influence current archaeological practice; and to see whether the study of the past actually has a future (on our world or any other). Above all it was hoped to view the profession from a new and (hopefully) refreshingly alternative viewpoint. I like to think that in all these we succeeded (though for an unbiased perspective perhaps you should really ask someone from the audience). I didn't see anyone in a total state of lecture-prompted unconsciousness, which, from my own experience as a lecturer, can usually be taken as a positive sign.

The three broad themes discussed at the 1997 TAG conference are developed further within this book. Here, Part One examines popular archaeological stereotypes from

Howard Carter to Indiana Jones and Lara Croft. Part Two focuses upon the written word in the formulation of the past and of alternative worlds. Part Three examines the future and the shape of things to come. The chapters contained within each part have changed, some out of all recognition, from the original conference papers, and certain new chapters have been added by those who were unable to speak at the time. Overall the scope, aims and vision of the original session have expanded and matured.

Special words of thanks must go to all the contributors to this volume, especially for those who have coped so well with my (usually well-meant) advice, requests and persistent nagging over the last three years. Thank you also to all the original conference (and immediate post-conference) contributors, who for whatever reason found that they were unfortunately unable to participate in this particular work. Thank you to all the 1997 conference organisers and facilitators and to all those institutions who gave permission to use particular images (especially: Bournemouth University; the Griffith Institute, Ashmolean Museum, Oxford; the JPL; the Kobal Collection; Malin Space Science Systems; the Massingheimer Collection; NASA; the NSSDC; Photo Multiphoto Paris; and the Sussex Archaeological Society). Special thanks must also go to Douglas Adams who, though unable to participate in the conference, generously consented to supply both a paper and a preface to complement and complete the overall feel of the book.

A huge debt of gratitude goes to Glynis Laughlin for reading and correcting the text (any errors that remain, of course, are solely my responsibility) and to Vanessa Constant for successfully combating the bibliography monster. Acknowledgement must go also to my wife Bronwen and daughter Megan, my parents, relatives and friends who have coped with my particular (and perhaps unhealthy) obsession with science fiction, some for over thirty years (which is well over and above the call of duty).

So, if you have ever pondered upon the importance of having archaeologists on the first deep-space mission, if you worry that there may be life on other planets (and if there is, how could we tell?), if you possess a burning desire to conduct an environmental impact assessment upon the moons of Jupiter, if you feel that the prospect of time-travel could seriously damage the cultural heritage, if you are worried that archaeological excavation is becoming less of a reality than cyber-space, if you believe that the Egyptian tomb you visited as a child may have contained a curse, or if you have ever entertained fears that fictional archaeologists might just lead slightly more interesting lives than the real thing, then welcome. There are many possibilities. Let us explore just some of them…

PART ONE

ARCHAEOLOGISTS IN FICTION

The perception of what archaeology is and what archaeologists do is perhaps shaped more by popular stereotype than by reality. More people have, for instance, seen the films *Raiders of the Lost Ark*, *Stargate* or *Curse of the Mummy's Tomb* than have ever participated in an archaeological excavation. More people have read *2001: A Space Odyssey* by Arthur C. Clarke than will ever read *Excavations at Much-Whinging-in-the-Marsh 1948–69* by A. Dull Archaeologist. Worried? Should you be?

Is the general perception of archaeologists in popular culture as thrill-seeking, tomb-raiding individuals close to the truth? Are those involved in archaeology secretly pleased by the heroic pose of fictional archaeologists such as Captain Jean-Luc Picard, Lintilla, Professor Bernice Summerfield or Lara Croft? Can anything be learnt from the way in which archaeological practice is portrayed within fiction and within in the public consciousness? Can (or should) the examination of a Roman cess-pit in London compete with the sheer stubble-jawed excitement of Indiana Jones?

Come, join us in this first stage of exploration. The exploration of inner space. The investigation of archaeology within popular culture.

1
Are we perceived to be what we say we are?
John Gale

Popular Culture finds voice and expression in a wide range of formats in both art and literature, which both digests and exudes material drawn from broader aspects of contemporary culture and society. This continuous creative cycle will at times happen onto archaeological themes, which can only therefore mirror contemporary perceptions of what those themes mean and or represent. Therefore the portrayal of archaeology and archaeologists in popular culture could be seen to be primarily derived from a perception of what those terms mean to the society that created it. If this is true then are we seeing a fair representation of what the term 'archaeology' means to the world at large, or is the image just a caricature? In either case should we (i.e. the greater archaeological body) be concerned with what this representation tells us about ourselves, and our profession?

This chapter is intended as a preliminary exploration into this disturbing issue. It will begin to examine the background, which underpins the presumption that popular culture has at its centre, a straightforward no-nonsense view of things, which exposes meaning in a raw incorruptible form. It will then look at the end product, by way of a very unscientific (but hopefully entirely relevant), selection of out-takes from mixed media to see what popular culture really has to say about archaeologists, and what archaeologists do. This will be further examined via the results of a small questionnaire survey which tests public awareness of archaeology. Finally it will briefly examine what we say we are by reference to what we produce for public consumption.

The end result and overall execution of this enterprise is not intended to have been exhaustively researched and consequently interpretation and methodology might be constructed on weak foundations, but then perhaps so are our collective efforts to pass on what we think we know of the past.

How are archaeologists perceived by the public at large?

Are archaeologists collectively and generally viewed as interesting – stimulating – eccentric – odd, maybe? Is what we do seen as a valued service which enriches our society and culture, or is it perhaps that we are tolerated by the masses and encouraged by a few, but are largely irrelevant to modern-day living? And whatever and however we are perceived to be by the public at large, does it matter anyway? Of course we can on reflection think of numerous arguments which both qualify and justify our venerable '..ology', both as an academic pursuit and a worthwhile profession, but if we do have value in the society in which we live, how is reflected back at us?

All these questions have from time to time no doubt played on the mind of most practising archaeologists, if only when challenged to justify expenditure, often when funds have to be drawn from the public purse. But how do we go about answering them? Primarily we have two options, we can pose suitably framed questions directly to the public, alternatively we can observe such impressions and perceptions indirectly through a third party or medium. In this paper I have attempted to do a little of both, neither method has been explored exhaustively, rather the emphasis has been to hold a preliminary investigation into the comparability of the data and the possible or potential inferences produced by the two methods.

In investigating the public perception of the archaeologist I begin with a premise, a premise which revolves around the question concerning what archaeologists are perceived to be about by contemporary society at large. The premise involves the investigation of this question by examining the portrayal of archaeology and archaeologists, via the popular medium of science fiction and the media more generally. The premise relies on the assumption that science fiction, however inventive is firmly rooted within the cultural environment experienced by the author, and consequently therefore will be reflective of it. It would of course have been possible to pursue a similar objective by the examination of any other facet of popular culture and media. However science fiction of all genres is consistently the one in which story lines are most likely to utilise characters and events, which feature archaeologists (with the possible exception of fictional crime). The reasons for this, one is tempted to suggest, is that both archaeologists and science fiction writers inhabit fantasy worlds and subsequently wish to be divorced from the constraints on creativity imposed by their own time. In reality both archaeologists and science fiction writers do at least share a common difficulty, which is that their depiction of past and future events is compromised more by their own cultural baggage than any real lack of factual data or creative imagination.

Cultural baggage whilst commonly viewed as problematical to the faithful analysis of past events and ancient cultures, can in this case be usefully investigated to explore contemporary views and opinions reflected in society by the work of science fiction authors. Using this idea as a foundation it should therefore be possible to conduct a reflective examination of what our discipline is perceived to be about, and to consider how accurate or recognisable this may be to ourselves.

Certainly the most influential and widely accessible science fiction material is that produced for broadcast by television. Over the last thirty-five years Anglo-American culture has increasingly produced a number of extremely successful science fiction television series which have captured the imagination of both science fiction aficionados, and the public at large. I have chosen to concentrate on two very different shows, which perhaps typify the breadth of the genre as a whole, and I have selected an episode from each of them where the story line has archaeology as a major theme.

Case study 1.

Series. *Dr. Who.* Episode *The Daemons.* First broadcast *1971*

Story line: An archetypal English Village is under the media spotlight because a nearby ancient burial mound is under archaeological excavation by a Professor of Archaeology. The television cameras are brought in to witness the live opening of an internal sepulchral chamber, with of course due attention to a modicum of preliminary hype. The media interest is accentuated by the presence of an amateur local historian and white witch who warns them of dire consequences should the tomb be opened. Our hero (The Doctor, or "Dr. Who" for the uninitiated) just happens to be watching a preliminary broadcast and is suitably intrigued. The archaeologist of course disregards the warnings of the local historian and opens the tomb. Daemons are subsequently released who then proceed to enslave the villagers with the assistance of the Master (the archenemy of the Doctor who is of course behind all this). The Doctor ultimately defeats the Master and his Daemons (who turn out to be aliens) and peace is restored.

Case study 2.

Series. *Star Trek : The Next Generation.* Episode *The Chase.* First broadcast 1995.

Story line: The principal character Captain Jean-Luc Picard whilst being the Captain of an Inter-galactic space vessel, was and is an archaeological scholar (transferable skills will obviously be applied with more conviction and alacrity in the 24th century). The Professor from his alma mater joins the ship with a mission for his long lost protege. The mission is to aid the professor in his life long research project investigating the potential commonality of origin of the major cultures currently spread throughout the galaxy. This has been done by the detailed examination of the DNA profile of the dominant cultures represented in the series (Klingons, Terrans, Vulcans etc.) plus the determination and sampling of older and extinct cultures, which are of course derived from archaeological investigation.

True to the series type, a large dollop of moralising on what is essential an inter-galactic racial debate with obvious parallels possible in modern contemporary society, draws to a satisfactory (if predictable) conclusion.

Analysis

The two series from which the above story lines have been extracted (*Dr. Who* and *Star Trek: The Next Generation*), have been among the most popular of science fiction programmes in recent years with viewing figures numbering millions, not only with science fiction enthusiasts but also with a wider public. As such, they are bound to be influential when we consider the number of people watching them, particularly as both shows have been syndicated and dubbed in many languages for broadcast globally. The two episodes that are under this examination are separated by a quarter of a century and in some respects, it shows. However the differences between the two are more concerned with production quality and the development of understandable technological advancements upon which the story lines are constructed. The depiction of the archaeologists, and more importantly of archaeology in both episodes, whilst fundamental to the plot can of course be entirely fictional and divorced from reality as it is set in a completely fictional context. But for the characters to be recognisable as archaeologists they have to tap in to what might be expected as such by the viewing public.

The 1971 Dr. Who episode featuring the excavation of a round barrow demonstrates excavation by the apparently unsuitable 'tunnelling' approach, where entrance to the foci of the barrow is enabled by excavation of a tunnel from the flank of the barrow. However the technique used is probably drawn from the contemporary excavations undertaken at Silbury Hill in Wiltshire by Richard Atkinson (between 1968–70), where for all practical reasons it was the only viable option in that case (Atkinson 1978). However it is not just the technical methodology employed which is of interest but the depiction of the archaeologist and what he is hoping to achieve. The archaeologist is depicted (fairly typically for the period) by a white male who is definitely on the advanced side of 50, who has a predilection for Harris Tweed. In addition he has a measure of arrogance, or perhaps more charitably we might see this a single-minded approach to his work, which precludes him from the normal quotient of social graces. You may well be able to identify such a character with a number of prominent late 1960's and 70's archaeologists … I could not possibly comment.

As to the professor's objective, it appears that he's after 'treasure'. If we are charitable we might interpret this as academic treasure, as the case is not clearly made either way. It would hardly be pertinent for the writer to have included a discourse on academic issues within the story line.

The second extract from Star Trek: The Next Generation, was only produced a few years ago, and subsequently one might expect it to be more up to date in the methodology and science of archaeology. And one has to admit that in those respects it does come up to the mark. Once again we have the aged professor, accompanied this time with the central character of the series Captain Jean Luc Picard, whom we are led to believe is an archaeology graduate. The professor is once again an aged white male – the Harris Tweed has gone but the appropriate level of arrogance is still there.

The subject matter this time is quite different. In the story line we are exposed to a number of recognisable scenarios, to which any archaeologist might be exposed. One such scene early in the story involves Picard in the identification and interpretation of an ancient artefact, which has been brought on board ship by his old professor. This we see the good Captain achieve, with a fairly faithful depiction of what we would all recognise, a logical and analytical exercise in classification of an ancient artefact, culminating in inferences on social and cultural meaning derived from symbolism embodied in the decoration and form of the artefact. The scene culminates in the artefact being presented to Picard as a gift, a slightly worrying development in that the aged professor is willing and apparently able to distribute largesse in such a Schliemann-esque manner. One almost expects Indiana Jones to burst onto the scene crying "That's an important archaeological artefact, it belongs in a museum".

What both episodes demonstrate is a fairly typical treatment of their contemporary archaeology, which highlights above all else the excitement of the discovery of long departed and strange cultures through their material remains. This is quite convenient because after all that is a fairly standard definition of archaeology anyway.

And elsewhere?

Is this supported by the portrayal of archaeology and archaeologists elsewhere in science fiction? For the most part I would have to say yes. Although I have dwelt on examples from the visual media, there is equally valid material which can be drawn from more prodigious literary sources.

Science fiction in print varies quite considerably from the comic book to what can be loosely described as the quality end of the market. A consistently recurring theme of science fiction novels, which incorporate archaeology within the story line, is the presence of archaeologists within teams of scientists exploring the galaxy. Arthur C. Clarke's *Rendezvous with Rama*, Greg Bear's *Eon*, and A. E. Van Vogts *The Voyage of the Space Beagle,* for example, all develop this theme, whereby the archaeological interpretation of extinct alien species is fundamental to inter-planetary exploration and its understanding. As a generalism, the depiction of archaeologists in these works, and what they do, is not dissimilar in content and relevance to that which is discussed above.

So, are we perceived to be what we say we are?

To summarise then, with the exception of a certain amount of stereotyping in the characterisation of archaeologists, what appears to be emerging is a model which portrays us as serious, single minded but ever so slightly mysterious quasi-scientists, whose discipline is liberally blessed with large dollops of excitement and discovery. These depictions will of course have been provided by the authors of the television shows and books that I have discussed, and will be grounded in *their* own perception of what we are. This interpretation will have been fed no doubt on some research, but is equally likely to be drawn from interpretations provided by previous incarnations from fictional sources, in a never ending cycle of media consumerism.

The role of the media in its widest possible definition is crucial when considering questions, which concern perception and influence in our society. The importance of the media in social engineering is very much a current issue across a wide spectrum of academia, but its impact is still very poorly understood. However it is generally accepted that the media exhibits a degree of influence on the formation of contemporary behaviour, and can therefore actively change personal attitudes, understandings and perceptions within society. The relevance of this to the question "are we perceived to be what we say we are?" should be clear. If the public receive most of their information on archaeology from interpretations provided from outside the discipline, then their understanding of what we are and what we do will be founded on such information.

A sociological imperative can be seen in the establishment of a view or definition of archaeologists driven not by archaeologists themselves but by the media (in its various guises). We are, in common with so many other areas of cultural life subject to what sociologists might refer to as 'media imperialism' (Giddens 1993, 559–60).

So what is the alternative? You may well suggest the archaeological documentary or its big brother the factual series, which in Britain is currently represented by programmes such as *Time Team* or *Meet the Ancestors*, would be the preferred medium for the portrayal of archaeology to the general public. Viewing figures for *Time Team* particularly, and its continuing presence on our screens, demonstrate its popularity with that most fickle of viewers, the armchair archaeologist (whoever he or she might be). However a recent rudimentary survey which I conducted seems to suggest that the impact of the media, particularly in factual programming, is quite limited. In a sample of just over 100 individuals polled at a Hertfordshire Comprehensive school (covering both students and staff), less than 10% were able to name an archaeologist (other than Indiana Jones). Of this 10%, *all* were from the teaching and support staff who represented only 10% of those polled. In the same poll only 9 individuals could name a factually based television programme associated with archaeology, and of these only 3 named *Time Team* (the rest were even distributions of televisual science magazine programmes *Equinox*, *Horizon*, *Time Watch* and even general news bulletins).

Incidentally, when asked which fictional programme they associated with archaeology, (which is once again dominated by Indiana Jones) science fiction has a relatively small quotient, with less than 10%. Although conclusions from such a small and crude survey are extremely limited, they do suggest that we are dealing with potentially a large number of people who do at least have some perception of archaeology and archaeologists.

What then of ourselves, what do we say we are? Well if I was to put that question to a dozen archaeological professionals or academics I would be likely to get a dozen subtly different answers. Obviously the next step is to do just that, but in the meantime perhaps its just easier to look at what we do, by examining what we produce.

We produce reams and reams of information, predominantly in report form and for the most part in an increasingly scientific manner. We have striven for objectivity and professionalism under the paternal guidance of our very own national quangos (such as English Heritage, Cadw and Historic Scotland) and most would say that we have managed to become quite good at it.

But, are we not becoming a little dull? A number of archaeologists have in recent years begun to explore alternatives to how we present our considerations either directly or indirectly (Hodder 1992, 263–73; Pitts and Roberts 1997). We are so preoccupied with qualifying our every breath, afraid that a metaphorical Brutus is about to strike (for Brutus substitute your relevant pet hate figure or organisation who has an element of editorial control over your work), that we go for safety and make even our most exciting discoveries sound bland and lifeless. Unless, however, we are trying to attract funds, then we all begin to wax lyrical and get embarrassingly enthusiastic, informing interviewers from the media that our particular piece of research or site is fundamental to life on the planet. The reasons we are able to cast off our conservatism at these times I suspect are because:

1   The interview is generally relegated to an obscure transmission time on an equally obscure local station.

2   Your comments will appear on page 22 of the local rag next to the article about budgie rustling being on the increase.

3   If any of your colleagues do hear or read your enthused comments you can always grin and say you have been misquoted or they will assume your comments are directed to the developer or sponsors and consequently are for their ears only, and will satisfy the demands for good public relations.

Most of our literary output is so constrained by its format, it is often dull even to ourselves. We are not as archaeologists often required to deal in rocket science, and although we make increasing use of science to recover data, when we present interpretation we increasingly try to do so in a quasi-scientific manner. We should perhaps endeavour to undertake our business and write about our ancestors in ways, which inform, not bore people to death. The past is a foreign country, with a difficult language to interpret but perhaps it's losing something in the translation?

The public face of archaeology represents excitement and discovery, whether this is derived from *Time Team* or *Star Trek*. It is this excitement which has helped produce in recent years, the burgeoning numbers of undergraduates reading archaeology at most UK Universities. Public interest in the past has probably never been greater, but does the public perception of what we do and are, match that which we ourselves recognise? I would have to suggest that for the moment, and for me at least, the jury is out.

John Gale is a Senior Lecturer in Archaeology in the School of Conservation Sciences, Bournemouth University, Poole, Dorset, BH12 5BB. His hobbies include teaching windsurfing to snails and dodo spotting. His favourite colour is Venezuelan meringue.

2
The Celluloid Archaeologist – an X-rated exposé

Steven Membury

The Celluloid Archaeologist has appeared in over 100 films, many of which have captured the public's imagination. Most of these are well known and need no introduction here, but a few films are shrouded in mystery. It is these dark and shameful chapters in the Celluloid Archaeologist's career that are explored in this particular chapter.

Figure 2.1 Harrison Ford as Indiana Jones in Raiders of the Lost Ark (1981): perhaps the most celebrated of all celluloid archaeologists. Here the good Doctor is about to escape with the prize desired by all adventurers in celluloid: a nice slab of golden loot © The Kobal Collection.

The modern reputation of the Celluloid Archaeologist is of a resolute character who challenges evil, whether it be the undead or Nazi storm troopers. He appears to live a life of whirlwind romances, exotic locations and terrifying encounters with ancient forces. Defeating mummies, snakes, giant aliens and evil geniuses are all in a days work for this champion of British stiff upper lip and fair play. His unflappable daring enables him to triumph even when faced with situations that would turn most members of the Institute of Field Archaeologists into quivering wrecks. Despite this, there lies a dark and sinister past that the Celluloid Archaeologist would rather be 'best left alone'. This secret history reveals a character revelling in racism and sexism, dabbling in the gangster underworld and is even being involved in the seedier aspects of the flesh trade! This exclusive glimpse into the murkier side of the Celluloid Archaeologist carries a Parental Guidance certificate so be warned.

Romancing the Stone Age

The Celluloid Archaeologist along with many of his real world colleagues has long had a fascination with Egypt. In many of his early films, therefore, he can be seen excavating ancient monuments in the desert. The earliest Egyptian film, *The Lure of Egypt* produced in 1921, concerns archaeologist Phillip Bellamy, who is accompanied by his wife Margaret on an expedition to find ancient Greek ruins in North Africa. However, when Margaret contracts desert fever, it is Phillip's assistant Bob Harding who cares for her while the alcoholic Phillip takes the last bottle of desperately needed medicinal brandy and continues his excavation. Unfortunately, the newly discovered ruins collapse with Phillip inside and he is left, presumed dead, by his guide Hassan who relays the news to Bob and Margaret. When informed of her husband's apparent demise, Bob and Margaret realise that there is no longer any form of marital barrier and confess their love to each other. However, Phillip suddenly returns reeling drunk and reeking of hashish. He accuses the couple of plotting his death and lashes out murderously. Luckily Hassan is on hand and saves Margaret and Bob by killing the drink and drug-crazed archaeologist, leaving the couple to enjoy their new- found love.

This is not the only time the Celluloid Archaeologist has marital problems and again only 5 years later Egypt is the location for our romantically challenged hero's second venture on the silver screen in *Made for Love* (US 1926). This time the plot revolves the archaeologist's wife who, feeling alienated by her husband's pre-occupation with his work, carries on flirtations with a veritable host of international lovers. The plot thickens when the archaeologist is given a book recounting a tale of two doomed lovers whose tomb he is excavating. These ancient Egyptians had suffered the cruel fate of being buried alive after revealing their forbidden love to the then ruling pharaoh. The archaeologist is also informed of a curse laid on despoilers of the tomb by the pharaoh some 4000 years previously. History is about to be repeated when the archaeologist and his wife are entombed after an explosion at the excavation site. This followed an argument because Joan, (the Archaeologist's wife) after a marital dispute, succumbed to the amorous advances of an Egyptian prince. This time however the couple are happily reunited after the prince's death while releasing them from the tomb.

The archaeologist's work obsession forcing their spouses to extra-marital dalliances is a reasonably common attitude for the Celluloid Archaeologist and is prevalent in many early films. Indeed it is the whole plot in a 1923 film *Borrowed Husbands* which, as the title suggests, involves an archaeologist's wife living a romantic double life involving many lovers, because of her real husband's lack of interest. Again there is the ever-present danger of a curse hanging over the Archaeologist but within this film the curse and marital infidelity is happily overcome. Romance is returned to the marriage so luckily the audience is left with their requisite Hollywood happy-ending.

It is interesting to note that some of the earliest examples of Celluloid Archaeology in films portray our hero as a man obsessed to distraction with his work. He is a heavy drinker and almost certainly a crazed drug user. This does make one wonder where scriptwriters got this stereotype idea (certainly this author knows of no individuals, currently involved in archaeology, that fit this particular description).

Howard Carter and Boris Karloff, a Double Feature

The storyline featured in the 1926 film *Made For Love* represented the first reaction in the cinema to an actual archaeological discovery, the excavation of Tutankhamun's tomb by Howard Carter in 1922. This had the most remarkable effect on films featuring archaeologists and it captivated the imagination of the western world with the discovery heralded as "The most sensational Egyptological discovery of the century" by the Illustrated London News, (Bacon 1976). The discovery heralded a preoccupation with things Egyptian throughout the western world and this influence can be seen in many aspects of social life in the twenties including; architectural and artistic design. Although early reports focused on the spectacular artefacts deposited within the tomb, the ensuing publicity following the death of Lord Carnarvon caused the public preoccupation with the curse myth, which was bound to find an outlet within the medium of celluloid.

The cinema's fascination by the subject of ancient Egypt is exhibited in the earlier films, *The Lure Of Egypt* (US 1921), *Made For Love* (US 1926), and contemporary 30s films, such as *Charlie Chan in Egypt* (US 1935), but with the release of *The Mummy* (US 1932) archaeological factors actually influenced the plot and even elements within the storyline itself. Although appearing ten years after the first press releases reporting Carter's discovery, *The Mummy*, directed by Karl Freud, and starring Boris Karloff, sums up many of the ideas the public held concerning archaeologists within the 20s and 30s and offered the Celluloid Archaeologist a great new challenge.

The film begins in 1921, (note the time link with Howard Carter's excavation), just after the tomb of the bandage swathed character Im-ho-tep had been unearthed. The story concerns a prematurely buried priest punished for his love for an Egyptian priestess Anck-es-en-Amon, (who's name was influenced by King Tut's Queen Ankhesnamon), and the setting free of a curse due to archaeologists despoiling his tomb. In the film Karloff in his role of Im-ho-tep, is revived after 3,700 years when

British archaeologist Bramwell Fletcher unwittingly reads the potent words of the sacred Book of Thoth. As he reads, the parchment eyes of the mummy slowly open, and leaving a trail of rotted bandages the mummy moves out of the tomb with the sacred scroll. Leaving Fletcher, (who probably never realised the archaeological interpretation really could bring the past to life) laughing insanely and crying, "He went for a little walk!" This little walk was not the last this resilient archaeological relic would take in the history of archaeology within the cinema.

The Celluloid Archaeologist is covered by two distinct characters in this film, these personalities recurring through out his career: the professor and the young assistant. Many other movies from this period show these characters such as: *Police Call* (US 1933), *Charlie Chan in Egypt* (US 1935), *I Live My Life* (US 1935), and *Mr. Moto Takes a Vacation* (US 1939). In these films the Celluloid Archaeologist is an upper-middle class, Oxbridge graduate and lover of obscure facts, who has spent his life wrapped up in researching even more obscurer facts in a dusty library. This arcane research has lead to the discovery of a "Key" which requires an expedition that leads to a confrontation involving supernatural powers. Of course the Professor will need a young archaeological assistant whose only distractions are the charms of the professor's daughter, or a particularly insistent mummified prehistoric Egyptian.

This two-fold image within the Celluloid Archaeologist is explicable in terms of storylines, as the professor role would not fit within the usual heroic stance, being too old and far too academic. The young Celluloid Archaeologist is generally an unwitting hero, whose work involves him in romance and whose study of archaeology enables him to combat supernatural powers (as he possesses an 'understanding' of all legends and mythologies). This leaves the old professor to the role of unflappable eccentric obsessive researcher with little contact with the 'real world', who supplies much of the brains behind the brawn. How one grows from one to the other is never detailed, but by the professor stage the acceptance of divine intervention and esoteric knowledge has become commonplace, so presumably adventures are part of a career in Celluloid Archaeology.

The set of films that followed *The Mummy* include *The Mummy's Hand* produced in 1940 when Im-ho-tep has become Kharis, a prince whose tongue had been cut out before burial and sustained in half-life by administration of tana leaves by priests. Needless to say the inevitable desecration of Kharis's tomb takes place in the form of Dick Foran and Wallace Ford who then have to combat a wretched shuffling monster hyped up on a potent brew of triple strength tana leaves. The mummy, although impervious to bullets, soon succumbs to the bane of most horror monster's lives, namely fire. In this case his incineration is affected by pouring a flaming vat of tana leaves over him. Unfortunately the film lacks the horror of the earlier classic, though it does show that not every aspect of cinematic disaster is down to the Celluloid Archaeologist. In this case the blame falls with cowboy actor Tom Tyler who was chosen to play Kharis because of his resemblance to a young Karloff. This was a necessary requisite since Universal studios lifted the early sequences of the movie from the original. Unfortunately crippling arthritis plagued Tyler and thus his monster's shuffle never really captured the menace of Karloff.

Lon Chaney Jr next put on the bandages as Kharis in the *Mummy's Tomb* (US 1942) this time Kharis is seeking out the now grey haired Foran and Ford at their hometown, Mapleton, Massachusetts. Again problems occurred with story continuity, the wholesale splicing from earlier films reaching a climax in this movie with the final burning scene, complete with torch-bearing villagers, being lifted entirely from the earlier horror flick Frankenstein. Further films followed in quick succession but all were similarly dire and all featured spliced flashbacks. These films, when combined with the Abbot and Costello meet the mummy movie in 1955, finally convinced Lon Chaney, the Celluloid Archaeologist and Universal Studios, that they were flogging a dead Mummy.

Hammer studios disagreed. In 1959 they recycled the whole genre with the imaginatively entitled *The Mummy*. This was basically a revamp of the 1932 film, and was the beginning of a run of sequels based on the original story. Each retelling was to feature archaeologists in their desecrating, 'better left untouched' role. Egyptian curses proliferate in this decade as more and more mummies "Go for little walks," ensuring that the mythology concerning Carter's excavation became a cinematic legacy

The films *The Mummy* (GB 1959), *Curse of the Mummy's Tomb* (GB 1965) *The Mummy's Shroud* (GB 1967) and *Blood from the Mummy's Tomb* (GB 1971), all follow a basic plot similar to the original, but none of these really live up to the class of the earliest mummy. *Blood from the Mummy's Tomb* (GB 1971) is interesting as it uses artefacts discovered within the tomb of Egyptian Queen Tera as the medium of evil power, not

Figure 2.2 Christopher Lee as bandage-swathed nasty "going for a walk" in The Mummy (1959). The image of the menacing undead Egyptian, awakened by meddling archaeologists, is one of the more potent established within the history of the cinema © The Kobal Collection.

the mummy itself. This is a reflection of the idea that King Tut's curse was not only limited to the individuals responsible for the opening of his tomb, but also extends to artefacts such as his death mask. This can be shown by press reports concerning the 'strange accidents', which plagued the crew of the aeroplane which ferried artefacts from Egypt in for the travelling exhibition.

These films involve the two archaeological characters seen in the original Mummy film, something which perhaps shows that despite the passing decades, the Celluloid Archaeologist had not changed his basic image. The two characters crop up in many other films including *Dark Streets of Cairo* (US 1941), *The Mummy's Shroud* (GB 1967), and the relationship between the two forms a part of the plot in *Indiana Jones and the Last Crusade* (US 1989). One of the most interesting points to these films is that the Celluloid Archaeologist is the protagonist in the drama whose foolishness in disturbing the dead leads to horrifying supernatural situations. It is in the course of the quest for knowledge that the ignorance of the Celluloid Archaeologist initiates the unleashing of supernatural forces but sometimes he shows a more devious trait, that of Treasure Hunter.

The Good, The Bad and The Archy

This murkier side to the Celluloid Archaeologist's character can be seen in his role in *The Dark Streets of Cairo* (US 1941). In this film our hero Professor Wyndham recovers the seven jewels of the seventh pharaoh in a Tin Tin type adventure that involves robber barons and other murky underworld gangster characters. The Professor eventually succeeds in evading the barons and smuggles the jewels out of Cairo to America where he has a triumphant reception in the museum. Fine archaeological effort, but very dubious legality.

Indeed our Celluloid hero shows a preoccupation with treasure and he can be found within many films as early as the 20s and 30s digging up and claiming priceless artefacts. For example *Buckin' The West* (US 1924), and *Riders of the Whistling Skull* (US 1936) in both of which the Celluloid Archaeologists considers himself the true 'owner' of the discovered artefacts. These two films also show the Celluloid Archaeologists contribution to taming the wild west, a previously undisclosed phase of his career! In *The Riders of The Whistling Skull* the Archaeologists, (a group of four men sharing equally ridiculous names, Cleary, Fronc, Brewster and Coggins), aid two women in their search for a missing father and discover treasure on the way.

The storyline trots along a recognisable path of find treasure map, lose map to men who wear black hats and spit a lot, get map back, find loot and finally an ending involving romance between members of the expeditionary party. The film contains few surprises but another facet of the Celluloid Archaeologists unpleasant character comes out, as instead of studying the indigenous peoples the four encounter they try to shoot as many of them as possible. Which is pretty outrageous as, apart from continually hindering the search for the treasure, attempting to sacrifice one member of the party and branding another, all the Native Americans are trying to do is protect their rightful heritage. Clearly the Celluloid Archaeologist does not believe that native people are able to 'understand' their past in the same way that western academics can. Which brings us to another unpleasant chapter in the Celluloid Archaeologist's career, that of archaeological theorist.

Going 'Walkabout'

The beginnings of modern political archaeological theory can be found in the early part of the twentieth century and the Celluloid Archaeologist was at the forefront of the new academic thinking. In Australia studies sought to describe aboriginal cultures as "relics" or "savage" members of humanity. Indeed the archaeological collection and curation of artefacts took place without the slightest regard for the peoples who had produced them. The basic view was to view aborigines as 'lower life forms' fit only to study in zoological terms. These ideas were further strengthened by observations of early theorists that noted apparent similarities between Neanderthal morphology and Aboriginal skull types. The Celluloid Archaeologist grasped these dubious theories whole-heartedly, especially in the film *Blond Captive* (US 1932). This was originally released as a 'documentary', with adverts carefully designed to appeal to public interest (including reviews of reported bloody rituals, none of which actually appear in the film). The film's plot was centred upon an archaeological expedition concerned with the finding of 'modern' Neanderthal man and featured a 'true story' about a white woman captured and held captive by an Aboriginal tribe. The Archaeologist, of course, had to step in, managing to lower the aboriginal population statistics during the course of a daring rescue mission.

Another film that shows the Celluloid Archaeologist dabbling with dubious theory is *Skulduggery* (US 1975). This stars the Celluloid Archaeologist as an adventurer who discovers a lost tribe of ape people. In this movie the hero (and his archaeologist partner) uses anthropological theory to prove the humanity of the 'missing link tribe'. At least our hero moves with the times, having obviously educated himself in anthropological theory in order to recognise a Homo species through taxonomic study. A further interesting aspect to this film is the appearance of a female Celluloid Archaeologist, a rare occurrence indeed if the cinema is to be believed.

Feminism and Celebrity Skin

The Celluloid Archaeologist's feminine side only appears in a few films and they are surprising in their diversity and in their use of character. The earliest film in which a female Archaeologist occurs is the western drama *Buckin' The West* (US 1924). In this movie she is portrayed as 'the woman in the white hat', who armed only with an intrepid name, (Xyethia Tomkins), a treasure map, and accompanied by her frontiers-man hero, Cal Edwards, (a sort of educated Clint Eastwood), she not only foils an international criminal's plot to steal Aztec treasure, but also finds love in the wild west. This story is a classic adventure that contains all the elements of later Spielberg epics; intrigue, international criminals, treasure, exotic settings, and of course romance.

While other films from the silent era also contain scenic elements of ancient Egypt, "love within the ruins", curses, and even the evils of drugs.

This particular Western drama involves a strong female character who is integral to the basic plot, not just a subsidiary feminine element thrown in so as to engage a male character's libido. Such a central character, as opposed to a mere assistant, does recur, with movies such as *Jurassic Park* (US 1993), and *Friends* (GB/F 1993), but not for another 70 years. Between these decades the female Celluloid Archaeologist is a marginal character with few lines (but plenty of screams and swoons). The appearance of such an early female Celluloid Archaeologist may therefore appear as a sympathetic suffragette figure. Unfortunately, in most films the female Celluloid Archaeologist seems fairly gratuitous, as no real use is made of the characters. Perhaps their profession was chosen by Hollywood in order to provide an explanation for their presence in exotic places and romantic settings. Films such as *Dos Dios Medre* and any number from the *James Bond* franchise, all use the female character in this way. It seems that the appearance of a female archaeologist is a marker for romance as the descriptions of wolves or ravens are for battle in Beowulf. The use of the female character as 'honey trap' for adventurers and heroic men clearly shows the true colour of the Celluloid Archaeologist's scriptwriters in a male dominated profession.

The exceptions to this role are the characters within the films, *Jurassic Park* (US 1993), and *Friends* (GB/F 1993), who play professional people, and are portrayed for specific purposes. In *Jurassic Park* a palaeontologist is used for her knowledge of dinosaurs and thus complements the film with instructive comments in the same way as her male counterpart. She is used in a sexual role, the two palaeontologists are lovers, but her primary position is one of an expert employed to 'try out' and asses the reality of the dinosaur theme park, and thus her survival is understandable. Within *Friends* the role is again as a palaeontologist but the character is portrayed as an escapist who is using the study of the past as a means of not facing the present.

Other modern films with female characters are generally Egyptian odysseys involving the living dead, and include a soft porn flick called *Desert Princess* (F 1994), and of course the absolutely appalling revamp of the classic *The Mummy* (US 2000). In the first of these the Archaeologist is a serious be-spectacled 'professional' who of course eventually tears her clothes, lets her hair down and removes her glasses to reveal a hidden glamour with inevitable consequences. This phase of the female Celluloid Archaeologist is a certainly a career low point. To be fair, *The Mummy* remake features a generally better character who, although not averse to utilising her womanly charms to get her own way, demonstrates her 'tough exterior'. She is educated, determined, and a more useful member of the exploratory party than the square jawed monosyllabic hero who accompanies her. It is a shame that she is the only redeeming feature in this exceptionally average movie in which the expensive special effects do nothing to hide a truly painful script.

It is in the seventies film *Carry on Behind* (GB 1975) that the female Celluloid Archaeologist, here played by Elke Sommer, made the deepest impression. Her aggressively sexual pursuit of Kenneth William's male archaeologist character shows that she did not take the apparent male domination of the profession lying down. The character of Professor Anna Vooshka can be described as the most pronounced concept of the female Celluloid Archaeologist. It is probably the highlight of her career, especially as she flirts her way through the film, oblivious to her colleague's obvious discomfort.

Post-Indiana Paradigm

Of course the most famous Celluloid Archaeologist of recent times is Indiana Jones, and this character has attracted huge audiences by appearing in a trio of films albeit in a more moral frame of mind than his earlier incarnations.

The effect of Indiana Jones cannot be ignored, not only upon the general public, but also upon professional Archaeologists, who constantly refer to the man within various publications (reviews of Indiana Jones films have appeared within archaeological periodicals such as *Antiquity*). The trilogy represents the best contract that the Celluloid Archaeologist has ever had, all three films having grossed over $109,000,000 on their initial release. Archaeologists are generally quick to write off any perceived factual basis to the foundation of the Jones character, in an attempt to distance themselves and the subject from the treasure hunting ideals central to each film.

The character does, however, possess some roots within the profession of archaeology, and he appears to mirror certain 19th century collectors of antiquities such as Giovanni Belzoni, who worked in the near East during the early half of that century. Belzoni worked in Egypt for the British Consul General where he 'collected' many archaeological objects for the British Museum. Some of Belzoni's own writings sound like a rough draft for a Spielberg production. He certainly made many enemies whilst engaged in his collecting business, but believed his motivation to procure artefacts for museums was correct. One of his adversaries was Drouetti, who worked for the French Consul in a similar capacity. These two characters frequently encountered each other, often with similar consequences as Indiana Jones' meetings with his nemesis Beloque.

One particularly memorable fracas ensued when Belzoni had secured the Philae Obelisk and was attempting to return it to Luxor. Here he ran into Drouetti's agents, (Lebulo and Rossignano) accompanied by about thirty Arabs. Lebulo began:

> "by asking me what business I had to take away an obelisk that did not belong to me; and that I had done so many things of this kind to him, that I should not do any more. Meanwhile he seized the bridle of my donkey with one hand, and with the other laid hold of my waistcoat and stopped me from proceeding any father: he had also a large stick hung to his wrist by a string.
>
> At the same moment the renegade Rossignano reached within for yards of me and with all the rage of a ruffian levelled a double barrelled shotgun at my breast, loading me with all the imprecations that a villain could invent; by this time my servant was disarmed and overpowered by numbers. The two gallant knights before me, I mean Lebulo and Rossignano, both escorted by the two other Arabian servants of Drouetti, both armed with pistols, and many others armed with sticks, continued their clamorous imprecations against me, and the brave Rossignano, still keeping the gun pointing at my breast, said it was time that I should pay for

all that I had done to them. The courageous Lebulo said that he was to have one third of the profit derived from the selling of the obelisk when in Europe, according to a promise from Drouetti, had I not stolen it from the island of Philae. I have no doubt that had I attempted to dismount the cowards would have dispatched me on the ground, and said they did it in defence of their lives, as I had been the aggressor" (Belzoni 1821, 366–367, source Daniel 1951).

This scene appears not unusual for the period, as agents from differing countries attempted to acquire objects for financial gain, often with the official government sanction. This form of archaeological reconnaissance was praised by later archaeologists such as Howard Carter, who stated that; "Those were the great days of excavating, anything which took your fancy was taken, and if there was a difference with a brother excavator, one laid for him with a gun". Thus the early 19th century represents a golden age in archaeology and the atmosphere of this time is captured in the Indiana films as the hero sets out to acquire objects about to fall into the hands of a foreign power. The time frame is different, however, and the foreign power in question is Nazi Germany, but the rivalry is the same and the technique of artefact collection also mirrors the attitude of European archaeologists well into the twentieth century.

An interesting aspect to the trilogy is that in the plot of the third film *Indiana Jones and the Last Crusade* (US 1989) both the two characters young adventurer and old professor appear and are related. Jones senior has fulfilled his academic ambition by finding the 'key' he has searched for obsessively and Indy is the dashing hero who can realise the ambition of acquiring the object, (in this case the Holy Grail), by

Figure 2.3 Harrison Ford and Sean Connery as Jones Junior and Senior in Indiana Jones and the Last Crusade (1989). For once the two stereotypical celluloid characters of "young (hero) adventurer" and "old (obsessive) professor" are actually related © The Kobal Collection.

performing the necessary legwork. That all the objects Indiana Jones attempts to acquire have religious connotations is perhaps a way of supplying mysticism to the quests and as a means of explaining the supernatural events which occur within each film.

That's A Wrap

The fictional Celluloid Archaeologists found within the cinema do not appear to represent archaeologists within the profession today. They do however reflect individuals that existed in archaeology within the last 150 years. The idea that the profession represented a source of fabulous wealth is exhibited within many of the films, and this concept appears to reflect an enjoyment of early archaeological investigations, when artefacts were taken by visitors to foreign countries and brought back to fill various private collections. The personification of archaeology and of archaeologists within the medium of cinema could therefore be termed 'The Schliemann Effect' as certain influential characters have shaped the portrayal of characters on film.

So we come to the closure of a career spanning a century of the Celluloid Archaeologist. Despite all the rapid changes of the modern world, it is perhaps warming to see that, despite his public image of moral crusader in television series such as Star Trek and Stargate: SG1, this character has in fact remained as fossilised as some of his finds. The Celluloid Archaeologist has had a long and illustrious career involving over 100 films and spanning almost the complete century. His modern image is one of a fair-minded chivalrous individual with a strong moral sense, who is willing to sometimes break the professional code or "prime directive", but only in the interests of natural justice. He is still however on the search for that elusive semi-mythical object and inevitably that quest will take him into a desert (even if the desert in question it is on planet Quarlex) and will involve some very unfriendly (possibly even undead) locals.

That's All Folks!

Steven Membury is Development Control Archaeologist for Somerset County Council. His interest in Celluloid Archaeology began when he realised there was an alternative to cramming archaeological theory to complete a student dissertation. This meant he could combine his love of B movies with his obsessive need to assess and catalogue everything around him. He now lives a double life in Somerset, by day a local Government archaeologist, but by night a rather overweight couch potato with a detailed knowledge of soap operas and a passion for popcorn.

3
Archaeology and *Star Trek*: Exploring the past in the future

Lynette Russell

Celluloid archaeologists tend to be more romanticised and swashbuckling than anything encountered in real life. Film, television and computer games have all, on occasion, featured archaeology and archaeologists, perhaps the most famous of all being the fictional Indiana Jones. The character of Jones has been established through a trilogy of movies which later spawned a television series (Young Indiana Jones), as well as a large number of comic books, CD-ROMs, computer games and teen-novels all devoted to the archaeological adventures of this particular fictional archaeologist.

In more recent times the "celluloid archaeologist" has been replaced with the digital archaeologist. Lara Croft of the computer game *Tomb Raider* has, in particular, generated an industry dedicated to *Tomb Raider* merchandise, books, novels and web pages. Croft, like Indiana Jones before her, pursues archaeology with little regard to the ethics of investigating the past. These two fictional archaeologists are more akin to treasure hunters and artefact dealers than true scholars. Each appears to be more comfortable in particularly harsh environments, hunting priceless treasures while being tracked by their enemies, rather than with the museums and libraries that can make up a substantial component of the modern archaeologist's working life.

The Indiana Jones movies were hugely successful and anecdotal evidence suggests that they were responsible for an increased interest in archaeology amongst the general public. As such it could be argued that the central focus of each of the three movies, that of a prized artefact, has been the cause of increased looting of archaeological sites (Bassett 1986, 25). A second effect may well have been to contribute to the rise in the number of students interested in studying archaeology at degree level. David Frankel of LaTrobe University undertook a survey of his undergraduate students in order to ascertain whether or not celluloid archaeologists had an effect on students subject choices. While the overwhelming majority of students stated that they were not influenced by fictional archaeology in their choices, those that did acknowledge a celluloid influence all stated that this was from Indiana Jones and the movie series. At the University of Melbourne, Antonio Sagona noted an impact on enrolment numbers in the years immediately after the release of the Indiana Jones films though this effect appears to have been relatively short lived.

Studying how archaeology is represented within popular culture could of course be used to develop models for the public perception of the discipline and its practitioners. Such models could be used to help inform decisions on a wide range of topics from guiding research projects to developing public programmes. How the archaeological profession is viewed by the general public should in addition be of interest to the practitioners themselves. Much archaeological research, which is funded by public money and popular representations, can, rightly or wrongly, inform particular funding decisions. Within Australia, although the popular media (in particular the daily newspapers) do seem to be interested in archaeological stories, there is often little discrimination between academic or management archaeology and fringe investigations, such as the quest for Noah's Ark. Few clues are often given in the reporting to show that topics such as these are not necessarily given equal status amongst the profession.

Topics surrounding archaeology, archaeological sites, archaeological ethics and 'fringe' archaeology also feature frequently within various genres of fiction, of which science fiction is arguably one of the most popular. In the immensely successful science fiction media phenomenon that is *Star Trek*, for example, archaeology and topics related to the study of the past are depicted on a fairly regular basis. Archaeological and historical themes have in fact dominated *Star Trek* since its inception in the late 1960s something which was in part due to the overt liberal humanist agenda of creator Gene Roddenbery. In addition series writers frequently looked to the past for inspiration and the original series *Star Trek* had many story lines which evoked an historical, often Greco-Roman, point of view. Within this particular chapter I am confining my observations to the televised sequel to the original series *Star Trek: the Next Generation* (STNG) which ran from 1987 to 1994. I am, however, at present engaged in a book length project on these particular issues.

Star Trek: The Next Generation

All over the world the words "Space. The final frontier" evoke memories of *Star Trek*. The four television series and the continuing feature film series attract enormous audiences indicating a cultural phenomenon which has no equivalent. Indeed *Star Trek* has become what Bernardi (1998, 11) describes as a "mega-text". This mega-text consists of much more than the Paramount studio produced videos and films, comprising, among other things, novels, internet chat groups, conventions and magazines (or fanzines) written and distributed by followers of the series. Whilst I do consider myself to be a fan, I am not what others might describe as a certified "trekie" or "trekker". I do not wear the Star Fleet uniform and neither do I attend any of the *Star Trek* conventions that regularly occur worldwide. Although I do have interest in following the debates amongst fans on internet chat groups dedicated to *Star Trek* and other science fiction, my interest is for the most part a concern for the representations of race, culture and species and the depiction of anthropological and archaeological concepts. That this interest results in me watching many films, programmes and videos in the name of research is merely a bonus.

In terms of archaeological knowledge my interest in STNG revolves around the following questions:

1 What form does the representation of archaeology take in STNG?

2 Why is archaeological knowledge considered to be an important component of the *Star Trek* canon?

3 What is the role of archaeological knowledge within the future as depicted in the series?

4 What, if any, are the ethics and controls applied to archaeology?

Digging in Space: archaeological characters

Numerous characters are described as being archaeologists in STNG. The first is Vash. A female archaeologist appearing in several episodes, Vash is depicted as unethical, devious and dishonest. She fully acknowledges that her interest in archaeology is primarily centred upon the profit to be made by the illegal and unsanctioned sale of recovered artefacts. The second character is the only other female archaeologist in the series, Federation officer Lieutenant Marla Aster. Aster is ship archaeologist onboard the *U.S.S. Enterprise* and her sole appearance is in an episode which sees her killed while undertaking investigations on a strange planet. Although portrayed as an ethical scientist, Aster is also depicted as cavalier and perhaps even a careless investigator whose relentless pursuit of her career leaves her young son orphaned. These two counterpoised images of female archaeologists provide a discursive space in which to consider the gender specificities of the representation of women and archaeologists.

The character of Vash is introduced in the episode *Captain's Holiday*. Here Vash is depicted as part of the archaeological fraternity, wearing a standard archaeologist's "uniform" of multi-pocketed pants, robust hiking boots and a well-worn backpack. Such attire ensures that she is instantly recognisable by the public as someone who is clearly an archaeological fieldworker.

The episode *Captain's Holiday* takes place on Risa, a planet well known throughout the Federation of United Planets for its sexually available women and artificially maintained tropical climate. Upon meeting Vash, the Captain of the Starship *U.S.S. Enterprise*, Jean-Luc Picard, recognises the opportunity for adventure, something which he would much rather pursue than a relaxing beach side holiday. Vash has in her possession a disc which apparently holds secrets to the ancient enigma known as the *Tox Uthat*. Time travellers from somewhere in the distant future arrive to tell Picard that he must help them retrieve the *Uthat* which is, in reality, a dangerous weapon. The ensuing chase sees Vash pitted against several dangerous adversaries, all of whom are trying to salvage the *Tox Uthat* for their own ends. Throughout the struggle Vash, is portrayed as untrustworthy, devious and utterly unethical. At the end of the episode, once Picard has destroyed the device, Vash apologises for having lied and reiterates that she is interested in archaeology only as a means of generating money. In short she sells artefacts. She is a futuristic version of a nineteenth century tomb robber.

As a romantic interest for Picard, Vash has a semi-recurring role in the series and she returns to STNG in the episode *Qpid*. During the course of this particular story the United Federation of Planets is holding its Archaeological Symposium on board the Starship Enterprise. Vash attends the symposium even though she is not herself a member of this prestigious professional association. Once here, Vash reveals that her interest is not in the symposium *per se*, but in potential artefacts from the nearby planet Targus III. Vash believes that she may be able to surreptitiously transport down to the surface and salvage material that she could then sell for an impressive profit. Under the guise of attending the professional symposium therefore, Vash intends to pursue her hobby of tomb raiding.

In both episodes (*Captain's Holiday* and *Qpid*) Vash is represented as sexually profligate and morally corrupt. Her ethical indifference, and overt sexuality renders her "available" and her gender enables her to use sexual favours as bargaining tools. Although she is self-empowered, in the episode *Qpid*, she is depicted as both treasure hunter and treasure trophy. In this episode Picard and the omnipotent being known as Q (Captain Picard's nemesis), offer her partnership. As competitors for Vash's affection, Picard and the all-powerful Q appear more equal than at any other time. Jean-Luc offers friendship, loyalty and an alliance based on mutual respect. Picard asks her to stay with him on board the Enterprise. Q offers Vash the opportunity to travel the galaxy and secure whatever archaeological objects she desires. A relationship based therefore on desire both physical and material. Vash's well known love of profit appeals to Q. In keeping with her characterisation, Vash accepts Q's offer and leaves to journey across the universe in search of treasure and other material gains.

In the episode *The Bonding*, Marla Aster, in her role as Ship's archaeologist, investigates the Koinonan ruins. During the course of this investigation Aster is killed when a bomb, an artefact from an archaeological site and set during the course of an ancient war which led to the extinction of all sentient life on the planet, accidentally goes off. The death of Lieutenant Aster has significant ramifications on board the Enterprise, most noticeably as Captain Picard has to advise and console her young son. Although himself a keen student of the past, Picard is extremely critical of Aster and her actions. He notes that she had a somewhat careless attitude and that as a mother she should not have left her child in order to investigate areas of unknown potential. By this reckoning Picard articulates a view many female archaeologists would recognise as being a popular one: that motherhood and archaeological fieldwork are mutually incompatible. Interestingly, even in the twenty-fourth century similar rules for fatherhood do not seem to apply.

The characterisations of Aster and Vash provide the audience with two dichotomies, the first between an ethical and an unethical scientist, the second involves the depiction of women within science fiction. Aster's position as the ethical scientist is compromised by her apparent neglect of her duties as a mother, while Vash, on the other hand is cavalier, reckless and unethical. Analyses of representations of women within popular culture and history have led to the development of several heuristic models. Feminist historian Anne Summer (1994) has postulated that within historical discourse women tend to be depicted as either sexually unavailable and motherly ('God's police') or as sexually available and potentially dangerous ('Damned whores'). The characters Vash and Aster can be seen as conforming to this dichotomous model with little room in which to manoeuvre.

The depiction of male archaeological characters within STNG is much less prone to stereotypes. As Deegan (1986, 221) has pointed out the women in *Star Trek* are always "alien". That is, they are other to the norm, which tends to be white and male. This comment more properly can be applied to the original series and the earlier episodes of STNG, as *Star Trek: Voyager* and *Star Trek: Deep Space Nine* both have strong women characters in positions of authority. Nonetheless, in the earlier series, Deegan notes that women are depicted as secondary characters who either "provide romance or reveal that "any woman's desire for power is abnormal" (Deegan 1986, 221).

The central character to STNG is Captain Jean-Luc Picard, a highly complex individual who is difficult to characterise. Throughout the seven seasons of STNG the series writers evolve Picard's character to become thoroughly self-reflective, unusually ethical and philosophically introspective. In the episode *Contagion* Jean-Luc Picard's love of archaeology is introduced. Here he discovers a planet which he believes to be Iconia, a mythical place where the ruins of a great lost civilisation are to be found. Picard decides to risk the possibility of a hostile encounter with the warlike Romulans in order to uncover some of the secrets of Iconia. For the Captain the thrill of archaeological discovery outweighs any immediate concerns that he may have for safety. Interestingly, in this case, the characteristics that Captain Picard displays are not dissimilar to those which he condemned within Lt. Aster.

It becomes apparent in numerous episodes that Picard's great love of the past had led him to consider archaeology as a career option, but he ultimately rejected this for a career in the Star Fleet of the United Federation of Planets. The dilemma of choosing a Star Fleet career over archaeology never truly leaves Picard and he frequently reflects upon it. Whilst strictly speaking Jean-Luc Picard is not a 'professional' archaeologist, he is a dilettante who frequently describes himself as an 'enthusiastic amateur'. Archaeology for all its appeal would not have suited Picard. He is used to total control and, as a Captain of a starship, his authority goes unquestioned within the militaristic structure of the Federation. A Starfleet Captain often has the power of life and death over many people and, however much he may enjoy archaeology as a hobby, it is unlikely to hold the same levels of total power that he otherwise enjoys.

The mission of *Star Trek* as a meta-narrative of colonialism is well known and has been extensively analysed elsewhere (e.g. Bernardi 1998, Hastie 1996, Ono 1996). The utopian future depicted in *Star Trek* has been described as based on "nineteenth-century essentialist definitions of human nature, building...on faith in perfection, progress, social evolution, and free will" (Boyd 1996, 96–97). The character of Captain Jean-Luc Picard is intimately wound into this imperialist framework. As the Captain of the U.S.S. Enterprise he is a man with "an ongoing mission". As an archaeologist he is a man with a passion.

Despite his amateur status Picard is asked to deliver the keynote address at the Federation Archaeological Symposium which is being held on board the Enterprise (in the episode *Qpid*). That he is extended this honour indicates his high status within the archaeological fraternity for it is clear that the request comes on the basis of his research and not from his status as Captain. Whilst the symposium is taking place, the Enterprise orbits a planet known as Targus III. Targan law has, for the last century, specifically refused to allow outsiders to access their archaeological sites, therefore Picard's address concerns the visible ruins of Targus III and his reassessment of the last archaeological survey work conducted there over a hundred years ago. His address to the symposium is dotted with clichés, such as mystery and detective story and, as such he embodies the popular view of archaeology which owes much to the celluloid stereotypes. Such a viewpoint rarely hints at the hours of monotonous sorting and measuring that usually accompanies the process of archaeological analysis.

Picard's thrill for archaeology and unbridled enthusiasm for the past recurs in the episode *Rascals*. This episode commences with Picard, on board a shuttle craft, returning to the Enterprise after a two week stint excavating an archaeological site. The Captain is seen to be boring the other crew members with his archaeological treasures (these mostly comprise of amorphous sherds of pottery). The patient and humouring crew are seen swapping furtive, knowing glances at one another and frequently rolling their eyes and smiling at the Captain's exuberance.

Immediately prior to their arrival on the Enterprise, a malfunction occurs in the operation of the transporter and this results in Picard and three other crew members being returned to the ship in the form of children. Despite the transformation, they all appear to have maintained their adult knowledge and memories. It soon becomes apparent to Picard that, in such a body he can not continue in his role as Captain. His newly diminutive size means that his orders are trivialised and the crew can not adjust to having a leader who is twelve years old. After stepping down from duty Picard ponders what he might do with his life and he settles on devoting his time purely to archaeology. This episode for the first time raises an important issue, for the writers of STNG frequently portray archaeology as dilettantism, an interesting hobby but one which is not a real career option.

Archaeology appears to be a glamorous and exotic hobby for Picard and a means of making profit for Vash. For the ill fated Aster it was clearly a career choice, though not a very long lived one. The one character who chooses and maintains an archaeological career throughout the programme is Professor Richard Galen. Professor Galen, Picard's mentor and former teacher, is a key archaeological figure in the series and although only appearing in one episode, he is frequently mentioned by Picard as a man of great influence. Galen is presented as a single minded inquirer of the past. A man whose archaeological quest is motivated by the highest ideals of the pursuit of knowledge. Galen is shown as an ethical scientist, he is also solitary, perhaps even sad (*The Chase*). It seems that the pursuit of professional archaeology comes at a price.

Ethics and Control

Throughout the archaeological discipline the issue of control and the "ownership" of the past has come to occupy a central position. The writers of *Star Trek* have embraced this concern and the issue of control and ownership frequently appears as part of the plot, though mostly as subsidiary storylines.

An interesting subplot to the main story in the episode *Qpid* involves Vash and her attempt to transport to the forbidden ruins of Targus III, at the same time that Picard is delivering his address to the Archaeological Symposium of the United Federation of Planets. Whilst Picard emphasises archaeological ethics and issues surrounding the "ownership" of cultural heritage, Vash is attempting to raid the Targan sites even though the Targans have chosen to effectively close their heritage sites to outsiders. Despite the embargo on foreign researchers, analysis does continue by way of concentrating upon the reinterpretation of previous excavation work (Picard notes that there have been some 947 archaeological investigations in the past). The rights of the indigenous population to control research on their history is promoted as a basic right, although this does not prevent scholars continuing to work on certain elements of Targan history.

The fundamental right of all species to control their own destiny is promoted as the highest ideal of the Federation. The Prime Directive, which the Federation holds to be its founding and guiding principal, states that no-one may interfere with the natural cultural development of a species. The rule of non-interference is considered to be the most important element of the *Star Trek* canon. Ironically while this prime directive is in principal not to be violated, it is frequently transgressed and the prime directive is often ignored as and when it applies to the past and the archaeology of non-human species. This raises the extremely interesting question of archaeological ethics and who actually owns the past. This issue is tied to the Federation's meta-narrative of colonialism.

Whilst it is never unequivocally stated in its entirety on the television series, according to the Internet chat list STREKL, the prime directive asserts:

1   The right of each sentient species to live in accordance with its normal cultural evolution is considered sacred.

2   No Star Fleet personnel may interfere with the healthy development of alien life and culture.

3   Such interference includes the introduction of superior knowledge, strength or technology to a world whose society is incapable of handling such advantages wisely.

4   Star Fleet personnel may not violate this Prime Directive, even to save their lives and/or their ship, unless they are acting to right an earlier violation or an accidental contamination of said culture.

This directive takes precedence over any and all other considerations, and carries with it the highest moral obligation The prime directive basically states that Federation members should not interfere with a thriving culture which is not aware of space travel. It is, however, only used as and when convenient, and is often forgotten when it would be seen to detract from the plot.

Interpretation of the Prime Directive can be extended to the archaeological past of alien species. This is most clearly depicted in a *Star Trek: Voyager* episode (*Emanations*). Here an "away team" study a series of emanations which are identified as coming from a peculiar asteroid. Once on the asteroid the team discovers a series of corpses covered with what is described as "a polymer resin", which is a by-product of the decomposition process. A dispute breaks out between the away team crew as the team-leader Commander Chakotay, a Native American, states categorically that no-one may study the remains with any type of mechanical device for he fears that the bodies belonged to a race "who obviously buried their dead with ceremony and did not intend them harmed". The other crew members in the group refuse to believe that a thorough scientific investigation of the burial ground can be undertaken without recourse to electronic scanning or physical examination. The commander's status as a Native American establishes his otherness within the mainstream of the crew. He is expected to feel empathy for "native people" (even aliens) and in this case he is the obvious choice to articulate the problem of archaeological ethics.

A similar concern for the rights of indigenous people and the ethics of studying other cultures dominates the episode *Who Watches the Watchers*. Here an anthropological field team, positioned behind a holographic "duck blind", has been studying the indigenous population of MinTarca III. An accident takes place which reveals the anthropologists to the people, thus "contaminating" their natural development and clearly violating the prime directive. In fact the accident causes the development of a new belief system within the native group, a belief in an all powerful being known as "the Picard". Refusing to sanction false beliefs Captain Picard sets about showing that he may be a highly evolved man, but a man nonetheless.

In an appeal to earth history and an unmistakable assumption of unilineal historical trajectories, he notes that, if left unchecked the belief will become a religion and this will result in holy wars and inquisitions. Picard does not want the burden of having caused such a future for the MinTarcans and so decides to take Nuria, a native leader to the Enterprise. Nuria is a leader amongst the MinTarcan people. Picard believes that once on board he will be able to show Nuria "how the magic works". Nuria is selected in part because Picard believes others follow her, but also because she is, in his estimation, more highly evolved than the others. Picard is in this instance convinced that rationality and science, as he defines it, will win out.

After describing the evolution of human society (defined as white European/North American culture) Picard suggests to Nuria that she too has come from a more primitive past. She agrees and describes her ancestors, who she notes no-one remembers, but whose evidence she has seen.

> Nuria: "Remnants of tools in caves. Our ancestors once lived there."
>
> Picard: "My people once lived in caves and in time we built huts and then one day ships like this one."
>
> Nuria: "Perhaps one day my people will travel in the skies."
>
> Picard: "Of that I am absolutely certain."

At no point in the episode do the writers reflect on whether or not the anthropologists should have been observing the MinTarcans. The closest they get to self-reflection comes from one of the MinTarcans who asks why would a people so evolved bother to study a people so primitive. We are assured that such studies are very important, though why and for whom is never made clear.

Patterns of evolution and historical trajectories

In terms of development, "unilineal evolution" is a dominant feature of the way that the *Star Trek* writers describe various species and species encountered for the first time are frequently described in terms of the European prehistoric phase system (Stone, Bronze and Iron Age etc.). An interesting example comes from the episode described above (*Who Watches the Watchers*) in which the people of MinTarca are described as a proto-vulcanoid race at the Bronze Age level of development. A unilineal historical trajectory is evoked which sequentially progresses from "stone age to space age" with all points known and already named.

A species encountered in the episode *Samaritan Snare*, are known as Pakleds. These are a people described as "a curious throwback". As Pakleds speak and walk slowly they are generally assumed to be less evolved than species within the United Federation of Planets. The android character Commander Data suggests that the Pakleds may however have simply developed complexity in areas other than communication. However the Enterprise crew under the direction of the first officer decide that the Pakleds "need to continue to develop", assuming that they are on a path moving towards a pre-known destination. Given enough time the Pakled will become like the Federation species, dominated as it is by humans.

Gene Roddenbery, creator of *Star Trek*, populated his universe with a plethora aliens most of whom are humanoid. Roddenbery believed that this was a reasonable assumption and had developed a theory of "parallel evolution", a process whereby similar environments produced similar beings. Such a view was he believed a distinct probability for "natural laws undoubtedly govern life development just as other natural laws govern time, space and atoms" (Whitfield and Roddenbery 1968, 207).

Parallel evolution is extended in the episode *The Chase*. Here Professor Richard Galen arrives on board the Enterprise filled with fervour and enthusiasm. Galen urges Picard to join him on an archaeological hunt which will have Galaxy wide impact. Once again Picard must confront the decision to pursue Star Fleet rather than a career in archaeology. For a while he appears genuinely uncertain and perplexed by the dilemma which Galen presents him, but finally chooses Star Fleet and rejects Galen's offer. Galen, angry and embittered, leaves the Enterprise and is later killed when his ship is mysteriously attacked. Convinced that the raid and Galen's death have some connection to the archaeological hunt, Picard decides to investigate. After examining all of his mentor's notes and findings, Picard realises that the puzzle in question concerns DNA patterns from all over the galaxy.

After transporting to a particular planet, the Captain puts the pieces together. He does this while the a series of overtly militaristic races, the Klingons, Romulans and

Cardassians, are squabbling over ownership and sovereign rights of the material, which they believe to be part of a powerful weapon. Only the humans are shown to be sufficiently sophisticated as to take charge of the situation and prevent the others from fighting. Galen's secret is finally revealed, in a message from a long dead race of humanoid beings. These beings were a race of "founders" who seeded their DNA codes through out the various homeworlds of the Galaxy. The great truth, the idea that Galen believed would have Galaxy wide impact, is that all species are descended from a common ancestor.

Several important issues are raised in *The Chase*. Firstly, the question of unilineal evolution, as discussed above, which appears commonly throughout the series, is restated and each species is shown to be a product of their own historical trajectory, having branched off from a single common ancestor in the distant past. Secondly, even though all the species involved in the "chase" are humanoid, only the human group comprising of Picard and his crew are most like the "founders" in terms of both appearance and behaviour. As such it is implied that the humans represent the pinnacle of evolution with the Klingons, Romulans and Cardassians apparently having some distance yet to climb up the evolutionary ladder.

Conclusion

In this chapter I have outlined some of my findings for an archaeology of *Star Trek*. Although brief, it is clear that archaeology, as a discipline and as a career choice, plays a vital role within the *Star Trek* canon. The overriding colonial narrative of *Star Trek* and the imperialist motives of the United Federation of Planets (see Russell and Wolski for an extended discussion) ensures however that it is an archaeology dominated by hierarchical politics.

It is apparent that themes derived from archaeological research in the real world, informs and directs many of the story lines within *Star Trek*. Even though the future portrayed is one that is technology dominated, it is also a future where the simple questions of culture history and understanding of historical processes are seen to be very important. However, though the catch-cry of *Star Trek* is "to boldly go where no-one has gone before", it is evident that many of the places and people the crew of the Starship Enterprise visits are in fact from the human (and more often specifically European) past.

The archaeologists depicted in *Star Trek* were identified as conforming to two representational types. These are the ethical committed scientist and the corrupted, unethical trophy hunter. Gender does not seem to be an impediment to being an archaeologist in the future, even if the two main female archaeologists depicted within the series clearly possessed major character flaws. If the *Star Trek* version of what is to come is even semi-accurate, then it may be comforting to know that archaeologists can at least look forward to increased employment opportunities in the twenty-fourth century.

Acknowledgements

This chapter has benefited from the input of several people, most notably Ian McNiven, Ron Southern and Nathan Wolski. Melinda Tursky, former president of the University of Melbourne *Star Trek* Club, generously shared her considerable knowledge with me. I developed the idea for the chapter when working on an earlier publication with Nathan Wolski. I must also acknowledge Tim and Myles, who have become sophisticated critics of science fiction in general and *Star Trek* in particular, whilst at all times maintaining their enthusiasm for viewing. I am also very grateful to archaeology lecturers Associate Professor Antonio Sagona (University of Melbourne), Dr David Frankel (La Trobe University) and Dr Jay Hall (University of Queensland) for discussing the impact of the Indiana Jones phenomena with me.

Lynette Russell is the Senior Research Fellow at the Centre for Australian Indigenous Studies, Monash University in Melbourne. Along with Ian McNiven and Kay Schaffer she edited the 1998 volume *Constructions of Colonialism* and has published on postcolonial theory and representations of indigenous Others. Her current research interests revolve around representations and representational theory, being particularly interested in how images of "Indigenous" or "Native!" peoples are transferred and adopted by science fiction.

4

The Myth Makers: Archaeology in *Doctor Who*

Brian Boyd

Archaeology and science fiction share a common heritage in that they are both manifestations of the western colonial encounter. In the popular perception, both are concerned with the discovery of the unfamiliar, the different, the other, the alien. In these unfamiliar contexts it is the role of the explorer/pioneer/archaeologist to describe, explain and interpret. What follows considers this perception, drawing upon depictions of archaeology and archaeologists in one of the most successful BBC television serials ever, *Doctor Who*, which ran from 1963–1989. Much has been written about the programme in recent years, particularly in the fields of "communication studies", with discussions ranging from the analysis of "fan culture" (Tulloch and Jenkins 1995) the construction of textual narratives (Fiske 1983). This short article focuses on just one main issue, encountering the alien, in both Doctor Who and in archaeology.

The image of the Doctor

One of the dominant images of the archaeologist within the public perception (and sometimes within the discipline itself) is that of the "archaeologist as detective", as a kind of Sherlock Holmes character (Shanks and Tilley 1987). We can construct an image of the archaeologist as the (gentleman) detective, piecing together clues in a logical, scientific manner, cleaning up mysteries and occasionally vanquishing tyrannical enemies. The image of the BBC's fictional, time-travelling maverick, Doctor Who, very much fits with this Holmesian ideal of the gentleman scholar and scientist, fighting crime, solving mysteries for the greater good of (western) civilisation. Several parallels can be drawn. First, there is the idea of the Doctor's foil or companion – akin to Holmes's relationship to Dr. Watson – who exists largely to ask questions, allowing our hero to periodically (and, often, cryptically) explain parts of the plot to any viewers who may equally be baffled. The companion's role is particularly crucial at the dénouement, when all the clues are pieced together explaining how yet another evil plan was thwarted for the good of humanity:

> "But how did you know that X was behind it all?"
> "Oh, from the beginning really. I first suspected when he /she…".

You get the picture.

Second, there is the regularly-returning arch-enemy. In Holmes's case, Moriarty, and in Doctor Who we have "The Master". In both cases, the very antithesis of the hero, equally brilliant but for all the wrong reasons, never totally defeated, always escaping to fight another day. And yet, each holds a begrudging respect for the other, an intellectual admiration, an almost sibling rivalry.

Then there is the Victorian/Edwardian influence. We have only to look at the costumes worn by the various Doctors: William Hartnell's Victorian/Edwardian gentleman scientist with black frock coat, ebony walking cane and *pince-nez*, Patrick Troughton's Dickensian hobo, Jon Pertwee's velveteen, ruffle-shirted dandy, and so on. To emphasise the point, we even encounter the fourth Doctor, played by Tom Baker – usually a mix of Left Bank Toulouse-Lautrec bohemian and Harpo Marx – abandoning his trademark wide-brimmed hat and unfeasibly long scarf for a deerstalker, cape and pipe in the 1977 story, *The Talons of Weng-Chiang*, a genuine Holmes homage set in a fog-bound Victorian East End London, complete with chirpy "Cockenese" (the local tribe, explains the Doctor to his Eliza Doolittle-type companion, the "savage" Leela), triad gangs, opium-smoking, "Good Old Days" music hall parlance, and bumbling bobbies whom the Doctor assists in the most brilliant, if patronising, of ways.

Victorian literary traditions and motifs – particularly stories in the Romantic/Gothic horror style – were frequently drawn upon by writers of the television series: *The Brain of Morbius* (Frankenstein), *Planet of Evil* (Dr. Jekyll and Mr Hyde), *State of Decay* (Dracula), and *Timelash* (several H.G. Wells stories), to name but a few. In fact, the programme's central plot device – the time machine – owes a large debt to Wellsian scientism, and this represents the major difference between Sherlock Holmes and Doctor Who as far as plot devices are concerned. The former is confined to a particular era and geographical location (later Victorian England for the most part, at least in the original novels), while the Doctor, thanks to his space-time machine, the TARDIS – camouflaged as a Victorian police box, a familiar object in unfamiliar settings – solves his mysteries throughout time and across vast regions of space. This gives an added, philanthropic, dimension to the character of the Doctor. He is an explorer, a traveller, an adventurer. This image is, of course, entwined with those other Victorian legacies: colonialism, imperialism and the anthropological encounter (outer space being the ultimate "periphery"), where the explorer set out to discover the unfamiliar and the different, and to describe and explain "it" for domestic consumption, with male-dominated mercantile and missionary objectives key factors here.

Archaeology and archaeologists in *Doctor Who*

Archaeology – another product of the western colonial encounter – has appeared periodically throughout the history of *Doctor Who*. Invariably presented as the adventurous, gentlemanly pursuit of knowledge, the subject and its practitioners are very much characterised as artefacts of the colonial era. An exception to the "gentleman scholar" depiction of the archaeologist can be found in the 1978 story *The Stones of Blood* in which the Doctor pits himself against some blood-draining standing stones. The location chosen for this was the Rollright Stones in Oxfordshire, "a sort of megalithic temple-cum-observatory", the Doctor tells his companion, Romana. The archaeologist in this instance is a woman – Professor Amelia Rumford, author of *Bronze Age Burials in Gloucestershire* ("the definitive work on the subject", according to the Doctor). Professor Rumford may well be scholarly and knowledgeable, but the writer, David Fisher, chooses to characterise her as firmly belonging to the elderly eccentric "formidable lady" category, so beloved of the BBC Sunday evening Agatha Christie "Miss Marple" slot. One fan-based website refers to her as "sublimely dotty". Clearly this downplaying of female authority while at the same time extolling the virtues of the eccentric but brilliant archaeologist are part and parcel of the overall colonial project. Criticisms have been levelled at the show on numerous occasions that the Doctor is "perhaps a bit sexist" (T. Dicks, former script editor, quoted from the BBC video *Thirty Years in the Tardis*), but this ignores the persistent gendering of the search for knowledge as a male pursuit, which underwrites Doctor Who (and much science fiction) as a whole. For excellent gender studies on the sci-fi genre, the reader should refer to, amongst others, papers in Helford 2000, Barr 2000, and Merrick and Williams 1999.

For the most part then, the imperial image dominates. By way of illustration, we can offer a selection of examples from the series, beginning with the 1967 story *The Ice Warriors* by Brian Hayles.

The temporal context in this story is the "near future", with the Earth in the grip of an Ice Age. Three archaeologists have made a discovery in the ice, and they are attempting to extricate their find, watched from afar by couple of local poachers, who have a clear disdain and suspicion for the whole business:

> 1st poacher: "They're not scientists, they're archaeologists".
> 2nd poacher: "Archaeologists?" (spits venomously).

Once taken back to base, the archaeologists' block of ice melts to reveal an alien, an Ice Warrior from Mars, who wakes and revitalises his fellow warriors who have been frozen in the ice for several centuries (since before humans inhabited the Earth, to be precise). They announce that they are the rightful custodians of Earth and that the humans must be destroyed. The Doctor (Patrick Troughton) arrives on the scene, with his companions Jamie, a young Highlander rescued from the battle of Culloden, and a Victorian girl named, somewhat unimaginatively, Victoria. The Doctor allies himself with the humans, and devises a plan to wipe out the Ice Warrior population on Earth (except for one which escapes, obviously). In the process, the Doctor also manages to halt the advance of the glaciers, thus saving Earth twice over.

We see here that while the desire for knowledge of the alien other is gratified by the scientists/archaeologists – they excavate and thaw out the frozen Ice Warrior – this ultimately leads to the destruction of the "indigenous inhabitant". This is a common theme not only in *Doctor Who*, but in a great deal of classic and contemporary science fiction.

To take another example, we can turn to the 1975 Gothic horror homage, *The Pyramids of Mars* (by Stephen Harris). Little needs to be said here about the enduring public perception of archaeology being primarily about "the pyramids" and "ancient Egypt", so long part of the Gothic horror film tradition and recently revitalised in Hollywood's recent blockbuster *The Mummy*. The exotic, eerie mixture of discovery and revelation, treasure and death, and the Howard Carter-type gentleman archaeologist places *The Pyramids of Mars* firmly in this genre.

The story is set in 1911, on the cusp between Victorian and Edwardian Britain. The drama begins with the excavation of a tomb in a previously undiscovered pyramid in a previously undiscovered valley. When the inner chamber is broken open by the (Oxford) Professor of Egyptology directing the excavation, we discover that trapped in the pyramid for centuries is an alien, known as Sutekh (the Destroyer), understandably intent on wreaking havoc once set free from "his ancient bonds". Sutekh had been imprisoned there by his family, led by his brother Horus, because of his evil leanings and desire for power. The various skirmishes across the galaxy culminating in Sutekh's capture and incarceration entered into mythology, thus forming the basis for the belief system of ancient Egypt. In *The Pyramids of Mars*, then, the whole cosmology of ancient Egyptian society is structured around the family history of an alien being. Enter the Doctor.

In a story replete with every ancient Egypt/pyramid/mummy/archaeology/imperialism cliché imaginable, including some remarkable racial stereotypes:

> Professor Scarman (on entering the antechamber): "Abdul, quickly man, your lantern". Scarman pulls back a red curtain to reveal a carving of the Eye of Horus which illuminates, causing the Arab workers to flee in terror. He calls after them: "Come back, I need your help. Superstitious savages…"

Here we see again how the archaeological encounter sets off a chain of events leading ultimately to the destruction of the alien other. Sutekh intends to destroy the Earth (and much of the cosmos) once released, something which the Doctor cannot allow. As a result, Sutekh is dispatched and the Earth is saved. Again, however, it is the unintended consequence of the archaeological encounter – in this case, the opening of the tomb – which facilitates the possibility of world destruction. The only way to avoid this is to get rid of the alien, silence its voice and deny its authority. Who is heard, Who silences.

Monsters and mechanoids

We have thus far identified a preoccupation with the subjugation of the other, of difference. Taking this further, it is instructive to consider how the alien other is physically represented in *Doctor Who*. Generally, there are two forms. First, what may be termed "the monster" (invariably of the green rubber suit variety) and, second, the "mechanoid/robot/cyborg", which may have some recognisable "human" component in its physiognomy. Both, however, rarely display any real "human qualities", which makes it easier to justify

    a) its innate evilness and
    b) its inevitable destruction.

An example of this comes from the 1972 story, *The Claws of Axos*, where the invading aliens initially appear human (or humanoid at least) in form and benign in nature. As soon as their true intentions are revealed (world conquest, naturally), the Axons revert to their true form, leathery-skinned, tendril-covered creatures with a lethal electrical touch, and are swiftly dispatched by the Doctor aided by Brigadier Lethbridge-Stewart's UNIT (United Nations Intelligence Taskforce) troops.

Probably the best known of the "human"-type monsters are the Cybermen (note the gendering, needless to say). These cyborgs were once human, gradually replacing their body parts and functions with electronic, mechanical features. They eventually became devoid of all human elements such as emotion, compassion and, it probably goes without saying, humour. In the 1967 story *Tomb of the Cybermen*, the TARDIS lands on the planet Telos, where an archaeological expedition is attempting to uncover the lost tombs of the Cybermen. Much aided by the Doctor, the archaeologists enter the tombs. Once inside, however, one of the party reveals that he – along with his equally unscrupulous business partner – plans to revive the Cybermen who, he anticipates, will help him achieve a position of great power and financial standing back on Earth. Perhaps unsurprisingly, the Cybermen have other ideas.

Indeed, the entire tomb complex has been designed as a trap for inquisitive intruders. Once ensnared, their fate is to be transformed into Cybermen. Outwitting this proposed reproductive venture, and despite having helped the archaeologists break into the tombs in the first instance, the Doctor then has to come up with a counter-plan to reseal the tombs and return the aliens to their frozen state.

Domination; and resistance is useless

So, we encounter a repeated denial of the alien voice – regularly expressed as a desire for domination over humanity – through the colonial encounter. But the Doctor, we should bear in mind, is himself an alien – a Time Lord. Nevertheless, he does possess, as the writers and producers of the programme were at great pains to emphasise, certain "human qualities" (very much like the character of Spock in *Star Trek*). Obviously this is to forge empathy between the lead character and the audience, particularly relying on the "liberal democratic humane scientist" (Fiske 1983, 75) of the western colonial era. Generally regarded as producer of one of the "golden ages" of Doctor Who, the early Tom Baker years (1975–1977), Philip Hinchcliffe is of the opinion that the Doctor should be the type of person who "forged the empire out of his own latent values" (interview in *Doctor Who Monthly*), occasional quips not-withstanding,

    The Brigadier: "Well naturally enough the only country that could be trusted with

such a role was Great Britain".
The Doctor: "Well naturally. I mean, the rest were all foreigners". (*Robot*, 1975)

We must remember, however, that the Doctor is also a renegade, an outcast from his own society. Unlike his fellow Time Lords – and flagrantly opposing their laws – he actively interferes in the affairs of other planets and other times. Yet, things are not so clear cut. Time Lords, they themselves decree, should merely observe, gather information and accumulate knowledge. This image is a fallacy, however, because in actual fact the Time Lords do interfere in external affairs, frequently using the Doctor as their unwilling and, often, unknowing agent (as seen in the stories *The Doomsday Weapon*, *The Curse of Peladon*, *The Three Doctors*, *Genesis of the Daleks*, *The Brain of Morbius*, *Attack of the Cybermen*, and so on).

This seemingly *laissez-faire* policy leads to a paradox where events and actions are regarded as predestined; to interfere would be to change history. This is the routine reason given by the Doctor for not becoming too noticeable involved in the events of Earth history. For example, he does little about the violent events surrounding the French Revolution; he allows the Great Fire of London to take hold – indeed he helps feed the flames with material from an alien spacecraft, the occupants of which he has left inside a burning building in Pudding Lane. He does, however, leave a memento for a (17th century) friend who has helped out in bringing the aliens to task:

> Companion: "What did you give him?"
> The Doctor: "a control panel from the Terileptil ship".
> Companion: "Won't that confuse the archaeologists?"
> The Doctor: "Ssshhhh…." (*The Visitation*, 1982).

Perhaps the best example is from 1982's *Earthshock*, where a massive bomb built by the Cybermen is due to collide with 20th century Earth and wipe out all life on the planet. The Doctor attempts to thwart the plan but is only able to change the time of the impact, not the location. He thinks he has failed, but then realises that the explosion will take place 60 million years ago, at exactly the time when the dinosaurs were wiped out. Naturally, he lets it go ahead so as not to interfere with established historical development on Earth (the explosion also kills all the Cybermen on board and, more bizarrely, one of the Doctor's own companions. Conversely, when the Doctor travels into the future of Earth, or to another planet altogether, he meddles away quite happily, regardless of the consequences.

We therefore have a contrast between the non-interference in the past, in Earth's history, coupled with the persistent meddling in unknown futures and on unknown worlds. The preservation of the past vs. the destruction of the unknown. This stands in contrast to the Doctor's quote (which opens this volume), "there is no past or future, only a multitude of possibilities". In fact, the effect of the colonial encounter reduces the multitude of possibilities, reduces the alien in the name of western science and imperialism, but this is masked by claims of objectivity through a spurious policy of non-interference in the affairs of other worlds and other times.

> "You and I are scientists, professor. We buy our privilege to experiment at the cost of total responsibility" The *Doctor* (*Planet of Evil*, 1977).

Some kinds of archaeologists may be seen as Time Lords, with a monopoly on the construction of history. They explore, survey, collect and analyse the material residues of past worlds, and produce accounts of those worlds through routine archaeological procedures. The histories produced through this encounter with an alien past seem, however, strangely familiar to us. We can interpret those alien worlds because through uniformitarian assumptions we can identify certain elements of behaviour, of "human-ness", which we regard as being universal. Time Lords claim objectivity through a policy of non-interference in the affairs and histories of other worlds. Archaeologists can no longer lay such a claim. The objectivity sought for by empiricism does not exist.

We are active in our interference. We construct representations (which we term history) through the destruction of the remains of material worlds, past worlds. We may think of ourselves as Time Lords, with an academic or intellectual authority over the past, over others' – and the other's – ideas about the past and histories: the misplaced, self-appointed authority which comes from academically/disciplinary-sanctioned practices – surveying, collecting, analysing, recording, presenting – but in so doing we are actively interfering and silencing. We are in fact the Time Meddlers, and as such our responsibilities and obligations are considerable.

Responsibility to ourselves within the discipline, and to those people who see archaeologists as providing believable and interesting histories, people who help fund the discipline is considerable. In particular, an obligation to recognise that our uniformitarian perspective is simply one of many possible ways of looking at the past, of constructing narratives and histories other worlds. The main obligation is therefore to avoid constructing histories based upon our own prejudices and interests, and to produce accounts of other times, places and peoples which are not grounded in uniformitarian assumptions but recognise as different those people whose material worlds we enter into, write histories about on their behalf, and use as the basis for our chosen disciplinary careers. Having said that, recognising "the unfamiliar" is but a first small step. The giant leap required to give full gratification to the desires of the other is fraught with difficulties, both of an intellectual and moral nature, as Bauman (1992) has so clearly argued.

That we must take responsibility for our own contemporary social constructions should go without saying. Giving full intellectual credence while at the same time avoiding superiority postures is another matter. This dislocation between archae-ologists' (our) theoretical premises and the actual nature of academic practice has been more fully discussed by Boyd (1996), and Meskell (1999), who points out that one of the difficulties in reconciling "disciplinary" and "alternative" voices may well be that although the aims of the two can be theoretically compatible, this is far from the case when it comes to praxis (1999, 89). The "multitude of possibilities" is thus much reduced. The time has surely come to fulfil our obligations to the people of the past, the present, and the future, and to increase those possibilities beyond the narrow confines of academic practice.

Acknowledgements

Many thanks to Zoë Crossland for useful comments, and to Miles Russell for his patience. This chapter is dedicated to Derek Torrance.

Brian Boyd is Lecturer in Archaeology at the University of Wales Lampeter. He writes mainly about archaeological theory and the prehistory of Israel and the Palestinian territories.

5

"No more heroes any more": the dangerous world of the pop culture archaeologist

Miles Russell

"The role of archaeologist appears to have devolved into the video games and Hollywood definition; one who is chased down corridors by boulders, having just desecrated the graves of the holy".
(Doctor Who Magazine, November 1998, 37)

"There's nothing more useless than a bored archaeologist"
(Douglas Adams 1985, 209)

Archaeologists are obsessed with context: the context of artefacts; the context of soils across an archaeological site; the context of archaeological sites; the context of ancient cultures and past societies. Paradoxically archaeologists are less aware of their own context, certainly with regard to how they are perceived, how they "fit in", and what their role within society is adjudged to be. In this chapter I will be examining the pop culture stereotypes, especially those of the goggle-box or television, arguably the most prominent and defining aspect of modern society, in order to ascertain the social context of the archaeologist in the late 20th and early 21st century.

Archaeology and archaeologists appear with surprising regularity on the goggle-box. Usually the appearance is in factual programming, and Britain particularly has seen a considerable rise in archaeologically-themed television throughout the 1990s (with examples like *Time Team* and *Meet the Ancestors* regularly receiving audiences of between 3 and 5 million), though their occurrence within fictional dramas, soaps and doccu-soaps is also quite noticeably prominent. Most people have access to a television set, or have watched one at some time (even if they later strenuously deny it) and however modern analysts argue and debate the significance of the flickering box upon our lives, there is no doubt that the television can dramatically alter and shape our perspective on the world around us. So, given the viewing figures for your average Saturday night, televisual extravaganza, what message is being beamed directly from the major T.V. studios, into the collective brain of the population?

The Fictional T.V. Archaeologist

The character of T.V. archaeologist, T.V. in this case standing for Televisual, (though Transvestite may equally be applicable given certain circumstances) is a common and reliable one. In fact the character, personality and career-path of the televisual archaeologist has become so well defined within western culture since the invention of the broadcast medium, that it has become deeply ingrained within the public consciousness as to be instantly recognisable, extremely comical and also perhaps also vaguely unsettling (at least to those who consider themselves to be REAL archaeologists uncovering the fascinating story of the past and conveying the reality to the unwashed masses and/or "just trying to do a job thank you").

Within televisual fiction there is a small, if very well defined, number of stock (male and female) characters to draw from:

1   There is the archaeologist driven by a single goal, considered mad by some, who will, through their discoveries, undoubtedly unleash a curse upon all humanity (perhaps even deliberately to get their own back upon the academics that ignored their work for so long – "ha ha!");

2   There is the archaeologist driven by pure personal greed, who, in the course of their quest for loot, will also undoubtedly unleash a huge, lumbering, bandage-swathed monster upon all humanity;

3   There is the gun-toting (and generally hard drinking) hero/heroine who pretends to be "in it" for the purist of reasons (i.e. protecting the cultural heritage from other alcoholic, gun toting loonies), but who is clearly motivated by the 'great discovery' and who will undoubtedly unleash something rather unpleasant upon themselves (usually in the form of a sudden and grisly death);

4   There is also the plain, if ever-so-slightly seedy (and generally comical) academic character, with an abiding, and usually incomprehensible love of obscure ceramics of the Late Byzantine World, who prompts contempt and boredom from his/her colleagues before unwittingly unleashing something unpleasant upon their immediate circle through the pursuit of knowledge (generally an indigestible 32 volume tome on the importance of Norse toe-clippings in 10th century Yorkshire).

So clear-cut have these figures become, that most broadcast serials or soaps, usually at a time when they are searching for a supposedly 'new idea', will often latch on to, and whole-heatedly embrace the character of pop culture archaeologist, further adding to the mythos and enforcing the stereotype. If you doubt this at all, watch such programming stalwarts as *Murder She Wrote*, *Columbo*, *The Avengers*, *Doctor Who*, *Star Trek* (in all its incarnations), *Lovejoy*, *Sliders*, *Quantum Leap*, *Babylon 5*, even, heaven forbid, *Scooby Doo* and *Goober and the Ghost Chasers*. Look around and see the stereotype everywhere.

The so-called 'gritty' realism of recent soaps and docu-soaps (a particularly nasty modern term) fares no better, be it *Brookside*, *Casualty*, *Eastenders*, *Coronation Street*, or even radio dramas like *The Archers*. Within such popular 'factoids' the stereotype has shifted somewhat from tweed-wearing Oxbridge type to tight-trousered popular hero (flying at great speed across landscapes accompanied by the latest in technology and a sure belief in their ability to overturn established theory armed only with enigmatic look and a Jean Michel Jarre soundtrack), or the idiosyncratic, intellectual 'mad-professor', poorly attired and hairdresser-free. The former has developed considerably since the late 1970s (evolving strangely from the monotone weird-beard of the academic T.V. twilight zone), perhaps feeding off the glamorous world of cinema (itself feeding from the heroic pose of the 19th century archaeologist-explorers of the eastern Mediterranean) while the latter has been with us since at least the early years of the 20th century (evolving from the scatter-brain world of academia).

Confused? Let me explain.

Adventurers and eccentrics

Whilst the modern investigators of the past come in many various shapes and sizes, the prime, stereotypical pop culture archaeologist usually conforms to the individual as "adventurer" or "mild eccentric". This image can be traced back to the earliest days of archaeology and antiquarianism, (for antiquarianism, in most cases, read treasure hunting). Heinrich Schliemann (1822–1890) represents, for many, the best example of the adventurer eccentric, combining equal amounts of both (often in seriously large doses). A pioneer in early archaeological excavation, the German born Schliemann amassed a considerable personal fortune through his business dealings, before retiring, at the age of 41, to devote his life to archaeology, beginning the excavation of, what he believed to be the ancient, and semi-mythical, city of Troy, in 1870. Schliemann was single minded and passionate. He may not always have been right in his inter-pretations, and some have since questioned his motivation, but he was certainly a powerful character at the cutting edge of 19th century archaeological discovery.

Other shapers of the adventurer stereotype include characters such as Giovanni Belzoni (1778–1821), Howard Carter (1874–1939) and Leonard Woolley (1880–1960: see also Membury, this volume). Woolley, whose extensive fieldwork experience included sites in the Aegean, Egypt, Syria and Mesopotamia throughout the early decades of the 20th century, probably helped, more than any other archaeologist of the time, to install the popular dress code of the televisual (and for that matter celluloid) archaeologist. In the many photographs that exist of him, the image of dust covered, pith-helmeted, khaki-short wearing investigator of the past, working amidst the shattered remains of some of the worlds earliest, and most interesting, civilisations is certainly a striking one. Association with contemporary adventurer/explorers such as T. E. Lawrence (later "of Arabia") who worked with Woolley as archaeological supervisor between 1912 and 1914, certainly helped strengthen the stereotype for a British, European and American public hungry for "Boys Own" style adventure in exotic locations. Such imagery was built upon further through early cinematic experimentation and through popular fiction, a good example of which is Agatha Christie's 1936 Hercule Poirot mystery *Murder in Mesopotamia* (Christie's second husband was in fact archaeologist and director of the British School of Archaeology in Iraq, Max Mallowan, who had earlier been one of Woolley's assistants).

Figure 5.1 Petra: "the rose-red city, half as old as time". Romantic images such as this, of the El Khazneh ('Treasury of the Pharaoh') in Petra, established the concept of explorers stumbling across the remains of exotic 'lost cities', and helped inspire many of the writings of authors such as Edgar Rice Burroughs and H. Rider Haggard. © Bournemouth University.

Explorers of unknown lands

A more extreme version of the archaeologist adventurer within popular culture is "archaeologist as intrepid explorer": an individual battling through strange lands, far from the luxuries of home. The explorer is one who hacks their way through dense vegetation or treks across uncharted deserts, struggles against potent natural forces (and sometimes aggressive lost tribes), in order that they may reveal the half buried remains of long dead (and long forgotten) civilisations. This is a particularly emotive image, which frequently appears within late 19th century fiction (see Cohen Williams; this volume) and early 20th century cinema (see Membury; this volume).

The origins of the intrepid archaeological explorer stereotype within popular culture may be traced back to a series of adventures into Africa, Asia and South America throughout the 18th, 19th and early 20th centuries by individuals such as Jean Louis Burckhardt (1784–1817) and John Seely (1788–1824). Seely, a young British captain in the Bombay Native Infantry, led an expedition to the caves temples of Ellora, now a UNESCO World Heritage Site, 400 km to the north east of Bombay, combating jungles, mountains, fast flowing rivers, bandits and tigers. Burckhardt, a Swiss born adventurer, was the first western European in centuries to explore the 'lost' cities, castles and

Figure 5.2 Hiram Bingham, the ultimate archaeo-explorer and inspiration for Indiana Jones, on campaign in the Peruvian Andes searching for "Vilcapampa" – the legendary lost city of the Incas © Photo Multiphoto, Paris.

monumental remains of North Africa and Arabia, including the famous "rose-red" city of Petra. The fact that this eight year odyssey of secret note taking, observation and recording was achieved by Burckhardt whilst disguised as an Arab trader (with the alias Sheikh Ibrahim), only enhanced his reputation as an explorer and intelligence gatherer *par excellence.*

The biggest impact upon the world of pop culture archaeology, however, was probably from Karl Mauch (1837–1874) and Hiram Bingham (1878–1956). Mauch, a German geologist and surveyor working on the eastern coast of southern Africa, was the first European to record the remains of Great Zimbabwe, a monumental complex of enclosed stone buildings dominating the high plains of modern Zimbabwe. Mauch was convinced that the remains were 'Ophir', city of the Biblical Queen of Sheba, a belief which the new European governments in Africa were more than happy to endorse. From a modern perspective, Mauch's interpretation was, to be polite, rather outlandish (and at least we can now show it was totally wrong: the whole site being entirely African in origin), but to begin with its effect was explosive: here there was evidence of the literal truth of the Bible. Stories linking Solomon and Sheba to Great Zimbabwe took a new turn when H. Rider Haggard used the site as inspiration for his book *King Solomon's Mines* (1885). On a more sinister note, countries like Britain, Germany and the Netherlands could now point to remains of Great Zimbabwe and use it to legitimise Judaeo-Christian colonial rule in Africa.

If anyone has claim to have inspired the character of Indiana Jones, then it must surely be Hiram Bingham. Born in 1878, the American Professor of professor of history and politics at Harvard and Princeton Universities was also a captain in the Connecticut National Guard, a distinguished pilot during the First World War, serving in the Aviation Section, Signal Corps and attaining the rank of lieutenant colonel, commander of the flying school at Issoudun, France until 1918, lieutenant governor then governor of Connecticut, member of the United States Senate, a member of President Coolidge's Aircraft Board and naval training school lecturer during World

War Two. It is for his exploits in South America, however, as director of the Yale Peruvian Expedition (between 1909 and 1912), that Bingham is perhaps most famous. In the course of these expeditions, Bingham and his team investigated the fortified Inca sites of Choqqequirau and Ollantaytambo, and discovered the 'lost' cities of Machu Picchu, Vitcos and Espiritu Pampa.

Officers and gentlemen

Parallel with the explorer stereotype is the officer/ex-military gentleman character, also searching for excitement, adventure and information on the past. Arguably two of the foremost examples of this variant were Augustus Pitt Rivers (1827–1900) and Mortimer Wheeler (1890–1976). Pitt Rivers, usually referred to as the father of both British and also of scientific Archaeology, began his military career at Sandhurst, at the height of the British Empire, rising eventually to the rank of Lt. General. His inheritance of the Cranborne Chase estate in Wiltshire allowed him to devote much of his time and energy to archaeological investigation and the development of recording techniques, much of which was disseminated through self published books and self financed museums.

Wheeler, served as a major in the British army during the First World War and as a brigadier in Italy and North Africa during the Second. After the war, he became Director General of archaeology in India (until 1948). Renowned for his enthusiastic and spirited accounts in print and on television (he was in fact voted British T.V. personality of the year in 1954), Wheeler did more than any other archaeologist before to bring the subject to the forefront of public attention. His passion, wit and (so I'm reliably informed) immense sexual presence also helped to enforce the "archaeologist as officer and gentleman-style adventurer" stereotype so fed upon by pop culture until the arrival of Indiana Jones.

Wheeler and his contemporaries on the popular 1950s T.V. quiz show *Animal, Vegetable or Mineral*, also helped to develop the image of the deeply intellectual and loveable professor, increasingly out of sync with the real, if ephemeral, world, but wholly in connection with the worlds of long dead civilisations.

Figure 5.3 Mortimer Wheeler: T.V. personality of the year for 1954. © Sussex Archaeological Society

Nutty professors

A pop culture stereotype that, though commonly employed, is difficult to combine with the rugged explorer or military type, is the academic, or "nutty professor". This is 'academic' in the very worst sense of the word, for this fictional variant is one who is not conducting research to help or inform others, nor even trying to educate or communicate ideas to the world outside, no, this is a dull and totally dysfunctional individual. Academics within pop culture are the antithesis of excitement and adventure. They speak in monotonous tones about subjects in which no one is really that interested. These are people wholly obsessed with wilfully obscure areas of research. People who cannot articulate their theories. People who cannot even communicate successfully with other human beings.

Within the Indiana Jones trilogy of films, the areas of conflict between academic and action hero proved so mutually exclusive, that no attempt to combine them was made. Dr. Jones moves effortlessly from intensely dull academic, intoning to his students, in the film *Raiders of the Lost Ark* (1981), about prehistory in a way that is totally non-conducive to learning (the "Neo-Lithic" lecture is particularly memorable in this respect), to fully fledged adventurer, apparently by changing only his clothes and removing his glasses (whilst simultaneously ruffling his hair and growing stubble). A truly Clark Kent/Superman style metamorphosis.

Conflict between academic and action hero is further emphasised in the film *Stargate* and televisual offshoot *Stargate: SG1*. In both, the action hero is a military rough neck, Colonel Jack O'Neill, the academic, an Egyptologist called Daniel Jackson. Jackson is, to begin with, almost totally dysfunctional. He is hyper-intelligent, but cannot communicate any of his ideas. He does not, in any circumstances, relate to society. He has not experienced *life* in any shape or form. O'Neill is every bit the opposite: a hard-talking, all action, rugged adventurer. The central premise in both film and T.V. series is that both extremes must co-operate and work together in order to survive. In doing so they find respect for one another (and who knows, maybe even love).

Tomb-raiders

The strongest influence on the way in which archaeologists are perceived in popular culture today, however, is that of Howard Carter (1874–1939), not necessarily from the man himself, talented though he undoubtedly was, but from the nature of his discoveries. At 4pm on the afternoon of November 26th 1922, Carter broke through the sealed door to the tomb of the Egyptian pharaoh Tutankhamun, and assured his place in history. The unparalleled richness of the artefacts preserved within the tomb caused a media storm around the world, making archaeology headline news and generating the new craze of "Tut-mania".

Carter's discoveries and the reporting frenzy that followed helped strengthen the image of the archaeologist in the public mind: archaeologist as intrepid explorer excavating in exotic locations; archaeologists battling against the odds (Carter had suffered a number of severe setbacks throughout his career); archaeologist as artefact hunter; archaeologists as despoilers of ancient tombs; and, perhaps most significantly

Figure 5.4 Howard Carter investigating the sarcophagus of Tutankhamun in 1923. © The Griffith Institute, Ashmolean Museum, Oxford. Photograph No. 770.

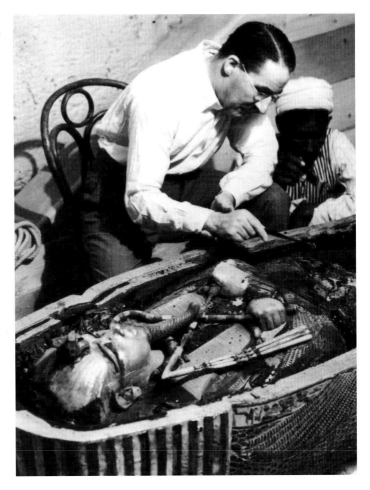

for the way in which the character would evolve within popular culture, archaeologist as doom-bringer.

Stories of a curse surrounding the resting place of the boy king Tutankhamun, were quick to surface. In 1923, a few months after the opening of the tomb, Lord George Carnarvon, Carter's employer and financier of the excavation project, died in Cairo. The exact cause of death remains uncertain, though many believe it to have been due to an infection caused by an insect bite. Needless to say, the press had a field day, and soon everyone around the globe was debating the nature of the ancient curse. There was a blackout across Cairo the moment Carnarvon died, it was said. On his estate back in Britain, his dog howled in despair and fell dead. King Tut, when he was finally unwrapped, was seen to possess a facial wound on the same cheek as the insect bite that felled Carnarvon.

By the mid 1930s, the media had credited a total of 21 fatalities to the curse of the boy pharaoh. These included Carter's personal secretary, and a number of Carnarvon's relatives. Strangely Carter himself, together with the majority of the excavation team and those present at the official opening of the tomb and the sarcophagus, appeared to emerge largely unscathed, Carter himself dying at the age of 66 in (what we assume to be) entirely natural circumstances. For the purposes of the story, however, this did not seem to matter. The ancient curse had arrived, and from this moment on archaeologists could simply do no good in the minds of the cinema going public.

The evil that archaeologists do

Pretty much all the early cinematic references to the archaeological community relate to tomb raiders: thoroughly nasty and unscrupulous individuals who are really up to no good. These images were so powerful, that we should not be surprised that they permeate all aspects of pop culture, so that the archaeologist of television, radio and the printed word is, more often than not, a doom-bringer. The doom-bringer/curse-invoker archaeologist is the stock character in many episodes of *Doctor Who*, *X Files*, *Star Trek* and other long running televisual syndications. Throughout the whole history of cinema and television, with the possible exception of Indiana Jones (whose case for the prosecution we will examine later), it is perhaps a sobering thought for those involved in the profession, that the pop culture archaeologist is systematically portrayed as "the bad guy".

Archaeologists, and those actively engaged in the pursuit of the past, may like to view themselves as public servants or (in some extreme cases) as heroes bringing the dead back to life, but the media continues to take this term somewhat literally. Archaeologists are the villains. They are tampering with forces that they do not understand. They are the people who raid the tomb, irrespective of the wishes and warnings of the local or indigenous population, awaken the dead, activate the curse, and bring down some immense supernatural nasty upon the world. Ultimately it is left to others, usually the FBI, the United Nations, journalists, time-travelling tourists, or Joe and Josephine Bloggs, to clean up the mess, destroy the curse and put the monster back into its sealed box.

In this popular and oft repeated televisual scenario, the archaeologist does not survive to the end credits. Usually they do not make it past the opening sequence. Their primary role is to disturb the monster, unleash the terror and die horribly (in fact they're usually the first in an ever spiralling body count). And what is the reaction to the doom-bringer's sudden (and wholly expected) demise?: "Good riddance". The bad guy gets it and everyone goes away happy.

Hunting the artefact: "Have you found anything yet?"

Another side-effect of Carter's and Carnarvon's Egyptian discoveries is the belief that modern archaeologists solely pursue artefacts. Not just scrappy bits of knapped flint or broken pot mind you, but the big gold, jewel encrusted rings, necklaces and diadems of ancient royalty. Who wants to know about the eating preferences of a 12th century peasant when you can gawp at some expensive bit of diamond-studded kit? Who wants Roman footwear when you can drool over a Roman emperor's gold plated jock strap (hopefully not whilst he's wearing it).

The obsession that the media has with rich artefacts and the acquisition of personal wealth, as exemplified by the monotonous series of "Man out walking dog finds 10 Million pound Roman coin hoard" or "Woman out jogging finds ring worth £6 Million!" style headline (best defined as National Lottery Syndrome), may be traced back to the earliest antiquarian investigators in Europe, Africa and the Middle East, and to a comment allegedly made by Howard Carter upon the initial breaking down of King Tut's tomb door in 1922:

> Lord Carnarvon: "Can you see anything?"
> Carter: "Yes, *wonderful things*."

Certainly the quantity and preservation of artefacts within the Egyptian tomb was amazing, and they took well over a decade to fully catalogue, but surely archaeology today means more than this? The contents of a tomb tells us how less than 0.0000001% of the population prepared for the afterlife. What about the ordinary mortals, the lesser elements in society. How did they live? What did they eat? What did they believe? Where did they defecate/copulate/educate etc? A rich tomb, coin hoard, or votive deposit cannot always be relied upon to provide such vital information. This does not concern "The News". Rarely does landscape archaeology, environmental archaeology, forensic archaeology or any of the other "ologies" that the profession are

Figure 5.5 "Wonderful things": View of the antechamber to Tutankhamun's tomb, with objects still in situ. © The Griffith Institute, Ashmolean Museum, Oxford. Photograph No. 712.

engaged in (and debate endlessly at conferences), impinge upon a good news story about how someone 'made it' thanks to the chance discovery of a long dead Viking.

This of course manifests itself in the ever common question directed to archaeologists in the field: "have you found anything yet?". Often the reply "Yes we've found 670 postholes suggesting the presence of a major Neolithic timber structure unparalleled in this part of the world", is met with a blank expression, embarrassed silence, quiet clearing of the throat and a "But have you found anything yet?". Have you found any nice finds, personal objects to link us with those who lived and died in the past? Found any gold/silver/or other precious things? Sad to say, but when I go to the hairdresser (I don't get this look by my own efforts you understand), I tend to avoid saying that "I'm an archaeologist" because this is guaranteed to provoke the response "Really? What interesting things have you found recently?" and I just know that the recording of a major prehistoric flint knapping scatter from the chalk hills of southern Britain really does not live up to the expectation that should have been battling Nazis in the African desert for control of an important Biblical artefact.

The legacy of Indiana Jones is immense. The trilogy of films *Raiders of the Lost Ark* (1981), *Indiana Jones and the Temple of Doom* (1984), and *Indiana Jones and the Last Crusade* (1989) have, as has already been noted, spawned a plethora of books, television series (especially *Young Indiana Jones*), radio shows, web sites, computer games as well as generating the expected 'look' of an archaeologist and generating a whole host of televisual imitators. Perhaps the most successful imitator of the good Dr. Jones has been Lara Croft, star of the *Tomb Raider* series of computer games (and soon to be a major Hollywood movie). Let's not beat around the bush here: Croft is a grade A1

Figure 5.6 One thing you can be sure of in the world of Pop Culture archaeology, be it Egypt, South America or Mars, is the certainty of pyramid-shaped tombs containing lots of luverly loot. © Photo Multiphoto, Paris.

psychopath. The computer game has been successful because it tapped into to what most game-heads want: adventure, excitement, lots of weapons and killing, oh and a heroine who appears to have a deep seated dislike of clothes (to be fair the same can be said of Dr. Jones who rarely seems able to keep a shirt on his back). Archaeology is here the backdrop, providing the initial drive to the story ("you must find the following") and the setting (tomb/lost city etc) within which a large quantity of wolves, dinosaurs, alligators and other humans may be mercilessly gunned down.

At the end of the day, both *Raiders* are about desecration of burial grounds and looting of artefacts. That may sound harsh, but although Jones and Croft may represent a rare case of 'good guys' in the realm of the Pop Culture archaeologist (good in that: "Yes so they may both be gun-toting loonies, but hey, at least they're saving important aspects of our cultural heritage from bad gun-toting loonies"), they are both obsessed with the single artefact above any other concern. The Ark of the Covenant and the Holy Grail represent two such 'things' that Dr. Jones wanted to possess (even if this can be justified as saving them from the clutches of the Nazis in order that they may be placed 'in a museum'). And what about that South American tomb at the beginning of the film *Raiders of the Lost Ark* (1981)? Did the good Dr. Jones record the context of the tomb or the nature of the wall carvings? Did he photograph anything? Did he fill in a context sheet? Did he ever take out his notebook and actually write anything in it? Did he buggery. I suppose that *Single Context Recorder* may well be a significantly more dull game than *Tomb Raider*, but at least it would be closer to what archaeologists really do.

What to wear on an expedition

It is important, when planning an expedition, to decide what you are going to wear. For the pop culture archaeologist the choice is simple: pith helmet and infeasible khaki-coloured shorts. Interestingly, no one has ever felt it necessary to ask *why* such archaeologists require unceasing quantities of camouflage (presumably, whilst on expedition, they really don't want to be seen by members of the public, who may ask them embarrassing questions). The pith-helmet and shorts, both covered in a liberal sprinkling of ancient dust, is of course a fashion stereotype not just of the archaeologist, but of the colonial explorer in general (early *Tarzan* movies often give the impression that at least half of Africa was populated by pith-helmeted types – perhaps it was?).

It is the archaeologist however, certainly in the days before Hiram Bingham and Indiana Jones gave us the leather jacket, hat and quasi-beard, who kept the pith helmet alive throughout the 20th century. If anything this particular piece of designer headgear has, in recent years, become the lazy shorthand for the archaeologist. Put one on a televisual, cinematic or cartoon character (as per the publicity for 1999 *The Rugrats movie*, based on a popular kids T.V. show, which contained an image of a 2 year old American child in a khaki outfit and pith helmet) and the implication is clear: 'Adventure', 'Exploration' and 'Excitement', possibly combined with a liberal dollop of 'Treasure'.

Today the clothing choice has expanded somewhat. We've noted the battered jacket

Figure 5.7 A well planned expedition will always provide a good supply of pith helmets, mummified bodies and native workers © Photo Multiphoto, Paris.

and hat of Dr. Jones and the tight-fitting costumes preferred by Ms Croft for their fieldwork, but recent pop culture archaeologists have also been noted wearing the multi-pocketed outfits so beloved by modern day explorers. In a way fiction does here seem to mirror reality, for the majority of those engaged in archaeological fieldwork in Britain throughout the 1980s and 90s were clearly (and distinctively) marked by the almost tribal use of disused military attire from NATO or former eastern-bloc countries. You weren't a REAL archaeologist if you did not possess at least one pair of West German issue combat trousers (part worn being best) complete with those air holes round the groin (what did German soldiers do that made them so sweaty in this area?), a Middle-Eastern style scarf or bandanna, an East German or Soviet style hat (complete with ear protection), big clumpy boots (taken from a parachutist) and a nice German or Czechoslovakian shirt with bizarre central logo. Oh and multiple facial piercings.

The pop culture academic (or arm chair) archaeologist has never really been confronted with such a worry over how to look. The majority of those appearing on film or T.V. felt secure in their corduroy or tweed jackets (with leather elbow guards), nice trousers and sensible shoes. Oh and if the look could be finished off with a good pair of steel-rimmed spectacles, to show how much reading and research you do, then that would be just peachy. Unfortunately the pop culture look for action or academic archaeologist has yet to translate to the medium of factual T.V. (the majority of documentary style, televisual archaeologists appear to have been plucked straight from a dodgy 1970s programme on the importance of whelk farming in Iceland).

How to dig and what to take on an expedition

So you've got your wardrobe sorted. What other things do you need to take on your archaeological pop culture exploration to Egypt/Abydos/Skaro? Multi-pocketed trousers or a back pack of some kind, are of course very useful for storing all those artefacts you hope to unearth (most pop culture archaeologists do not appear to possess finds bags or any other form of storage container), but is there anything you may require in order to help you actually find that lost city or break down the doors to that alien pyramid?

The pop culture archaeologist apparently suffers from a severe lack of modern technology. Conversely (perhaps perversely, seeing that most pop culture archaeologists conduct their work in *the future*) the world of the contemporary archaeologist has benefited greatly from the latest technological advances, from geophysical prospection to Global Positioning via Virtual Reality. The fictional, pop culture archaeologist has no geophysical plot to help them locate their site. They do not possess robotic excavators. They do not have transmat beams to instantly teleport sensitive artefacts to the conservation laboratory. They do not, in some cases, even appear to have a compass.

The pop culture archaeologist works in narrow, irregular sized (and often dangerously deep) trenches, most apparently having been dug at random (though having said that they do seem to be worryingly good at finding things). Even in the futuristic worlds of *Star Trek*, there are no new ways to investigate buried remains. Traditional shovels and pick axes would seem to be the height of the sophisticated Starfleet tool repertoire. Curiously the trowel, a tool so beloved by archaeologists today, is almost always curiously absent from the pop culture archaeologist's kit (or if it is present it's the kind of trowel that could safely move an entire spoil heap in one single flick of the wrist). They do not record things as they dig through them. There are no cameras, planning frames or context sheets. There are sometimes notebooks, but these are more akin to diaries, recording their own personal, subjective viewpoint, rather than objective ways of noting changes in soil colour or texture.

Weaponry? Now that's a different matter entirely. If you want to arm yourself prior to commencing your dig (and lets face it, if you're wearing combat gear, why not go the whole hog?), then there's lots on offer. Rifles, pistols, Uzi 9 mm's, lasers, stasers, death-rays, quantum torpedoes, pop culture archaeologists have got the lot. They also seem to possess an unending amount of alcohol which, though actually (if rather unfortunately) a rather accurate reflection of REAL life, is not the sort of thing you really want around if you intend to carry huge quantities of lethal hardware with you on your expedition.

The most recent brand of toy produced by the toy manufacturer Lego perhaps demonstrates, more clearly than anything else, what is expected of a pop culture archaeologist on expedition. The *Lego Adventurers* range has, for its main character a stubble-chinned, battered hat and khaki-uniform wearing explorer, by the name of *Johnny Thunder* whilst the female of the species, *Miss Pippin Read,* wears green pith helmet, uniform and lipstick. He raids tombs in Egypt. She raids tombs in South America. Both possess the kit necessary for fieldwork in these areas, namely rifles, pistols, dynamite, magnifying glasses and a shovel (they don't seem to be carrying alcohol, but then hey this is a kid's toy). Other stock characters in the expanding *Adventurers* range include *Dr. Kilroy*, an elderly professorial type with big white moustache and sideburns, *Dr. Lightening*, a white-suited (and white pith helmeted), monocle and bow tie-wearing, academic, *Senor Palamar*, a villainous art collector type in Panama hat and cream suit and *Rudo Villano*, another baddy who seems to have the same basic fashion sense as *Johnny Thunder*, but (in classic Western-style) favours a black hat, greater stubble, more intense frown and a nasty facial scar.

Reality check

Factual archaeological programming in Britain has gone some way to, at least partially, dispelling the myth of the pop culture archaeologist. *Time Team* and *Meet the Ancestors* have shown the importance of survey, the nature of digging and interpretation, as well as the often laborious, though no less important, world of post excavation. *Time Team* is also notable for bringing a new word into the English language: 'Geophys'. Somewhere between 3 and 5 million regularly watch these programmes in Britain (though I'm told the numbers are rising), so the message of what the profession is about, as well as showing that "it is quite fun and exciting thank you" (entertainment and education not always being mutually exclusive) *is* getting across at last, especially to those who would not normally visit an archaeological or historical site.

The influence of *Time Team* on society may also be detected within the framework of pop culture itself. In 1999, a few episodes of *Coronation Street*, the most successful and long running soap opera in Britain, contained an archaeologist. The character that appeared was not the stereotypical clean cut, upper class, tweed-wearing, dysfunctional academic buffoon that used to be wheeled out as a typical archaeologist in British pop culture, neither was he a gung-ho action hero of the Hollywood genre. No, the important thing with this gem from recent pop culture was that the fictional archaeologist portrayed was a down-to-earth, scruffy, dishevelled (but loveable), intellectual with a keen wit and, perhaps most significantly, a regional accent. If one wants to assess the impact of the new archaeologies upon T.V. (especially *Time Team*), then one need look no further.

Admittedly the *Coronation Street* character was affected by all the usual problems that a pop culture archaeologist faces with regards to recording (and the general lack of it). His 'site' was a real sight, which no self-respecting professional could tolerate. He had no understanding of current legislation or Planning Policy Guidelines (though this could be said of many people working in the profession today). He was also, as with most fictional characters, blessed with incredible powers of interpretation, being able to deduce the presence, not only of a Roman military unit known only as the

"Nero garrison" (whoever they were), but also the "villa and bath house of Paulinus", and all from just two pieces of pottery, an animal bone and a piece of rusty iron. With insight like this he should be offered his own T.V. series.

So What?

A recent discussion on an archaeological related internet mailbase became extremely heated when the topic of fiction came up. "So what?" seems to have been the current consensus of opinion: "So what if the public sees archaeologists as heroic Indiana Jones figures?"; "So what if the media thinks we're only after gold?"; "So what if the writers and broadcasters of fiction see us as villains and bad guys?"; "It doesn't matter. Its not real life".

Yes *Coronation Street, Eastenders, Emmerdale, the Archers* and other pop culture soaps aren't real life (well done for noticing by the way). They are fiction. Most people who watch and avidly follow these series know this, but prefer fiction to the daily grind of real life. Most followers of *Star Trek* and the *X-files* know that the worlds within these programmes aren't real, but find them a useful substitute for real life. The main issue in this respect is that *Coronation Street* regularly attracts an audience in Britain of around 30 million. *Star Trek, Doctor Who* and other syndicated SciFi dramas attract significantly more through broadcast repeats and sales around the globe. More people watch and digest these stereotypical views of 'the archaeologist' in these prime slices of televisual pop culture, than will ever see the reality of the professional at work.

Stereotypes are, by their nature, merely exaggerated versions of reality. Stereotypical doctors, estate agents, law enforcers, fire-fighters, teachers and solicitors all appear with great regularity within pop culture, especially within the world of televised fiction. Most stereotype professionals, however unrealistic these portrayals may be, are deeply ingrained within the public consciousness, to be regurgitated again and again by the writers of fiction. In the majority of cases, however damaging the stereotype can be, we can safely acknowledge that: "Doctors/teachers/solicitors etc aren't actually like that", because in most of our daily lives we encounter doctors, teachers, solicitors etc on a very real basis. At least 98% of the population probably do not regularly encounter archaeologists, so the reality (or unreality) of the stereotype cannot ever be satisfactorily, or indeed objectively, assessed.

If the public perception of what an archaeologist is and what they do is coming primarily through fiction, rather than solid fact, then what, if anything, should archaeologists be doing to counter such rampant negativity? Archaeologists could acknowledge the fact that their pop culture representative is a treasure hunting hero/ gun toting psychopath/doom-bringing villain and perhaps work within this (although perhaps not to the extent of wearing battered leather jackets and carrying whips on site), educating people through this emotive imagery, towards the reality of genuine discovery: "The past is a vibrant and exciting place for a modern audience, and you don't need Indiana Jones to provide unnecessary and wholly artificial hype". Alternatively, the archaeological community could openly reject the pop culture character, explain why and attempt to create an image that they are happier with and which they find closer to reality. To some extent, the recent spate of archaeological and anthropological television programming (both terrestrial and satellite) is successfully achieving this particular aim, bringing archaeological discovery to the fore and altering the whole nature of the fictional pop culture persona.

Or, archaeologists could (as the majority have traditionally done) totally ignore pop culture, only sticking their heads above the spoil heap long enough to scoff "It's just fiction – REAL archaeology isn't like that at all". After all, the pop-culture archaeologist lives in a world of adventure and excitement. They are thrill-seeking egotists, obsessed with the importance of their own discoveries and their own personal fame. They destroy the career of anyone who gets in their way. They desire vast personal wealth through the accumulation of prized artefacts. They are people who refuse to communicate their ideas and discoveries to the public. They are people who care not one jot about society, and who could quite happily endanger large numbers of people just so they could dig the site/tomb/burial ground they wanted. They are totally dysfunctional. They are scheming, violent and frequently veering close to alcoholism. They are villains. They are misfits. They are intrinsically evil. And we know that, in reality, archaeologists just aren't like that.

Are they?

Miles Russell is a senior Lecturer in Archaeology in the School of Conservation Sciences, Bournemouth University. He is obsessive about *Dr. Who*, industrial music and Neolithic flint mines (usually at the same time).

PART TWO

PAST, PRESENT AND PARALLELS

And so we leave inner space. It is now time to examine alternative places and timelines. It is time to visit new worlds containing strange and wonderful, and even sometimes strangely familiar places, customs and people. It is time to leave our world and move on.

6

A novel prehistory

Julia Murphy

The novel using prehistoric scenarios first arose from the post-Darwinian Victorian era, when authors visualised their explorer characters stumbling upon ancient civilisations. Over a century later, archaeologists have very different understandings of prehistory, but to what extent have novelists taken on board these new interpretations?

How do we perceive a past which has no written history, a past which is created through heterogenous networks of concepts and media – from primary sources of material culture to secondary sources such as guidebooks and Hollywood films? What is the relationship between the stories that archaeologists tell and the stories that the wider public understand? Instead of arguing for wholesale subscription to the "universal truths" of prehistory (the totality of which we may never understand), I will in this chapter consider why public consumption of prehistory often fails to reflect the diversity of past possibilities. Notions of cavemen clubbing their womenfolk over the head, or white-hooded druids performing sacred rituals at Neolithic sites still abound, and whilst regular press releases or television documentaries all strive to expose these myths, they still persist and refuse to be pushed easily away.

Of course, there are many reasons why people tend to believe the stories of this mythical past. One reason is because media interpretations derived from film-makers and writers of fiction would have us believe in fantasy worlds where, for instance, humans and dinosaurs lived side by side (as in *The Flintstones* or *The Land That Time Forgot*). More philosophically, this is also because of the way we view 'the other', this era about which little is generally known and which is therefore strange to us. According to Ricoeur (1984) we write the past in terms of the same, other, or analogue, and these three tropes of historical writing are distinguished by their differing relationships between past and present. If I elaborate on this using *The Flintstones* again, here we have two nuclear families living in the framework of nine-to-five jobs with familiar hobbies such as bowling, and the latest in prehistoric home appliances; altogether a very familiar scene. The unfamiliar past would be the representations of prehistoric humans as grunting hairy savages, although it could be argued that aspects of the familiar are bound to creep into these representations, because after all common themes emerge such as the need to eat, something every human understands and identifies with.

In this chapter I will ask whether are we destined to tell the same stories again and again, as products of our own time. Will we always impose our present day ideologies onto interpretations of the past? Can we escape the gender stereotypes that appear far too often in archaeological writing? In order to consider these questions, I will compare the reconstructions of the prehistoric past in the form of novels to the methods of writing stories of the future, works of science fiction. The similarities between science fiction and novels reconstructing prehistory already exist: the tale set in an unpleasant place where populations are controlled by terror or brainwashing; the lone rebel standing up to an oppressive social order; and the increasing technological sophistication could be the plot of Jean Auel's *Clan of the Cave Bear* as much as it could describe George Orwell's *Nineteen Eighty-Four* or Aldous Huxley's *Brave New World*.

Whilst sifting through several commentaries on science fiction, I frequently came across authors who appear to believe that the genre of writing is a male domain. For example when Edward James comments in the introduction to *Science Fiction in the 20th Century* that he will "not use 'she' and 'her' as the generic term for authors and critics because it is inappropriate when women remain in the minority in both professions" (James 1994). The reasoning behind this assumption is not stated, although it is a common preconception of science fiction, but maybe there lies a belief that men and machines must go together. So what happens when the magnificent machines or industrial wastelands are absent from a work of science fiction? Of course that depends on how science fiction is defined, but in the case of novels that reconstruct prehistory by imagining different worlds in different times with different technologies from our own, they are generally classified as works of historical romance, especially if written by a woman, and particularly if the publisher chooses to use the words "sweeping" and "epic" on the book's cover.

I will here consider three particular novels that reconstruct prehistory. Each maintains some use of archaeological evidence to a certain extent, but each author uses the archaeology to create very different pictures of the past. The first novel I will look at provides an interpretation of the Neolithic, whilst the next two are based on the emergence of modern humans. Considering that, like the authors of science fiction, the only boundaries to the type of societies that these authors create are placed there by their imaginations, the interpretations they present are often quite familiar.

Novel 1: Early in Orcadia

The first novel is *Early in Orcadia* by Naomi Mitchison, published in 1987. This is an incredibly thoughtful novel with a lot of author intervention and honesty about the limitations placed on those who interpret the past, and as such she presents a variety of possible models for the small scale societies she reconstructs, cleverly woven in with the evidence that the prehistoric Orkney Islands have left behind. Unfortunately, I am about to do this book no justice at all by tearing out the main themes, but it necessary for the overall picture.

Life for the inhabitants of Orkney five to six thousand years ago revolved around desperately and constantly finding things to eat, sex and child-birth, an awareness of death and spirits, story-telling and singing, a gendered division of labour, and a curiosity about what was over the sea which was coupled with a slow process of innovation and invention. These people lived with a great sense of urgency because of the constant struggle to find enough food and wood for their fires, and this involved the men looking for wild beasts great and small, whilst the women's role included doing the cooking, searching for wood in the forest while the men went along to protect them from the wild animals, making pots, bread and porridge, because "Grain was the women's thing" (Mitchison 1987, 15). This did not stop the men begging for grain every now and again so they could make it "come alive so that it sang in their heads" (Mitchison 1987, 16). When some of the people do venture to a nearby island, the first thing they do is make preparations for food, rather than explore their new home.

Although throughout this novel it is clear that it is written from a female's point of view, as Mitchison is sympathetic to the women's excessive labouring whilst the men are often depicted as lazy, she still falls back on stereotypical gendered divisions of labour (i.e. man-the hunter, woman-the-gatherer), and this even shows in the characters' names. The men have names of action, such as Hands, Hammer, Great Hunter, Catcho and Fishfish, whilst the women have names pertaining to their appearance or relationship to men, such as Thinlegs, Barebum, Sister, Sweetlips, Lovelove, and even Metoo. With the gradual innovations, it is a man who develops the model of the boat, and a woman who sees a possibility for darning or weaving with wool.

This is not to say that women lose out in terms of power relations, although at first it does seem that the head of the community is, by lineage, always a male, and the impression given when the newcomers arrive at The Shining to find just one woman and her children is that without the menfolk she is incapable of building a proper burial place, or maintaining the livestock, or remembering the proper rituals. However, Mitchison does give us a variety of societal models where the most revered in a society may be either The Big Woman who is also the Good Woman, or the Sun Man, or the Moon Woman, or the Headman, but it is interesting to note that this implies a blatant hierarchy amongst the tiny populations.

Each village contains a community which has a strong sense of their own past, which emerges in the stories they tell, the songs they sing, the rituals they act out, and their explanations for doing things in particular ways: because it has always been done that way. Special songs and words accompany important actions such as sowing seeds and setting out to sea. Singing is a communal activity and both story-telling and dreams hold important places in the society, with hazy boundaries between these and reality, so that there is always a fear that speaking dreams out loud will mean they come true.

This superstition of fear emerges most strongly in the rituals connected with the dead. Although the people have no fear of death themselves, because it is so common amongst their society and more babies die rather than survive, the fear is generated by the stone-house where the bones are left out for excarnation. It is thought that the spirits will be reborn in new children, and there is later a scene describing a young pregnant girl being led into the tomb to feel for an artefact that was placed there along with a set of bones, and the artefact she picks means that its previous owner will be reincarnated in her baby.

Along with these superstitions and rituals is mention of the Orkney Islanders worshipping eagles, but only the most prestigious members of the community know the real significance of this, and it seems to be a way of suppressing the rest of the population by fear. This is an attempt by the author to link her story to the evidence from the Orkney Islands, which includes the eagle relics found in tombs and Isbister. In fact Mitchison must have paid close attention to the archaeological research when writing her novel, for she is accurate in her interpretations of climate and the stone tombs, but there are conflicting areas such as "the wild animals in the forest" theme, because the severe Orcadian winds would have prevented dense forestation, and there is no evidence of the dogs, bears and wolves that she mentions.

Moreover, there is a greater emphasis on the burial monuments than the famed Neolithic domestic architecture of Orkney, which is one of few surviving examples in Britain. So it seems that although Mitchison demonstrates the threads of common humanity which link us to these past ancestors throughout her novel, it is the differences, particularly the strange mortuary rituals, that she spends her time explaining.

Novel 2: The Inheritors

In the second novel, *The Inheritors* by William Golding, first published in 1955, we see a great difference in how the subjects of the book are treated by the author. It is set in a time when the Neanderthals may have co-existed with anatomically modern humans. Golding writes from the viewpoint of the Neanderthals, but relies heavily on the popular stereotype that has taken over from archaeological reality. His Neanderthals cannot think coherently or logically, an interpretation which owes more to the grunting caveman of comic-books and films than to the evidence which shows us that Neanderthals had larger brains than modern humans, something which would not have evolved if it did not have some use. His Neanderthals move and look like animals, and even the babies 'mew' instead of crying. They use natural rocks and twigs that are lying around instead of fashioning tools, and rely heavily on their incredible sense of smell. They do bury their dead, and have an earth mother goddess. The role of the women is linked to this goddess and the ability to produce life, whilst the men are responsible for making plans and issuing orders.

There are many ironies at work within the novel though, when it is not taken at such blatant face-value, one being that the character Lok, who finally becomes the leader of the tiny band of Neanderthals, manages to contribute to their destruction by choosing to ignore the wiser suggestions of his mate Fa. Golding is addressing much wider issues than those related to the disappearance of the Neanderthals, which is perhaps why he chooses to emphasise the differences between them and the new people, to which he attributes mannerisms and characteristics that would not be out of place in a modern romance or adventure novel. What is interesting though is that Golding saw the Neanderthal issue as an ideal vehicle on which to convey his concerns for modern society.

Both *The Inheritors* and *Early in Orcadia* rely heavily upon gendered hierarchies based on biologically determined oppositions, so that the women's major role of being associated with the domestic sphere is an emphasis of our society, because after all the material evidence does not tell us whether the men did the cooking or the women shared the chore.

Novel 3: The Clan of the Cave Bear

The third novel I will look at is *The Clan of the Cave Bear* by Jean M. Auel. It was first published in 1980, after the author had carried out three years of writing and research, which included a survival course, and these facts are mentioned at the beginning of the book so that the reader is well aware of the lengths Auel went to in order to "capture the flavour of the prehistoric past" (Auel 1980, 3). The story itself is about a Cro-Magnon girl called Ayla, who at the age of five, is separated from her people by an earthquake, but rescued by a group of Neanderthals who are searching for a new cave. They are a group of twenty with a strict hierarchy which dictates the order in which they process across the landscape, and have a male leader, as "Maintenance of the fire could only be entrusted to a male of high status" (Auel 1980, 28).

Iza, who takes in Ayla, is a medicine woman, yet Creb, the deformed magician, is of higher status because "A medicine woman was only an agent of the spirits, a magician interceded directly with them" (Auel 1980, 30). The reasons for this are explained: "The women relied on their men to lead, to assume responsibility, to make important decisions. The Clan had changed so little in a hundred thousand years, they were now incapable of change, and ways that had once been adaptations for convenience had become genetically set" (Auel 1980, 35). Auel seems to be denying free-will and the individualism amongst the Neanderthals, and relies heavily on out-dated inter-pretations of hairy stooped hominids, in spite of her years of research for the novel.

Indeed this seems to be emphasised in Auel's explanation for the large brains of the Neanderthals, as she postulates that the extra parts of the brain could store memory, which "made them extraordinary". In them, the unconscious knowledge of ancestral behaviour called instinct had evolved. Stored in the back of their large brains were not just their own memories, but the memories of their forebears. They could recall knowledge learned by their ancestors and, under special circumstances, they could go a step beyond. They could recall their racial memory, their own evolution, and when they reached back far enough, they could merge that memory that was identical for all and join their minds, telepathically (Auel 1980, 40). These memories, we are later informed (Auel 1980, 49) are "sex differentiated", because women do not need to know about hunting, and men do not need in-depth knowledge of plant-lore. Hunting is the ultimate symbol of masculinity, and boys become men when they make their first kill during a hunt (Auel 1980, 80–92). Auel treats the Neanderthals as ancestors of modern humans, but as an evolutionary dead-end who are co-existing with Cro-Magnons and yet are ultimately doomed as a species.

There are elements of individualism in some of the characters that Auel focuses on, but none is so particular as the focus on the blonde-haired blue-eyed Ayla, the seemingly sole surviving modern human of the earthquake. She is the free spirit who has to learn to succumb to the order of the Clan's hierarchy, where the birth of a girl is announced with regret (Auel 1980,138), and women cannot challenge the men's commands or demands. Females have to be, after all, "docile, subservient, unpretentious and humble" (Auel 1980, 195). Women have to refrain from all contact with men when they are menstruating, because their spirits are battling and could be harmful to the men.

Spirits feature quite heavily in the lives of the Clan members, and each person has a totem to protect them, the totem being a male animal. Ayla is set up to be a feminist heroine. However, although she is accepted as part of the Clan, her individuality is often emphasised, not just because she wants to do things differently, for example secretly learning to hunt with a sling when women are forbidden to even touch weapons, but also because she looks so different to the bow-limbed cave dwellers (by their standards ugly and too tall). To the modern reader, however: "her chin had the hint of a cleft, her lips were full and her nose straight and finely chiselled. Clear, blue-grey eyes were outlined with heavy lashes a shade or two darker than the golden hair that fell in thick soft waves to well below her shoulders, glimmering with highlights in the sun" (Auel 1980, 365). Not only does Auel describe a vision of an archetypal beauty, but her language also indicates that the reader is supposed to recognise Ayla as this romantic vision.

Her individuality and difference means that ultimately she is never really accepted by the Clan, in particular the son of the leader who is destined to be leader himself, Broud. Broud's character encompasses all that Auel sees wrong with the male of the species, as he is the man who most often exercises his rights to beat women when they disobey his commands, and he is the character that "relieves his needs" with an unwilling Ayla in a drawn-out and violent scene (Auel 1980, 371–373). When Ayla realises she is pregnant, she is suddenly fulfilled, as it is her, along with all the other women in the clan, ultimate desire to have a baby, and she thinks about "warm, cuddly nursing babies and her own warm, cuddly nursing baby" (Auel 1980, 382).

Because of their aims at individuality – in Broud's case a selfish desire to excel and be recognised as special, and in Ayla's case the natural curiosity of someone who is part of the forward-looking evolving hominids – both characters find themselves on the edge of their community, where achievements are usually for the common good of the Clan. This attitude is exemplified by the leader Brun, who puts the Clan before his personal glory. Auel hints throughout of the inevitable doom of the Neanderthals brought about by their unwillingness to change, and Broud is a personification of this stubborn refusal to adapt.

The Clan of the Cave Bear does demonstrate knowledge of prehistoric techniques, with detailed descriptions of, for example, flint-knapping, although this sits uncomfortably with the flights of fancy that Auel embarks on at times. These include the importing of modern notions and ideas which Auel projects back on to this prehistoric society. For example, at the Clan Gathering, the event where once in every seven years the various clans gather together, a cave bear is sacrificed , as this animal is the great protector of all the clans. Everyone has to drink some of the blood of the bear, and eat some of its flesh, to "be one with the Spirit of Ursus" (Auel 1980, 494) a ritual which is a reflection of the Christian symbolised ceremony. Each clan also has to compete against another in a Neanderthal-style Olympics, so that they may gain status, and "The men vied in wrestling, sling-hurling, bola-throwing, arm strength with use of a club, running, more complicated running-and-spear-stabbing races, tool-making, dancing, story-telling, and the combination of both in dramatic hunt re-enactments" (Auel 1980, 450)

However, Auel also ties in interpretations of evidence of her own stories, for example when describing the burial of Iza, the medicine woman. Because Iza had important status, she is buried in the clan's cave, and the tradition, so it seems, is to bury the dead with their tools so that the ghosts of all these buried things may walk in the place of the spirits, where they believe the dead go. However, Ayla insists that Iza's tools were not in the pots and bowls she used, but instead the flowers and plants she used in her medicine. Ayla ventures outside and gathers together some of the plants with which Iza made her "healing magic", but "she selected only those that were also beautiful, with colourful, sweet-smelling flowers (Auel 1980, 532). She finds them difficult to carry back to the cave and binds the flowers into a garland, which she then lays in the trench next to the crouched, foetal-form of Iza's body. Auel here has used the well-known example of what archaeologists have termed the "flower burial", from the cave site of Shanidar in Iraq, where pollen grains were found around the buried body.

When we are told about how flints were knapped, the tone of the writing changes to one which is more "text-book", because Auel zooms in on a specific focus rather than adhering to her narrative format. This touches on one of the possible problems of conveying archaeological information in the form of a novel: that the narrative form demands a linear structure and a progression of a story which cannot entirely exclude speculation and fictional passages. In a sense, however, all archaeologies are fiction, telling particular stories depending on the interests or focus of the author, and expanding on the bare skeletons of evidence using different models.

Creating a fiction

Although the novel is an interesting medium for conveying information about the prehistoric past, it can be seen that they frequently rely on stereotypes, and they also encourage us to understand the past by seeking out the familiar and safe, the same rather than the other, if we follow Ricoeur's categorisation of historical writing (Ricoeur 1984). The major themes that emerge are discourses we recognise because it is the way we order our lives, and the authors concentrate on the shared areas of humanity such as the need to eat and the practice of burial rites rather than areas that are not so easy to understand.

The past is appropriate to reinforce present social positions, so that when we ask why women are expected to prepare the family's meals, we look to these inter-pretations of the past and are told that it is because it has always been so. However, can we really imagine a past that is so different from our own experiences of living and being in the world? Can we dissociate ourselves from the baggage of our own existence in order to imagine something which may be so far removed from our own lives? To write a history as "other" rather than "same", we should not be looking for the similarities between past and present, but rather it should be an attempt to recover temporal difference. However, was the past really so alien? Surely there are essential aspects of humanity that remain, such as those we can imagine on an individual basis: the discomfort of being cold and damp in an incessantly rainy climate, or the ache of hunger when there is no food.

Ricoeur's third category of historical writing is analogy, where our present day efforts only capture elements of the past and construct them into a narrative, so that it is the structure of the methods of story-telling which dictates how that story is told, rather than aspects of historical reality bursting through and ordering themselves into narrative (Riceour 1984). What is written is not an attempt to reconstruct the past, but rather something symbolising the past. It can be seen that the novels show that the past is the same and the past is different, but to analyse them in this way merely sets up a dichotomy of same/difference. Can we define the methods of writing the past in this way as "past-as-analogue"? Novels are certainly different in communicating their ideas and messages from textbooks, which often veer away from constructing their contents as narrative. Chapters and pages are broken down into sections to segment and characterise topics such as trade or domestic architecture. This artificial segregation of the fragments of past life often gives no clearer picture of the past than the novel, which is even honest enough to proclaim itself to be a work of fiction. After all, we are creating our knowledge of the past rather than finding it through the fragments of material culture.

However, the key to escaping the restrictions of writing about the past as defined by Ricoeur (1984) could well be found in feminist science fiction theory, which naturally leads on from the questions that science fiction has always tackled, for instance what it means to be human. These exciting theories propose methods which archaeologists could use to escape the reliance on explanation using, for example, gendered division of labour, and a move away from the stereotypical roles so often assigned to the unknown people of the past. Science fiction offers opportunities to explore societal models other than those caught in the binary oppositions of patriarchies and matriarchies.

Authors such as Donna Haraway and Vonda McIntyre see this escape from gendered characters through the use of cyborgs, whereas C. J. Cheeryh creates a character who is a genetically engineered human and blurs distinctions between human and alien. Octavia Butler uses "shapeshifter" characters who can be either male or female, and Ursula Le Guin writes of humans on a far planet who are hermaphrodites except when they are in season. The marginalised "others" of gender and race are primary concerns of these authors, so that definitions of otherness are broken down and are no longer appropriate. William Gibson's "cyberspace" metaphor gives us a conceptual space in which gender and identity can be reconsidered (Wolmark 1994).

Of course I am not proposing that we use shapeshifters in our interpretations of the Bronze Age. Rather that archaeologists take on board the possibilities that exist for the wealth of different societal models instead of merely displacing our societal model, generally a default of patriarchal society, and using it as a framework to build up a picture of the past from the material culture. Archaeologists often categorise material culture as gendered items when there is no evidence for this. Outside of burial archaeology, objects cannot be associated with male or female activities, and yet there are still cases where the archaeological record shows evidence of weaving activities, for example, and archaeologists interpret this as evidence of "women's work", where there is no reason for this assumption aside from the archaeologists' own experiences. To escape this trap of assigning gender roles in prehistory, a different approach to archaeological writing needs to be taken.

Similarly, when archaeologists interpret the prehistoric past, there cannot be any characters, only individuals, that may be identified from burial remains or even preserved footprints and fingerprints pressed in clay, and yet we know the past was peopled with numerous individuals in their different societies. Ursula Le Guin believes that there is a similar lack of character in science fiction, and that they exist as "masses" waiting to be "led by their superiors" (Le Guin 1989, 83). Where there are characters, they often exist because they are different, and Le Guin asks "what about the cultural and the racial Other? This is the Alien everybody recognises as alien, supposed to be the special concern of SF" (Le Guin 1989, 84). If we look at the way characters are dealt with in the novels about prehistory, there is a general tendency to view the lead characters as different in some way, and the story often takes place against a backdrop of dramatic change, such as the last of the Neanderthals or the shift from hunting and gathering to agriculture. Ayla in *The Clan of the Cave Bear* is an alien creature to the Neanderthals who raise her, and as a result she is alienated.

Novels differ from the text book writing of archaeology because they concentrate on individuals, even if these characters are symbolic. It is not possible for authors to give these people personalities from the archaeological evidence. We have to zoom in, as Auel does in her flint-knapping descriptions, on the material evidence which is left in the archaeological record, and ponder and recreate the technologies at the exclusion of the individual whose hands chipped the stones together, irrespective of whether those hands were female or male.

The problem of character in stories recreating prehistory can be overcome if the author concentrates on a commentary which is generalisation, with characters who are representative rather than uniquely individual, as Ayla in the *Earth's Children* goes on to be in subsequent novels where she alone is responsible for many of the innovations in prehistory such as the domestication of animals and the invention of new tools. But we are still left with stereotypically gendered interpretations.

Naomi Mitchison's *Early in Orcadia* overcomes some of the obvious problems associated with the structure of the novel by presenting a variety of societal models, all of which could be possible interpretations of the material evidence. However, as I have demonstrated, these novels rely on a familiar view of the past, in much the same way that science fiction writing of previous generations used recognisable societal models and largely existed in patriarchal worlds. The view from the present, whether to the past or the future, was largely a reflection rather than a consideration of alternative societies. But science fiction has found a way out of the reliance on gendered stereotypes and the see-saw of power struggles between women and men.

This is not to write women or men out of prehistory, but rather to halt the false assignment of gendered tasks onto the unknown members of past societies, which authors of fiction and archaeologists alike seem compelled to do.

Indeed through politicising the understanding of science fiction, "it has drawn on feminist analysis of the construction of gendered subjectivity in order to suggest possibilities for more plural and heterogenous social relations and power structures continue to marginalise women" (Wolmark 1994, 2). In addition to this, by projecting onto the past the assumption of gender determined by biological sex, there is no allowance for the multitude of possibilities that might have been, with gender no dependent on biology, but as transient phases in different societal set-ups.

The application of feminist theory to science fiction has led to traditional binary oppositions being challenged, such as the dual definition of 'alien' as other and of the other as always being alien, and this notion reinforcing relations of dominance and subordination (Wolmark 1994). This means that the excluded can then be included by breaking down the boundaries that have previously existed and dominated the writing. Wolmark (1994, 3) hopes that this will lead to a redefinition of "the female subject outside the confines of binary oppositions that seek to fix gender identities in the interests of existing relations of domination."

Archaeological writing already shares much with science fiction. This description of science fiction sounds familiar: "Science fiction, then is a literature of supposition. It makes one, or many speculative leaps, but it always endeavours to provide a logical rationale for its speculations" (Evans 1998, 2). By encompassing the question "what if…?" that is the essence of science fiction, archaeology allows fictions to jostle for viability, with the ridiculous falling over the precipice, and the possible standing up to be roughed about in the ongoing debate that is archaeology. Archaeological authors can learn much from the examples of feminist science fiction, where stereotypes are challenged and oppositions are broken down.

Julia Murphy is currently defying the laws of space/time by teaching history and English in Oxford and finishing a MPhil in the Department of Archaeology, University of Wales Lampeter.

7

Imaginary Places Real Monuments: Field Monuments Of Lancre, Terry Pratchett's Discworld

Martin Brown

The Discworld is a construct of best selling author Terry Pratchett. Since 1984, the flat world, which floats through space, supported on four elephants standing on a turtle's shell, has been the location for over twenty-five adventures at once parodying and developing the fantasy genre. Despite its unusual foundations Discworld bears a surprising similarity to our own world and its societies and technologies owe more than a little to our own terrestrial past.

The following chapter will focus on the mountainous kingdom of Lancre as a case study in the use and abuse of northern European archaeological monuments and folk traditions in the creation of a place. Management of these monuments will also be considered, as will attitudes to ancient remains. There will also be a consideration of the role and value of these archaeological sites in the fictional land both as plot devices and as elements in a larger complex landscape. The historic nature of the land and the concept of landscape on the Disc will also be considered with especial reference to Weatherwax's thinking in this area that landscape is far more than geography (Pratchett, 1988; Pratchett, 1992). Although Lancre, the setting for four books, will be the prime focus of this study the consideration of wider issues will necessitate occasional consideration of other places on the Disc. The field archaeology of Lancre will also be considered alongside the archaeology to be found on this planet, particularly within the British Isles.

Field monuments of Lancre

There are three principal monuments known from Lancre: the Standing Stone, the Dancers stone circle and the Long Man, an unusually arranged complex of barrows. Other monuments are occasionally referred to in the text but the three sites that will be considered in depth are described by Pratchett in some detail and provide the setting for key scenes in the stories.

The Standing Stone appears as a minor character in *Wyrd Sisters* (Pratchett 1988). The monument is to be found "on the crest of the moor" (Pratchett 1988, 68). Its size is described as being about that of a large man and it serves a current purpose for the witches who congregate there as it "stood roughly where the witches' territories met...". Like many megaliths encountered during fieldwork on planet earth, this monument has had beliefs and stories attached to it over time: "It was considered intensely magical because, although there was only one of it, *no-one had ever been able to count it.*" (1988, 68). Further evaluation of the site reveals the extreme difficulties that can face the archaeological fieldworker in Lancre "...all three witches arrived at the standing stone early; it was so embarrassed by this that it went and hid in some bushes".

This standing stone draws on a rich European folklore tradition for its magical qualities. There are numerous legends in Britain, and further afield, notably Brittany, where megaliths are said to behave in similar ways to that described above. Famously uncountable stone circles include Stanton Drew in Somerset and The Rollright Stones in Oxfordshire, while it is said that ill-luck falls on anyone who can count all the stones of Stonehenge (Hayman 1997; Grinsell 1976). The idea that stones move is also widespread in western Europe. In Britain allegedly mobile stones include the Long Stone at Minchinhampton, Gloucestershire, which is said to run around the field in which it stands (Grinsell 1976) and the Wimble Stone in the Mendips which Pratchett himself suggests as the inspiration for the Standing Stone (Pratchett, Pers. Comm.). Associations between witches and megaliths can also be found, particularly in Scotland, at locations such as Auldearn (Grinsell 1976). This association may have developed in popular culture from an ecclesiastical policy of discouraging curiosity by associating sites with evil, an idea which will be discussed below.

Evidence also suggests that the Lancre witches are also well within a European tradition in not only using a standing stone as a meeting place but also regarding the stone as a boundary marker between their territories, although the ease with which the place is found, despite the movement of the marker does suggest that it serves only as an indicator rather than a necessary fixed point. The use of monuments as markers and boundary points is well-known: they appear, for example, on Saxon land charters and on parish boundaries (Grinsell 1976) and in most cases, except in a fantasy novel, a megalith would suffice, being a solid marker that is unlikely to move. A second, recumbent, stone has also been noted on the gnarled moorland in the Lancre uplands.[1] This monument serves as a landmark in an otherwise confusing landscape (Pratchett 1998). Nothing is known about its origins or history.

The Dancers stone circle is central to the action of *Lords and Ladies* (Pratchett, 1992). At numerous points in the text it is made clear that this is not an impressive piece of monument building, more akin to the Greywethers of Dartmoor in appearance than, for example, to the Stones of Stenness: "The stones weren't shaped, they weren't positioned in an particularly significant way. There wasn't any of that stuff about the sun striking the right stone on the right day. Someone had just dragged eight red stones into a rough circle." (Pratchett 1992, 8).

The circle has been designed to mark ground and/or do a job but its function is the most important consideration in its construction: the necessity of its building, as becomes apparent in the story, over-rides any other factor. This circle may be compared with other examples of megalithic architecture around Lancre and further afield on the Disc: there are many other circles to be found in the surrounding Ramtop mountains. These appear to be of druidic origin and are used as weather computers and since replacement is often cheaper than upgrading a circle, the obsolete examples are left on the ground (Pratchett 1992, 8). The stone circle as druidic computer is also referred to in 69 *The Light Fantastic* (Pratchett 1986), but it is apparent that human sacrifice is also practised here, though not always successfully. Here Pratchett happily subverts two popular myths of later prehistory, including the wise proto-scientist druids and the bloodthirsty, half-savage pre-Roman priests.

The Dancers serve a simple, but important purpose: to mark a boundary between the world of Men and that of the Elves, or Lords and Ladies. In Lancre, it appears that such circles mark weak points in the frontier and that they have been marked in the past by the appearance of a phenomenon akin to the crop circle. Indeed, evidence from the Disc suggests that increased crop circle activity indicates weakening of and/or pressure on, the boundary between the worlds. This is demonstrated in the appearance of the circles in Pugsley Ogg's mustard and cress and in Archchancellor Ridcully's hair in the days before the Elvish invasion (Pratchett 1992). The use of the particular stones used for this monument suggests a deep awareness of their qualities in dealing with elves: their high iron content and strong magnetism form an ideal boundary designed to enclose the iron-hating elves. This choice of stones may be seen as echoing the apparently careful choices made by the builders of megaliths in Prehistory at sites such as Avebury (Burl 1979) where it has been suggested that the different shapes in the Avenue there are significant, symbolising male and female forms (Malone 1989).

By their very nature stone circles delineate space. The circles mark out an area, perhaps distinguishing sacred from profane or proclaiming restricted areas to those who built them. They may be excluding the everyday world or, as one sees in *Lords and Ladies*, enclosing and controlling some sort of power, be it real or imagined. The age of this class of monument and their prehistoric origin makes interpretation difficult: perhaps here one sees one of the values of fantasy writing, where interpretations can be played with and twisted, unconstrained by the testimony of the spade and where, amongst the wilder theories, one may chance upon something applicable to our own heritage. Whatever the origins of these monuments they have an importance that extends beyond their value as archaeological monuments. They are important visible landscape features and have accrued a large amount of cultural baggage from folk-tales to New Age belief via Romantic art work (Hayman 1997).

The cultural and political life of the most famous British megalithic monument, Stonehenge, has been well documented, demonstrating the differing interpretations of the monument and messages read into it over time (Chippindale 1983; Bender 1993). Changing interpretations of such monuments are exemplified by the notion of the stone circle as computer. This reading of Stonehenge was promoted during the 1960s and demonstrates how contemporary preoccupations and ideas will affect reactions to a monument (Hawkins 1965). Terry Pratchett has taken up this still-popular interpretation, coupled with the antiquarian idea of megalith builders as druids on more than one occasion (Pratchett, 1986; 1992). In *Lords and Ladies* one of the more recent theories concerning the origin of some stone circles – that they mark the sites of crop circles – appears as the circles materialise in both hair and mustard and cress.[2] However, Terry Pratchett has stayed away from the idea of ley-lines; maybe some ideas are considered too strange even for the Discworld, or perhaps it is a plot device that remains, as yet, unused.

There has been active management of the Dancers site in the past, including clearance of scrub. Like the comparable activity on British archaeological sites this procedure is carried out partly to open up the monument and to draw attention to it. However, unlike Britain, the ultimate purpose of making the monument more prominent is to alert people to the presence of the stones and to quietly suggest that they might be better off somewhere else, rather than to excite interest. The stones themselves are apparently heavily magnetised and this could present problems when using tools too close to them.

Difficulties in management can also be seen when the boundary between the two worlds indicated by the Dancers is weak; at such times there can be breaches from outside. In the past these incursions from Elfland have included flint arrows, known as elf-shot, and, notably, a murderous unicorn (Pratchett 1992). While the occasional gamekeeper, farm dog or field of bullocks may hold assorted delights for the archaeologist working in Europe they are as nothing when compared to the possibility of being dragged into the world of the Elves, a place which is far less attractive than it sounds.

The Lancrastian stone circle is known as The Dancers. Its name parallels British traditions in which names reflecting music and dancing are not uncommon; a well-known example being the Merry Maidens circle in Cornwall. According to local legend this monument is said to be a group of girls turned to stone for dancing on a Sunday (Grinsell 1976). Stones included in the Lancre Dancers are named the Piper and the Drummer (Pratchett, 1992), names which also echo the Merry Maidens, where a small stone group called The Pipers is situated close to the main circle.[3]

Although such legends are said to be very ancient, Hayman has suggested that these names and legends of punishment for Sabbath-breaking were invented in the post-medieval period by Protestant divines to discourage impious and curious locals from visiting sites associated with paganism (Hayman 1997). A similar situation is apparent at the Dancers, where the Lancrastians are meant to know about the stones, recognise their power and stay well away from them. However, forgetfulness, the power of the stories about glamorous Elves and the lack of knowledge of the reality of Elvish behaviour results in numerous visitors to the circle (Pratchett 1992).

The third major monument described in Lancre is the Long Man, a configuration of three burial mounds, one long and two round. Their arrangement suggests phallic references and may be paralleled by the use of long and round balloons in the suggestive arrangement common in British offices around Christmas-time. Oral testimony from Ogg demonstrates not only the difficulty of determining this configuration from the ground, but also the usefulness of aerial survey: "The first time I saw 'em from the air…I nearly fell off the bloody broomstick for laughin'" (Pratchett 1992, 303). To date, attempts by the Royal Commission on the Historical Monuments of England to employ witches to conduct low-cost, environmentally friendly air photo surveys have been unsuccessful. Examination of the monument on the ground reveals the long mound to include a chambered tomb marked with petroglyphs:

> "The sulphurous glow revealed a flat rock with crude drawing scratched on it. Ochre had been rubbed into the lines. They showed a figure of an owl-eyed man wearing an animal skin and horns. In the flickering light he seemed to dance. There was a runic inscription underneath…" (Pratchett 1992, 305).

Further investigation reveals the passage of the grave to lead into the Kingdom of the Elves, where the interior of the tomb becomes an elven sweat lodge whence the king of the Elves will emerge to roam abroad (Pratchett 1992). It is also apparent that the Long Man performs a psychological function, expressing important ideas through the medium of the landscape. The configuration of the earthworks has prompted intense debate concerning the messages embodied within the monument, challenging cherished views of the past. This view is clearly expressed by Casanunda the Dwarf: "I thought the people who built mounds and earthworks and things were serious druids and people like that…not people who drew on the privy walls with 200,000 tons of earth." (Pratchett 1992, 303). He later develops this argument, suggesting that all the ancients were doing was proclaiming their own potency: "I've got a great big tonker." (Pratchett 1992, 303). This notion is further elaborated by Ogg, who suggests that the Long Man is an embodiment of the landscape itself (Pratchett 1992). In mountainous terrain, as is encountered in Lancre, it is not surprising that monuments there have such potency, as they reflect the spirit of their creators and of the environment from which they have grown.

The name of the Long Man and its arrangement parallel not only European barrow types but also two English hill-figures, the Cerne Giant and the Long Man of Wilmington: one lends his name, the other his phallic qualities. However, there is no more definite link than that: when asked if he knew of the two round and one long barrow above the Long Man of Wilmington Terry Pratchett replied that he knew of the giants and the rest came from general knowledge and invention (Pratchett, pers. comm.). However, the phallic nature of the monument also alludes to a major interpretation of Neolithic monuments, that of the symbol of power. In its crudest interpretation the monument may be regarded as the manifestation of patriarchal, phallocentric 'Big Men' claiming, dominating and marking land (Clarke, Cowie and Foxon 1985).

The long barrow included in the Lancre Long Man is clearly a chambered tomb, which Nanny Ogg and Casanunda are able to enter. The entrance to the tomb is decorated with petroglyphs enhanced with red ochre, an image that echoes The Sorcerer, a Palaeolithic image found at Arièges in the Ardèche, France (Bahn 1997). The use of red ochre to enhance the image also comes from documented prehistoric practice and its association in Lancre with this phallic monument seems remarkably appropriate (Bahn 1997: Taylor 1996). As the characters enter the tomb fantasy is reintroduced: the characters go down into the earth, passing into a different world to meet the King of the Elves. Pratchett draws on both archaeological material and the myths that have become attached to them over time.

There is a long tradition of the prehistoric tomb as home for supernatural beings or creatures, including dwarves at the Scottish Dwarfie Stane (Hayman 1997, 13:) or ghostly blacksmiths in Wayland's Smithy (Grinsell 1976). In addition to the tradition of tomb as home there are the idea of the 'hollow hills' and of prehistoric mounds as entrances to other worlds (Grinsell 1976). In consequence, it should come as no surprise to the reader that the Elven King lives beneath the mound, for such people are the usual occupants of large mounds, such as Willy Howe in Yorkshire, in the British folk traditions (Grinsell 1976). This idea has also been re-explored by Pratchett in his 1998 novel *Carpe Jugulum* with the appearance of a goddess, strongly resembling a prehistoric Venus figurine, who lives beneath a chambered tomb.

A further version of this 'hollow hills' tradition, in which heroes or knights sleep beneath the barrow until some unspecified day, is also alluded to at the Long Man. When Nanny Ogg and Casanunda descend into the tomb they come across a chamber where "some old king and his warriors" are at rest waiting to be woken for some final battle (Pratchett 1988, 308). This and the comic interlude which follows draw heavily on ideas found in western Britain where King Arthur is said to sleep surrounded by his knights: examples include King Arthur's Cave near Hadrian's Wall (Embleton and Graham 1984). Such fantasies of the tomb as threshold to another world or dimension are explicable, as anyone who has sat in the darkness of a chambered tomb should be able to appreciate: in the darkness the dimensions of the monument are invisible and unknown and side chambers could, just possibly, plunge off into the earth to places unknown.

Excavating the imagination

What then are we to say for these monuments? Like earth-bound sites the monuments of Lancre embody many things, including the creative urge, constructional ability, symbolic power and ritual practice. Like their counter-parts on Earth the Lancrastian monuments are also associated with many stories and, because this is a fantasy creation, those stories live in an even more palpable sense than they lived for our own forebears. However, these monuments do have an archaeological potential, just like their terrestrial counterparts. They are remnants of bygone times and may be the subject of investigation.

There is no tradition of archaeological fieldwork in Lancre. The locals, although aware of the rich archaeological resource in the country will not go digging "reckoning in their uncomplicated way that it was bad luck to have your head torn off by a vengeful underground spirit" (Pratchett 1998, 191).[4] However, Venter Borass of The Unseen University of Ankh-Morpork, is recorded as having begun to consider the origins of the Discworld. His work has touched on geological strata and palaeontology but his theory that rocks are arranged by age rather than colour has found little favour with his brother wizards who remain firmly set in their view that "any god worth bothering…who had anything to say about Creation…would write it all down…and would have too much respect for their creations to expect them to go grovelling around in some kind of cosmic game of Hunt the Slipper." (Pratchett and Briggs 1995, 26–7).

Borass claimed to have discovered remains from the skeleton of a "Really Big Lizard" but these have had doubt cast upon them by suggestions that the fossilised bone is really part of a spoon handle (Pratchett and Briggs 1995, 25–7). However, there are other stirrings of antiquarian activity on the Disc, news of which has reached Lancre. Indeed, Nanny Ogg is able to use the activities of these individuals as a threat when bargaining with the King of the Elves: "I'll get em to dig into the Long Man with iron shovels, y'see, and they'll say, 'why its just an old earthworks,' and pensioned-off wizards and priests with nuthin' better to do will pick over the heaps and write dull old books about burial traditions and suchlike, and that'll be another iron nail in your coffin" (Pratchett 1993, 311–312).

Borass's work and the reactions to it of his peers are obvious parallels of the early days of archaeology and geology when archaeo-geological study led to the replacement of a creationist-diluvial paradigm by gradual processes (Torrens 1998). His suggestions concerning the fossil lizards in the strata of the Discworld also carry echoes of the Piltdown Man affair, where, in the early years of the twentieth century, the "missing link" (the skull of an alleged hominid) was created by forgery and passed off as evidence of the antiquity and primacy of the English (Curwen 1954; Somerville 1996). Nevertheless, it appears from Ogg's words (quoted above) that there are other antiquarians at work on the Disc. Her description makes it clear that these men conform to the traditional view of European antiquarians, barrow diggers and pioneer archaeologists, although for wizards one should substitute other professions.

The reference to the "iron nail" in the coffin of the Elves warrants further consideration: the rich tradition of folk-tales associated with ancient monuments has been discussed above and it may be argued that archaeological investigation of these sites has stripped away the myths, replacing them with a scientific truth, or at least interpretations. Indeed, the effects of science were recognised by some of the antiquarians themselves and resulted in the collecting of folk culture (Lower 1861).[5] The elf shot referred to above is a useful example here. In the past prehistoric flint arrowheads were called fairy or elf shot by the ordinary people of England (Merrifield, 1987). Today we know their origins and methods of manufacture; they are catalogued, classified and captured. Nevertheless people still delight in their chance discovery and in the objects as something ancient, as artwork and as the source of old legends. They are not usually interested in academic archaeological detail. Yet Nanny Ogg is correct: once the barrow has been shown to be a burial mound and once the folklore has been collected and classified the living tradition of myth ceases to exist. Rather than retaining its character in a vibrant shared local heritage the barrow or the folk-tale become the property of the intellectual (Boyes 1994).

It is easy for the ordinary person to feel excluded and even disinherited by professionals and archaeologists have not been good at communicating their theories and results. Thus, archaeologists should not, perhaps, be surprised if, having dispelled ancient myths with science the public have used some science and parts of the interpretations to create new myths. Furthermore, when in Lancre we should do as the Lancrastians and take heed of a witch's words: when Nanny Ogg refers to the antiquarians' books she dismisses them as dull. Perhaps the writers who are creating new (and New Age) myths are responding to a market which few archaeological books have filled, where the author tells an accessible, exciting tale of people and places in the past.[6] Perhaps this is also the secret of the fantasy genre. Does it help us recapture the magic of the past in a way which much archaeological writing does not? Should we also ask whether the rise of fantasy writing, and perhaps of fringe archaeology, should be seen as a development from or reaction to the decline of belief in organised religion? Having largely abandoned God do people now seek to replace the wonder and mystery in their lives with the geography and inhabitants of fantasy worlds?

Archaeological monuments do play an important role within the conception and realisation of the Discworld. Although the place is only a figment of one author's imagination, it must draw on actual experience and place to appear real. This aspect of the use of the past in science fiction and fantasy writing has already attracted comment elsewhere (e.g. Irwin, 1994; 1995). It appears that authors regularly use the past to give foundation to their own imagination: the success of, for example, Tolkein is that he was drawing on an established tradition and known world to create an elaborate, inspiring and believable fantasy. However, it is also clear that the physical remains of past activity in a fictional place have other uses.

Where monuments exist they may be agents of plot, as has been seen at the Dancers stone circle, but they also serve to give distinctiveness to the landscape. The moving standing stone of Lancre is an amusing, incidental character to the reader and an irritation to the witches on one level, but it is, in a deeper sense, an important piece of landscape character (without it the moor would not be the same). Indeed, the stone tells us that we are not in a normal place because here our own legends have become very real and, in consequence, anything could happen. Yet the remains do more than just provide character for a landscape traversed by witches, dwarves and elves. They also tell the reader that this is an ancient place with foundations, layers and histories.

In *Carpe Jugulum* this idea is clearly expressed:

> "The kingdom had been there many years, ever since the ice withdrew. Tribes had pillaged, tilled, built and died. The clay walls of the living houses had long since rotted and been lost but, down under the moundy banks, the abodes of the dead survived." (Pratchett, 1998, 191).

Although Terry Pratchett invented the Discworld, in part, by combining various established terrestrial myths he has given it its own history, archaeology and geography. This is essential, for without a past there can be no ruined temples for the muscle-bound hero to loot or ancient burial mounds for the protagonists to enter. In addition, there is a further, important reason for the Disc to have (to need) a past and its physical remains. Without a solid background into which the reader feels they might be able to enter and through which they could walk, the plot, however good, will lack an important component. Unless the action is anchored in a believable landscape, be it Hardy's Wessex or Pratchett's Discworld, the reader will feel that something is missing and this will detract from the power of the work.

Unless the reader knows the environment where the action is taking place, and has entered into that world then something of the intention and power of the author will be lost. One could say that the same is true of our own world. It has been argued that lack of connection with the environment, lack of understanding of its time-depth and failure to comprehend the relationships underpinning it can lead to dislocation. This may, in turn, foster lack of care for the environment, thoughtless development and exploitation of both people and place (Brown and Bowen 1999). These relationships and the layers which build up a landscape and a place have also been expressed by Terry Pratchett in the words of Granny Weatherwax as she explains to the Queen of the Elves that there is a deep relationship between humans and the land which the elves, as outsiders, will never understand (Pratchett 1992). The idea of past as an anchor and as an integral part of one's identity has been explored elsewhere by Terry Pratchett in *Strata*, where his first flat world appeared (Pratchett 1988). Here, although worlds are constructed, history is built into the design and everyone appears to be searching for roots and history.

Imagined worlds and real people

The archaeology of the Discworld is very much like the archaeology of parts of our own world. This should not surprise anyone as every author draws inspiration from somewhere, usually the places, people and books with which they are familiar. That the monuments have been given the qualities ascribed to our own archaeological sites should interest the archaeologist. This allows the traditional stories to live on even after the scientific approach has dispelled the fairies.

The fictional world also demonstrates the cultural baggage that archaeological monuments trail behind them because of their power as ancient, inexplicable, powerful places. Furthermore the elves, pixies and so on are manifestations of our desire, as a species to have magic and the unknown in our lives. The appearance of the monuments described above in these books also shows how important the ancient lumps, bumps and rocks are in our own world: these remnants of our forebears shape our environment and our understanding of it; they tell us about the history of our lands and of the people who came before use. Such remains provide inspiration and enjoyment to the artist and to the consumers of their work, which, in turn, contributes to the unseen aspects of a place, the layers that we as a culture, recognise, create and enhance. You can walk on the land, but a landscape is in the mind.

Above all, the archaeology of the Discworld is like that of Earth, in that it should be experienced at first hand. Reading a commentary on the Discworld novels is like reading the guidebook to a major archaeological site. There is no substitute for visiting the place oneself. You can visit the terrestrial sites mentioned in this paper using conventional modes of transport and you can visit the Disc by the simple method of a trip to your local library[7] or bookshop. In both realms you will be able to connect with strange and distant places and with people who were in some senses, just like us, but who are, in other senses, utterly different. Whether on the page or in the landscape the remains of a distant past contribute to the current appearance of the place and to our conception of it.

Martin Brown is the Assistant County Archaeologist for East Sussex, based within the Transport and Environment Department, East Sussex County Council, County Hall, St Anne's Crescent, Lewes BN7 1UE

Notes
1   The reader should, of course, be aware that almost all of Lancre is upland, although some parts are gnarly (Pratchett 1999).
2   The author cannot offer a reference to support this assertion but he has heard the theory put forward by members of the public on several occasions.
3   An alternative name for the Maidens is Dawns Men, which derives from the Cornish for Dancing Stones (Hayman 1997).
4   Even the more unpopular English Heritage Inspectors don't normally have to contend with this.
5   Lower suggested that the railway would drive away the fairies and witches. The comments of the witches are not recorded.
6   Julian Cope's recent book *The Modern Antiquarian* (Thorsons, 1998) is a good example of such a book which mixes archaeology and fringe ideas to create an attractive, if unorthodox product. For archaeological comment on this book see Darvill 1999.
7   Always be nice to the librarian! If you don't know why wait until you've read one or two of the books. N.B. not all librarians like bananas.

8

Under Old Earth:
Material Culture, Identity and History
in the Work of Cordwainer Smith

Alasdair Brooks

The Cordwainer Smith short story *Alpha Ralpha Boulevard* opens with a rhapsody to the recovery of the past:

> "We were drunk with happiness in those early years. Everybody was, especially the young people. These were the first years of the Rediscovery of Man, when the Instrumentality dug deep in the treasury, reconstructing the old languages, and even the old troubles. The nightmare of perfection had taken our forefathers to the edge of suicide. Now under the leadership of the Lord Jestocost and the Lady Alice More, the ancient civilisations were rising like great land masses out of the sea of the past." (Smith 1993, 375)

This paper uses the speculative fiction of Cordwainer Smith as an allegorical parable for exploring the role of material culture, identity and history within archaeological theory. As with all parables, this paper ultimately presents a deeply personal, and perhaps slightly quixotic worldview; it would be wrong to pretend otherwise. Nonetheless, it should be stressed that the choice of author was not made on a passing whim. Cordwainer Smith, one of Science Fiction's most enigmatic writers, often addressed themes in his work that are strongly relevant to archaeological theory. In this chapter I will discuss how Smith often explicitly acknowledged the central importance of material culture not only in the construction of the past, but also in the formation of social and cultural identities. Perhaps more impressively, in the classic short story *A Planet Named Shayol*, Smith implicitly explored the social and cultural implications of a world almost utterly devoid of material culture in any form.

An introduction to Cordwainer Smith

Cordwainer Smith was an important figure in the history of science fiction, but he is at best something of a cult figure today. A brief summary of his life, background and work is therefore necessary. "Cordwainer Smith" was the science fiction pseudonym of Paul Myron Anthony Linebarger (1913–66). God-son of Sun Yat Sen (who named him Lin Bah Loh: "Forest of Incandescent Bliss"), professor of Asiatic politics at Johns Hopkins University, World War II intelligence operative in Chungking, lapsed Methodist but devout Episcopalian (Pierce 1993) and author of what was for decades the definitive book on psychological warfare (Linebarger 1948), Linebarger led an extraordinary life even by the extraordinary standards of the 20th century. The Cordwainer Smith stories make up what is undoubtedly the most baroque and deeply symbolic collection of work in science fiction. One anthology editor's introduction to the story *On the Storm Planet* describes the Smith stories as:

> "A ... cosmology unrivalled even today for its scope and complexity: a millennia spanning Future History, logically outlandish and elegantly strange, set against a vivid, richly coloured, mythically intense universe where animals assume the shape of man, vast planoform ships whisper through multidimensional space, immense sick sheep are the most valuable objects in the universe ... and the mysterious Lords of the Instrumentality rule a hunted Earth too old for history." (Dozois 1994, 94)

The Cordwainer Smith stories are remarkable enough as straightforward fiction, but they also contain deeper threads and themes. Each story forms part of a deeply symbolic narrative that eventually combines elements of Chinese philosophy, Episcopalian theology and respect for the traditional Marxist sense of historical destiny. These elements are frequently meshed and hidden within ornate oriental narrative structures. Pierce's introduction to the short story collection *The Rediscovery of Man* contains an excellent summary of Smith/Linebarger's world view.

Linebarger was "A social and psychological thinker, whose experience with diverse cultures gave him peculiar and seemingly contradictory ideas about human nature and morality" (Pierce 1988). These contradictions are best illustrated by an incident from the Korean War. During this conflict, Linebarger was faced by the problem of how to persuade Chinese soldiers to surrender without losing face or honour. He developed leaflets which told the opposing army to shout the words 'love', 'duty', 'humanity' and 'virtue' in Chinese. Pronounced in that order, these words sound very much like the English for "I surrender". Linebarger considered this successful technique to be the single most worthwhile act in his life (Pierce 1988).

Linebarger's worldview and morality was also affected by his theological perspective. From about 1960, Linebarger's Episcopalianism became increasingly devout, and his fiction increasingly turned to Christian concerns. The term "Instrumentality of Mankind", used by Cordwainer Smith to describe the enigmatic rulers of the universe, has distinct religious connotations; in High Church theology "the priest performing the sacraments is the 'instrumentality' of God himself" (Pierce 1988). But unlike the deeply orthodox Anglican science fiction allegories of C. S. Lewis (Lewis 1990), Linebarger was not simply a Christian apologist. As Pierce has noted, "Behind the invented cultures, behind the intricacies of plot and the joy or suffering of the characters, there is Smith the philosopher, striving ... to reconcile science and religion, to create a synthesis of Christianity and evolution that will shed light on the nature of man and the meaning of history" (Pierce 1988).

Within this context, Smith's stories entail an attempt to reconcile the competing sides of what can be termed the 'supra-theoretical dialectic'. This piece of jargon simply refers to a recognition of the ongoing and inevitable debate in Western thought between the objective and the subjective, the material and the ideal. Bertrand Russell, for example, held that the history of Western thought is based on the opposition between the objective and the subjective (Russell 1961, 41). William James similarly postulated that the history of philosophy was a clash of human temperaments, including the intellectualist and the sensationalistic, the idealistic and the materialistic, the dogmatical and the sceptical (Sprigge 1995, 869).

In archaeology these competing worldviews are represented by processualism and post-processualism respectively, but competition and interaction between these perspectives is inherent in any academic discipline. Archaeology could perhaps learn from Smith's attempts to reconcile the two opposing ideological perspectives. Yet while Smith's interaction with the supra-theoretical dialectic is no doubt interesting, this paper focuses on more specific elements of archaeological theory. Specifically, how Smith's fascination with the meaning of the past led him to explore themes on the construction of the past that the theoretical archaeologist will find deeply familiar.

The Construction of the Past

There are only a few direct, explicit references to archaeology in the Smith canon. Prominent amongst these is the Lord Crudelta's reconstruction of a fifteen thousand year old 'Paroskii and Murkin' rocketship, "a beautiful piece of engineering and archeology [sic]" (*Drunkboat*; Smith 1993, 349). Other examples include the explanation of how archaeologists helped the neo-British to reconstruct the proto-historic Cambridge University attended by Helen America in the early years of space exploration (*The Lady Who Sailed The Soul*; Smith 1993, 101) and the quote at the end of this chapter from *On the Gem Planet*.

Yet beyond these examples, an awareness of the importance of the past and its mythic elements can be found throughout Smith's work. The rigid obsession of the Norstrilians to remain true to Australia, Her Majesty the Queen, and their 'Old Old Earth' character – despite century-long lifespans and immeasurable wealth amassed from giant mutant sheep that sweat immortality (Smith 1988) – stands as a particularly vivid example. But Norstrilia is hardly unique.

Other examples include the interstellar ship *Wu-Feinstein*, home of the legendary Go-captain Magno Taliano, and a precise replica of "an ancient prehistoric estate named Mount Vernon" – the home of George Washington (*The Burning of the Brain*; Smith 1993, 177–185). There are stories of an entire Empire destroyed by the mythic force of a legendary golden ship ninety million miles long (*Golden the Ship Was – Oh! Oh! Oh!*; Smith 1993, 215–221), and of a sunboy living fifteen thousand years in the future who re-enacts the life of the pharaoh Akhnaton (*Under Old Earth*; Smith 1993, 289–325). And finally, we can read of the Palace of the Governor of Night, an indestructible, invisible, yet surpassingly beautiful precise replica of the temple of Diana of the Ephesians (*Norstrilia*; Smith 1988, 59–62). But it is in the stories that deal with the movement named 'the Rediscovery of Man' that Smith dealt most directly with themes relevant to archaeological theory.

In brief, 'the Rediscovery of Man' is a socio-historical movement of *c*.16,000 AD wherein the Instrumentality unleashed chaos, disease, death and disorder on the universe in order to save humanity from millennia of corrosive decadent stasis. The movement relies on the reconstruction and imposition of ancient cultures and civilisations in order to provide structure and meaning for humanity (e.g. *Alpha Ralpha Boulevard*; Smith 1993, 375–376). The imposition and manipulation of the past by elites and other groups is, of course, an issue that has been widely explored by archaeologists. This examination has taken the form both of general discussions of the use of archaeology in constructing national identities (e.g. Wailes and Zoll 1995) to examinations of specific examples, such as the use of archaeology to reinforce the ideology of Nazism's theory of Aryan racial supremacy (Arnold and Hassmann 1995).

The Ayodhya mosque in northern India has been the site of a politically significant sectarian conflict between Muslims and Hindus, many of whom hold that the *Ramayana* reveals the Ayodhya site as the birthplace of Rama (Rao 1994:156). In his discussion of the symbolic construction and legitimisation of different pasts at the site, Rao states that:

> "The past is created from and in the image of the present. History and archaeology are entirely malleable, depending as they do on interpretative reconstruction ... There is a very fine line between historical/archaeological 'fact' and myth, with the distinction being made essentially in relation to contemporary issues and in the contemporary context. The past is thus continually recreated". (Rao 1994, 154)

Bond and Gilliam meanwhile state that "social constructions of the past are crucial elements in the process of domination, subjugation, resistance and collusion" and that "Representing the past and the way of life of populations is an expression and a source of power" (Bond and Gilliam 1994, 1). Historians and educators have also dealt with these themes, for example, through discussions of "the invention of tradition" (Hobsbawm and Ranger 1992) and the manipulation of American schoolchildren's ideological outlook through textbook content (Loewen 1995).

Cordwainer Smith's work explicitly addresses these themes, although it is quite clear that Paul Linebarger would not have fully agreed with Rao or Gilliam and Bond. Certainly Smith/Linebarger saw that the representation of the past could come about through an expression of power; the Rediscovery of Man is led by the ultimate power elite in the form of the Instrumentality. While the latter might not be entirely omnipotent, they usually might as well be. This is a 'government', that has ruled Humanity for untold millennia under the paradoxical slogan "Watch, but do not govern; stop war, but do not wage it; protect, but do not control; and first, survive!" (*Drunkboat*; Smith 1993, 341).

Furthermore, the malleability of the past is actively addressed in the short story *Alpha Ralpha Boulevard*; the main characters go into a hospital and come out French, they speak French, they read the first French newspapers to have been published in millennia, but there is an awareness that the reimposition of the past is not absolute. After all, "when the diseases had killed the statistically correct number of people, they would be turned off" (*Alpha Ralpha Boulevard*; Smith 1993, 375–376). Thus the past is reimposed to deal with "contemporary issues" and "contemporary context", just as Rao asserts – although in this case contemporary means a fictional world about 14,000 years in the future, and the issues and context are no less than the preservation of the entire species.

Cordwainer Smith would, however, have found the relationship between constructions of the past and "domination, subjugation, resistance and collusion" far more problematic. In real life, Paul Linebarger's fascination with Communism's "sense of vocation and conviction of historical destiny" is a matter of record (Pierce 1988), but he was neither a Marxist nor a Communist; it is hard to believe that he would have held to such a simplistic and rigidly Marxist definition of the construction of the past as expressed by Gilliam and Bond. Certainly the Rediscovery of Man is initially imposed from above, but this imposition is not blindly followed by ordinary men and women.

The plot of *Alpha Ralpha Boulevard* (Smith 1993, 375–399) revolves around the main characters' search for advice from the Abba-dingo (an ancient computer), advice that they hope will define whether they have free will in their new status as 'French', or whether they are simply "toys, dolls, puppets" of the Instrumentality. Furthermore, the Instrumentality is not acting out of a desire to reinforce its own control, as a rigid Marxist interpretation might suggest. While the Instrumentality might choose to unleash history on humankind, they have no control of the direction of that history or the meaning ascribed thereto by the people who live within it. This is indeed a central motif of Smith's work – that while elites may attempt to unleash or control social movements, they find it much harder to control the meaning thereof. Nowhere is this better illustrated than in the surreal civil rights/Joan of Arc allegory *The Dead Lady of Clown Town* (Smith 1993, 223–287), where attempts to suppress the animal-derived Underpeople backfire spectacularly.

The Instrumentality is, of course, an entirely fictional power elite, the distinction between social movements and the meaning thereof is nonetheless vitally important. It is important for archaeologists to recognise that the construction of the past and social identity is not a negative process, nor a simple hierarchical one involving the imposition of power. It is instead an impartial, inevitable process that, while it can indeed be manipulated by the unscrupulous or the powerful, can also provide structure and meaning to both social groups and individuals. Indeed, it is clear that Smith intended the reintroduction of the past to be seen as a positive process: "Everywhere, things became more exciting. Everywhere, men and women worked with a wild will to build a more imperfect world" (*Alpha Ralpha Boulevard*; Smith 1993).

It is important to reiterate that this is a fictional example, but many archaeologists will no doubt sympathise with Smith's openly stated opinion that without the invention of past, without a sense of identity and destiny, and therefore within an existence devoid of culture and meaning, humanity's existence itself becomes meaningless. Within the Smith canon, this viewpoint is most vividly expressed by the Lord Sto Odin, the Lord of the Instrumentality who journeyed under Old Earth to the Gebiet and the Bezirk, who saw the Sun-Boy dance to the music of the congohelium, and whose death was one of the causes of the Rediscovery of Man:

> "We are sworn to uphold the dignity of man. Yet we are killing mankind with a bland hopeless happiness which has prohibited news, which has suppressed religion, which has made all history an official secret. I say the evidence is that we are failing and that mankind, whom we've sworn to cherish, is failing too. Failing in vitality, strength, numbers, energy" (*Under Old Earth*; Smith 1993:292).

The Role of Material Culture

Remarkable as it may seem to the archaeologist, Smith's exploration of the meaning of the past was by no means restricted to fairly abstract, philosophical, meta-theoretical levels. Time and time again, there is a recognition of the importance of material culture in structuring both the constructed past, and its interactions with everyday socio-cultural identity.

In *Alpha Ralpha Boulevard*, the main characters sit down at a neo-French restaurant, and when they pay they "put imaginary change in the tray, received imaginary change, paid the waiter an imaginary tip" (Smith 1993, 383), but an awareness of the artificiality of the material culture (in this case, coins) itself fails to make the characters less French in their own eyes. At what point does awareness of the artificial symbolic content of material culture cause it to lose its symbolic power? Arguably, as Cordwainer Smith implied, it rarely does.

A contemporary archaeological example serves to reinforce the point. Gullible tourists aside, it is surely common knowledge today that the modern kilt and the concept of clan tartans are relatively recent developments popularised by Sir Walter Scott during George IV's 1822 visit to Edinburgh. Nineteenth century Staffordshire potters later appropriated images of this mythic Celtic past to decorate transfer-printed pottery vessels, further helping to transmute created myth into concrete reality (Brooks 1997). Yet awareness of the utter artificiality of the clan-tartan relationship has not destroyed the kilt's symbolic power as material culture. Indeed, tartan, for better or for worse, might well be the most recognisable symbol of modern Scotland. Similarly, Lady Llanover's utterly artificial 'traditional' Welsh costume featuring the now-familiar bedgown and beaver hat also found its way onto nineteenth century pottery (Brooks 1997), as did representations of an artificial, peacefully bucolic Britain that never was (Brooks 1999). Today, we recognise the artificiality of these mythic pasts, but as Cordwainer Smith so accurately assumed, knowledge of the artificiality of this material culture's past has not necessarily lead to a rejection of its symbolic importance in the present.

There are many other examples of Cordwainer Smith's recognition of the importance of material culture. The Department Store of the Heart's Desire is run by the last clinical psychologist in the Universe – a fantastically old, intelligent, genetically altered humanoid cat. Amidst the shop's ancient toys, coins, machines, weapons, and Cape of Good Hope triangular postage stamps, Rod McBan the 151st finds a 15,000 year-old bust of Old North Australia's long lost Queen Elizabeth II. Rod McBan's reaction is telling: "...she was a pretty and intelligent-looking woman, with something of a Norstrilian look to her. She looked smart enough to know what to do if one of her sheep caught fire or if her own child came, blank and giggling, out of the travelling vans of the Garden of Death" (*Norstrilia*; Smith 1988, 192).

Given that it is highly unlikely that the Queen has ever grown giant mutant sheep, or faced the possibly fatal telepathic screening of her children (as all Norstrilians do), Rod McBan's reaction may seem rather optimistic. However, it is made extremely clear in the Smith canon that the Norstrilians have given the colonial Australian past a mythic force all its own. Stuck for 15,000 years in a worldview rooted in the 'White Australia' of the 1960s, it is no surprise that Rod McBan sees the bust of the long-dead Queen as the embodiment of his Norstrilia. Similarly, in our own world, it seems perfectly natural that the embodiment of Scotland is often seen as kilted Highlanders – who before the nineteenth century were a geographically and culturally isolated minority persecuted just as fiercely by the Stewart Kings in Edinburgh as they were by London post-Culloden. Once again, the facts of the past, whatever they might be, rarely interfere with the symbolic power of that past in the present.

Ironically, however, the most astonishing example of the importance of material culture in a Cordwainer Smith story lies in a work about a world almost devoid of material culture in any form. *A Planet Named Shayol* (Smith 1993, 419–450) is an astonishingly original piece of rare power, and is undoubtedly one of the landmark short stories of science fiction. The action, if it can be called action, centres on one of the most terrifyingly bleak planets ever imagined. Shayol, named after a Jewish hell, is the punishment planet of the far future. It consists of virtually nothing except a monotonous, ginger-yellow desert landscape. The latter is broken by only three things: a herd of naked prisoners, the cabin of the planet's caretaker, and the immobile man-mountain of the Go-Captain Alvarez, the discoverer of Shayol, whose feet alone are the height of a six-storey building. The planet has a single indigenous life-form, the dromozoa, who manifest themselves as brightly-coloured lights. These are the cause of the Go-Captain Alvarez's grotesque form, and the sole reason for the presence of the herd of prisoners on the planet. The dromozoa actively seek out the herd of prisoners, and cause extra body parts to grow on the humans – heads, arms, torsos, and healthy internal organs growing externally. These parts are harvested by the caretaker, and then sent up to a medical satellite for use in transplant technology.

After an initial scene in the medical satellite, very little happens in *A Planet Named Shayol* for a very long time, at least in the sense of conventional narrative. There is a vague sense of huge quantities of time passing, but no real clues as to how much. It is a fiction cliché for a new prisoner to ask "Who are you?" and then be told "Names mean nothing here", but on Shayol, Smith manages the feat of making that cliché wholly believable. The characters are almost completely dehumanised. This dehumanisation is emphasised the virtual total lack of material culture on the planet – the caretaker's cabin and an inscription on a rock being the sole exceptions. When Mercer, the closest thing to a main character in the story, joins the herd his first action is to discard his clothing.

Thereafter, there is nothing else, nothing to distinguish the characters as human, as cultural beings interacting with a meaningful environment. Within an existence devoid of meaning, humanity's existence is itself rendered utterly meaningless. If the stories of the *Rediscovery of Man* are about redeeming humanity through the reinvention of the past and the power of material culture, then *A Planet Named Shayol* reveals the logical opposite extreme: the complete, final, and total dehumanisation that occurs when all forms of culture are stripped away. Nothing else remains.

Conclusion

The Cordwainer Smith stories are hardly unique in science fiction with dealing with the mythic sweep of the past. But they are arguably unique in doing so in a manner so relevant to modern archaeological theory. For example, Olaf Stapledon's *Last and First Men* (1978) and *Starmaker* (1979) are epic meditations on the philosophy of history, not on the construction thereof (and are far more agnostic in theme). Philip Dick's *Galactic Pot Healer* (1987) is probably the only science fiction novel to feature a ceramicist (and is thus dear to this author's heart), but while it deals with a mythic past, it is more the paranoid musings of an acid casualty than a coherent worldview. As this chapter has made it clear, Cordwainer Smith was very different. Yet it is worth noting that while Paul Linebarger had a firm grasp of the importance of history, identity and material culture in the creation of the past, he probably would have emphasised other elements in the Cordwainer Smith stories, particularly the theological and civil rights themes. But just because these were the themes closest to Paul Linebarger's heart, does not mean that the other issues that affected his work are diminished in importance.

Time and time again, in the examples cited throughout this chapter, the Cordwainer Smith stories demonstrate that Paul Linebarger had an intuitive understanding of the importance of the creation of the mythic past, and the role of material culture in that creation – in the form of objects both mundane and fantastic. Indeed, the Cordwainer Smith canon serves as a useful reminder to archaeologists that their theoretical battles over the creation of the past and the role of material culture remain firmly rooted in universal themes that can be found throughout Western Culture. That one of the more engrossing explorations of these themes is found within a regrettably obscure collection of science fiction short stories is one of the twentieth century's more curious ironies.

> "This was the second century of the Rediscovery of Man. People everywhere had taken up old names, old languages, old customs, as fast as the robots and the underpeople could retrieve the data from the rubbish of forgotten starlanes or the subsurface ruins of Manhome itself" (*On the Gem Planet*; Smith 1993, 451).

Alasdair Brooks is a Research Fellow in the Department of Archaeology, La Trobe University, Bundoora, Victoria 3083, Australia.

9

The Explanation

Philip Rahtz

This chapter is in three parts: the first two are by way of an introduction, expositions of well known themes; the third is a science fiction story which relates the first two; it provides a commentary for the first and an explanation for the second. The theme is that of determinism in archaeology, and the extent to which this is a viable philosophical concept in theory.

Archaeological theory has wavered between two extremes, firstly of total determinism; and secondly complete human control of the world. Since archaeology is by definition anthropogenic, former attitudes to the past were largely about hominid achievement and material progress, resulting in material residues reflecting human activities. Graham Clark's famous work on *Prehistoric Europe – the economic basis* (Clark 1952) has swung the emphasis towards *humans in the environment* as the proper study. Eric Higgs, also of the Clark School at Cambridge, went so far as to advocate the excavation of contexts, notably caves, where environmental factors could be studied which were unpolluted by human activity. The argument has in some quarters moved even further in the recognition that hominid development cannot be divorced from that of other animals – indeed all life forms.

A holistic view was implicit in some aspects of the 1970s "New Archaeology"; a systematic approach, the study of process, sought to integrate all facets of human and natural activities and explore interrelationships between them. This proved not only too difficult, but also engendered considerable opposition, the principal reaction among its detractors was that such holistic approaches belittled the achievements of the human species, and tended to the view that hominids were 'just another animal'; subject to the buffeting of nature, as well as its boons. Hence the success of cognitive studies, which sought to put back humans as the prime movers in their destinies, notably because of the convolutions of their minds. Determinism, and especially environmental determinism, is a frequently dirty word, expressed as such in numerous archaeological publications.

There has recently been some counter reaction, though it tends to be less vocal than that of cognitives. A major influence here may prove to be the attempts by Professor

Mike Baillie to trace the courses of human catastrophes – a famine, plague, depopulation, even the rise and fall of whole dynasties, as the result, if not of asteroid impact, then the outcome of volcanic eruptions, witnessed by the impressive coincidence of dendrochronological, ice-core and other evidence with historically documented events. With that preamble, we may return to first principles and an *Explanation* of certain phenomena.

Exposition A: Can we help it?

The debate on determinism and free will is over two millennia old. To philosophers who belong to the determinist school (the most recent exposition is by Professor Ted Honderich (1988), the theory is as follows:

Since there is no effect without a cause, any effect must be preceded by a cause or causes. If all these were known, the effect could be predicted before it happened.

This is self-evident in simple cases like natural phenomena such as the weather, what will happen to a golf ball when it is struck, or to a plant if it is watered. It is less obvious when applied to advanced living creatures such as hominids: at least in relation to their conscious modes of thought and action, notably in decision-making. Yet even at this level, if a total data set concerning a particular person were available to a totally detached third party (in this study inhabitants of another advanced planet), the decision reached in any particular situation could be predicted.

The fact that such a data set is not available does not affect the theoretical argument; the data does exist, even if unverifiable, and the decision is determined by precedent factors, which our non-terrestrial observers seek to evaluate.

It follows that no-one is really free to make any decision that is not predetermined by factors existing at the moment of choice; therefore free-will is an illusion. It is a necessary illusion without which we could not survive. The conviction that we are free to make any decision we want to is part of our apparatus for complex living. It is part of the process of natural selection in hominid evolution.

If this argument is accepted then certain social consequences follow:

1   We are not in any real way responsible for our actions

2   Pride in achievement, or guilt at failure, are unjustified

3   Reward or punishment are equally meaningless, however much they appear to ease the way society operates. Success or failure can no more be helped than having red hair (this found literary expression in Samuel Butler's *Erewhon*)

4   Hominids have less control of their environment than they would like to believe.

Most people would not admit to being in any way determinist in their thinking or acting, though some elements of the consequences of such a belief are present already in social reform in Britain: ameliorating of prison conditions; unwillingness to allow anyone to starve, even if it is wholly the result of their own 'stupidity', or 'laziness' or 'criminality'. Even the most ardent reformers would, however, probably not follow the consequences of determinism to their logical argument.

Disbelief in the above arguments is expressed by some philosophers and others in the following assertions:

1 Effects do not necessarily always follow causes; some things seem to happen without causes. This is a belief bolstered by Heisenberg's 'uncertainty principle', based on the discovery of apparent 'random motion' of certain sub-atomic particles. Such a random process might therefore be operating in our own brains, and allow us to be 'free' to make decisions not in accord with precedent factors (this view was attractive to some, but repellent to determinists who prefer to live in an ordered universe where effects follow causes).

2 Even if determinism *were* true, it is quite irrelevant to human society, since all the factors governing decisions can in practice never be known, each of us being intuitively convinced that we *are* free. We live in a society where a strong feeling for freedom is present in everyone. A society which has, moreover, evolved largely on the assumption that humans *do* make free decisions.

Nevertheless, there is limited acceptance of the idea that there is variation between human beings in their ability to cope with the demands of society, and that 'welfare', to a small or massive degree, should be a social responsibility exercised by central authority and/or benevolent individuals. A greater or lesser sympathy with determinist principles characterises the contrast between left and right wing politics. The left have favoured limited rewards and caring for the 'less fortunate' or less competent, while the right favour strong competition in which the more able have a higher standard of living and the less 'able' need not expect more than the nominal human compassion that is offered at any particular time. There is a similar tendency of greater or lesser support for environmental determinism. There are also left and right wing archaeologists. Do they have equivalent views on determinism?

Exposition B: Can we dream about the future?

The mystery of dreams is a universal human dilemma. Why, in the subconscious state of sleep, do we experience events and feelings that do not always seem to be related to our everyday life? Sequences of events and places sometimes seem as if they are something external to ourselves; we can be observers or participants. Events seem sometimes to be out of control. In extreme cases of nightmare we wake up in a fright.

Explanations of dream images are legion: that we enter an 'alternative universe'; that we enter into telepathic communication with the minds of a wider range of people; or, more prosaically, that it is all in our minds, drawing on a range of experiences that we have had, but forgotten. Another explanation is, however, that, at least in part, we are witnessing events that have not yet taken place. That in our dreams we are given glimpses of a future which is in some way fixed – in other words, a sleeping vision of the already determined future.

This view was expounded in a widely discussed book published in 1929: J. W. Dunne's *Experiment with time*. As a result of his own and certain friends' personal experiences, he was convinced that there was a relation between certain events in dreams, and things that later transpired hours, days, months or even years after the dream. There was a series of case studies to back up his belief. It was, of course, in Dunne's view important to *record* the dreams by writing them down on waking. These diaries were then periodically re-read and correlation with later events noted. The latter part of the book was a less successful attempt to explain the phenomenon, by reference to the present being a dot moving along a fixed line of time, rather like a traveller on the Trans-Siberian railway who knows all the places that have been traversed. Each new one along the line is, however, unknown until the moment it is seen, but it has been there all the time.

Dunne did not really explain *how* glimpses of future events got into our dreams, except in a woolly way. His book was well known in the years immediately after it was published, but has generated little interest since. Dreams tend to be regarded now as fodder for psycho-analysis, much exploited in popular journalism and films, but personal interest in them remains, at an anecdotal and family/friends level.

Story C: A Conversation on Computus

Computus is a planet of the Sirius star system with a history and biomass very similar to Earth, but with a developmental sequence some four million years in advance of that of Earth. Patras and his son Filofax are found in an elegantly designed living unit, with the familiar array of winking lights, manipulation keyboards and three-dimensional viewing screens. A similar conversation between Matras and her daughter Filafar must be imagined as taking place in another such unit in the same complex. Sexual dimorphism is thus apparent, even in this advanced society. The time is the present. They converse in a slightly stilted way, having been brought up in a Socratic mode.

> Filofax: Well, I am now 500 years old, and you have always impressed on me that at this point I put away childish things, and embark on my life's research. So perhaps you can now put me in the picture and give me some idea of the history of this initiative, which clearly dominates life on Computus.

> Patras: Yes, this is a great moment for you, and I have been looking forward to expounding to you the background to what you are about to undertake.

> F: Can we go right back to the beginning, to early prehistoric times? I've never been clear how it all began.

> P: The big breakthrough was achieved about 3 million years ago by scientists working in different areas. In the previous million years we had reached the limits of optical and electromagnetic scanning. We had a good idea of the extent of the visible universe mapped in this way. Our space craft had explored the parts of the galaxy which were within the limits of our cryogenic life-spans. As you know, we failed to find any star-system with a history similar to ours. Nor did we locate any planet with anything we could call a life-form.

But then came the Sirian Ray. This was able to probe much further than manned or even unmanned space probes and was an extremely sensitive analytical tool. It was developed to the point where it could assess the physical character of any planet scanned; its atmosphere, its climate, its natural resources, its year-length and the presence and character of any life-forms. For a while the results were disappointing. Planets were too hot, too cold or unstable, and there was no sign of any life-forms. But about 3 million years ago, one of several planets in orbit around the minor star Sola caused great excitement on our screens. It appeared to be remarkably similar to Computus in almost every respect, even in its proportion of seas, land masses and atmosphere. We named it Terra.

F: And what about life-forms?

P: Naturally we were optimistic, since we were devotees of generalising laws: that on a planet with a similar character, the evolutionary processes might have followed similar paths to our own; and as we focused in at larger scales, this proved to be the case. There was clearly a very diverse range of life-forms. They swam in the sea, flew in the air and lived on the land masses. They ranged in size from a few sirimetres to huge creatures much bigger than ourselves.

F: What stage had they reached in the evolutionary process?

P: As far as we could tell, they were at the stage recorded from our earliest prehistory. A wide variety of forms, with mammalian species showing signs of more sophisticated self-consciousness and brain capacity.

F: Could anything like ourselves be discerned at this stage?

P: Yes. Again we could find analogues with our early prehistory. One species had developed an upright stance, had begun to use tools and complex linguistic and social systems, had control of fire and, although still aggressive, also had some elements of food-sharing and collaboration in hunting other species.

F: So much for the first big step. What happened next? Did these more dominant creatures develop in the same ways as we did?

P: Yes, and that was a source of absorbing interest to us in the next 2 million years. We could observe the slowly increasing success in controlling the environment, ensuring survival and a longer life-span. We were of course able at every stage to interpret these, and to some extent predict the next stage, by analogue with our own prehistory.

F: But all this was merely observing, and a far cry from what goes on today. It sounds like no more than elitist research.

P: That brings us to the next major development, brought about by the steady advancement of computing. By a million years ago we were able to feed all the information into our world data base and gradually, again using our own history, we could predict, first general trends over the whole planet, then regional sequences, then events in very small areas, with some accuracy. This was not too difficult, as development on Terra was heavily associated with environmental opportunities and constraints at that time.

F: This all sounds a bit impersonal. Study of systems is all very well, but what about the study of the individual? Could you get round to anything cognitive? What was happening in the minds of the Terrans?

P: That was a further significant advance. Again, because decision making in all species starts from "How do we eat tomorrow?" it was easy to predict even what one individual of this advanced mammalian species was about to do. At this stage, with refinement of scanning, we were able to characterise every individual, both physically and psychologically. This therefore became very personal. At this point we named our Terran individuals Hominids.

F: This must have taken a lot of computer time?

P: Yes, but the study was so fascinating that it became a universal Computan obsession. Some indeed suggested that we were becoming more interested in Hominids than ourselves. The study was, however, recognised as intellectual research of the highest order, exercising our minds and developing our scanning, computing and interpretative techniques to the utmost. And remember that the total number of Hominids to be studied did not at this time exceed a million. This gave us time to perfect our techniques in preparation for the changes we knew would inevitably come with increasing acceleration.

F: Did these come about in the same horrific way as here on Computus?

P: Rather worse, if anything. Self-consciousness gave the Hominids an intensified conviction that they were the *most important* species, rather than just different. This brought about, in the last hundred millennia, an acute awareness of death (emphasised by special modes of disposing the dead), and a pondering of whether death was in fact the end. This also brought about, as in our own society in its early days, the search for some purpose to it all, some exterior guiding intention. This was the beginning of religion and the invention of a wide variety of deities. These, it was thought, could guide and interfere in Hominid affairs, and bring rewards and punishments in accordance with mysterious aims (as you will see, we developed this for our own purposes later on). You will remember how long it took us to realise that the sole purpose of life was reproduction of species – a wholly natural product of evolution and natural selection. Not realising this, even the very mechanism of reproduction in Hominids by intra-sexual copulation, was elevated to a mystique, subject to taboos and regulations as were eating and power seeking.

F: That sounds like trouble reminiscent of our own dark ages!

P: Indeed, fighting over resources was, of course, endemic in the survival struggles of all life-forms, as was predation in one form or another, though this was initially self-regulating and formed a sort of system in its own right. But the superior inventive abilities of Hominids brought about ever more competition for land and the resources this provided, and fighting with more destructive weapons, as happened here. Similarly, success in reproduction and an increase in life-span brought exponential increases in population, and consequential diminishing of resources and damage to the environment itself.

F: You spoke of the analysis of individuals. How detailed did that become?

P: Initially it was fairly simple, but became more difficult as the Hominids themselves became more complex. Fortunately this only acted as a stimulus to our own research and again we had our own development to use as a predictive model. By ten millennia ago we were able to probe the very biorhythms of the human brain and see what each Hominid was thinking. Since we had by that time total knowledge of the entire Terran environmental processes, our computers could match precisely the cognitive processes and decisions to their external world. As we expected, there was a direct relationship between genetic make-up, social influences and the environment.

F: Hominids on Terra were not, of course, aware of this?

P: A few began to suspect it, in recent millennia, but since one of the results of natural selection was to inculcate a feeling of individual free will and an ability to 'get on' by one's own decisions, such beliefs made little headway. Personal responsibility was a paramount concept, with its familiar dreary concomitant notions of guilt, pride, savage punishment, material reward and exploitation of fellow Hominids and other life-forms alike.

F: Could nothing be done in the light of our own experience to save them all the horrors that we went through?

P: At last you have come to the point. Could we do this, and if so, should we? Was it ethical to interfere in the 'natural' development of another world? We hoped, in any case, that they would, after further millions of years, arrive at our own stage of balanced harmonious world with the dynamic intellectual life we enjoy. A fierce debate ensued in our institutes. Finally, probably due to intellectual curiosity rather more than compassion, it was decided to attempt very limited inference to try to improve matters and save the Hominids from some of the trauma that we had experienced.

F: But surely to observe and to interfere are two very different things. Did not this involve radical new scientific tools?

P: Yes, and these have been steadily developed, but are still in their infancy. One major purpose of the study you are about to be involved in is the gradual perfection of these techniques over succeeding millennia. Firstly we discovered, quite by accident, that scanning of an individual's biorhythms and brain activity did, in a few cases, appear to induce a reaction, a sense of something odd happening in thoughts, and this could be monitored as a 'blip' in the day-by-day predictions for each person. This effect seemed to be more acute if the individual was drowsy or asleep. The sub-conscious areas of Hominid minds were clearly more receptive to our scans.

F: There is still a big step though between such a reaction and our being able to use it.

P: This was not too difficult. We were able to superimpose sound and vision pulses on the Sirian Ray, and these could then, in favourable circumstances, reach the mind of the individual, especially in dreams.

F: Did they not find this rather disturbing?

P: Yes, when this began, about seven millennia ago, we recorded numerous reactions to strange things in dreams, and attempts to interpret their meaning. Were they messages or warnings from particular deities? Were they the result of lobster supper or stress? In an acute form, the strange dreams were called 'nightmares' and here perhaps our image transposition went too far.

F: This doesn't sound much like *helping them*, only causing confusion. But I think I discern here the start of us being visualised as external god-like beings.

P: This also worried many of us, but we were unable to build on this by combining our ability to invade the mind with a way of predicting precisely what was going to happen to that individual. This initiated what are still rather undeveloped attempts to transmit rather lurid pictures and words of what was about to happen if things continued in their pre-directed course.

F: But didn't that negate the whole process of prediction, if we became *part* of it? An external factor.

P: Indeed, this is the great paradox of the interaction between the observer and the observed and that is one of the principal reasons why we have not yet got the balance right.

F: Do you think that there was any realisation of what was going on?

P: Yes, from the start this was one of the interpretations of dreams; that they foretold the future, and that such a future could be avoided. Rather surprisingly, some took this as an indication that time as we perceive it had no meaning. That the future existed as truly as the past, and that these dreams gave glimpses of it. The idea that this was *prediction* by a 'super-computer in the sky' was not suggested, though the theoretical possibility of such a computer was used by some Terran philosophers in the last two millennia to support concepts of a regulated, determined world.

F: Only limited success here then, but where does my part come into all of this?

P: After a long period of very limited success, we realised that progress could only be made by the intensive study of one Terran Hominid by one of ourselves. A kind of adoption on a one-to-one basis. Each person, on reaching the age of 500 years, is therefore assigned a Hominid just conceived, so that intense understanding can be achieved from the earliest possible moment. All this is done in the earlier years under the guidance of one's father or mother, so I shall have a considerable part to play in your work.

F: The observer then must become heavily involved with a Hominid for several decades?

P: It is indeed a great responsibility to be so linked to another individual on a different planet. This can cause acute distress, and occasionally one of us has to be taken off the study. It is perhaps absurd to talk of it as an emotional relationship, but this is what it can become.

F: Looking ahead rather, can one go beyond vague and uncertain warnings in dreams, and actually exercise influence?

P: Here we are on dangerous ground. Yes, a few gifted individuals have not only penetrated dreams, but have almost entered the mind themselves, in an attempt at direct action. This is strongly discouraged, as the consequences can make matters worse on Terra than they would otherwise have been. Some two thousand years ago, one of our young even succeeded in 'taking over' the mind of a Hominid so completely that the Terra thought that he was a god 'sent down' by his father to 'save' his fellow Hominids. Needless to say, this did not endear this Terran to his fellows, and he got himself prematurely killed. This and other similar cases are not in themselves so disastrous, but they have given rise in recent millennia to an expansion in the belief in supernatural deities to the point of the establishment of religions so powerful and widespread as to the cause of numerous wars and the loss of millions of lives. In some compensation, it must also be said that belief in external deities has brought hope and consolation in bad times, and has given rise to some really remarkable works of art, architecture, literature and music which we see as harbingers of a future similar to that which we now experience here.

F: Is there no other form of benevolent interference we can bring about to relieve Terran suffering?

P: In some related disciplines, knowledge of cellular evolution has led to attempts to use the Sirian Ray to affect this too. Very occasionally these have succeeded. We have been able to cure illnesses, to change water into wine, to increase the food supply, or even reverse death. Unfortunately these have been seized on by the extremists we talked about just now, to enhance their god-like pretensions (for this, sadly, has become a matter of pride). These changes have thus come to be associated with the religions I have described and with the particular individuals whose minds have been taken over. The trouble is that once a 'miracle' (as they call such occurrences) has happened, everyone sees that as the answer to their troubles. Being already dimly conscious of their supernatural mentor, they identify him or her with a deity who is able to bring about such miracles, and, in times of trouble, offer up prayers for such external influence to avert illness, to win wars, or even to give them power over others! So, as you discerned earlier on, we have become personal gods!

F: I don't like the sound of this at all. We appear to do more harm than good. I think I'll stick to dreams!

P: It might be wiser, but these are, as I say, early days and we must seek a solution to the problems of misguided interference. In the end, if our research is successful, we may either genuinely be able to help Terrans to accelerate progress to our present state, or we may eventually give up and leave them to their own fate. Even if this is one that we can see all too clearly, it will be difficult for us to distance ourselves completely. They are so much like us in essence, being the product of similar processes, that we have developed a great sympathy for them.

F: Is this a difficult time for me personally to begin my work?

P: Yes. In recent years the Terran condition has deteriorated so fast that we have been quite powerless to affect it at all. Nuclear fission threatens the planet itself with all its life-forms, as does air and water pollution. There is hardly any part of their world in which there is not war or famine and, ironically, Terran success in medicine has brought about the emergence of minute life-forms which threaten to kill millions, so you are coming in at a difficult time.

F: It is a daunting prospect, but I will undertake it. How do I start?

P: I have here on the screen this array of babies who have just been conceived on Terra. Shall we look it over?

Philip Rahtz is Emeritus Professor of Archaeology in the Department of Archaeology, University of York. He has written many times on the subject of archaeology and science fiction, most notably in his 1986 book *Invitation to Archaeology*.

PART THREE

THE SHAPE OF THINGS TO COME?

And so we reach our final destination. We have examined our world and the parallel worlds around us. Now it is time to consider what the future holds for us.

Can we accurately predict the shape of things to come with regard to architecture, fashion, technology and culture, or does science fiction just reflect and enforce the outlooks, beliefs and prejudices of its own era? Can ideas and concepts outlined within science fiction enlighten us as to the way forward for archaeologists and archaeological fieldwork? Is there life on other planets and, even if there is, how could we realistically tell? Has our solar system been visited by alien life forms (and if it has, why didn't they bother to leave us a note?). Do archaeologists have a future, or are they doomed to live their lives as Cyber-Diggers, locked forever within a Virtual-Trench?

10

A Quick Sketch of the *Enterprise*: Graphic reconstructions of the future

John Hodgson

"Which is farther from us, farther out of reach, more silent – the dead, or the unborn? Those whose bones lie under the thistles and the dirt and the tombstones of the Past, or those who slip weightless among molecules, dwelling where a century passes in a day, among the fair folk, under the great, bell-curved Hill of Possibility?

There's no way to reach that lot by digging."

Towards an Archaeology of the Future
Preface to *Always coming home*
Ursula K. LeGuin

Over the past 50 years the science fiction establishment has occasionally congratulated itself on its inventiveness, and strongly suggested a high degree of prescience in its predictions of the future of technology. Sometimes, this has been taken to the point where one might imagine the actual discoveries of 20th century science as being made by the transcendent inspiration of writers, while a drab bunch of mundane scientists tag along behind to construct the boring but necessary proofs. While this chapter cannot claim an exhaustive coverage of the literature and cinema in question, the sample available to most of us through the popular culture of the last 50 years suggests that this may be a very partial reading of the situation.

In the first instance – just as with fortune-telling or past editions of *Tomorrow's World* – it is very easy to remember the correct predictions and forget the howlers. The space-station shaped like a gyroscope, which has been popular from the days of *Dan Dare* right up to *Deep Space Nine*, is still cited as an brilliantly innovative idea for generating artificial gravity, although nobody is much closer to actually constructing one. The howlers – those elusive "atomic engines" which are not much like a plasma rocket, or the space-suited heroes who lose their helmets but are fine so long as they hold their breath – are mentioned less often.

Secondly, the writers and artists in all media who construct these scenarios are in the wonderful position of doing their building in non-space: in the dimension of the imagination. Here, there is the intoxicating freedom to borrow any interesting concepts from the sciences and extrapolate them, while ignoring the boring "nuts and bolts" factor of actual engineering practicability. After all, if you put that wonderful atomic engine inside a streamlined box, with perhaps a few pipes poking out of the side, there is no necessity to demonstrate how it might actually work.

It is, of course, possible that an illustration in the present may become a factor that influences the future; a design idea that was purely an imaginative exercise may be taken up and embodied as an actual artefact. At present there seem to be few instances of this, partly perhaps because writers and illustrators have now jumped so far beyond what is technically possible at the present moment. Engineers can hardly be inspired to build a space station the size and complexity of *Babylon 5* or *Deep Space Nine* when they have only just got as far as keeping *Mir* in the sky – for a time, at least.

Although ideas may be influential, the visual artist has to convey them by representing things – including artefacts; and the design process of these is still conditioned very much by the state of the technology rather than the limitations of human imagination. In fact the visual arts, as compared to literature, have a number of disadvantages in the realms of futuristic prediction. To a large extent, these are related to the mechanisms that they use to convey information.

Representation and the creation of icons

Representative illustration functions in a way which is analogous to the mechanism of reading. Rather than deciphering words letter by letter, the brain builds up a visual vocabulary of commonly encountered words which are recognised by their shape on the page; only unknown words are 'spelled out'. This process can be very clearly observed in children who are learning to read aloud. Similarly, a representative picture contains a complex system of visual clues and references to things in the "known world"; icons which can be recognised as part of the normal environment of both the artist and the audience. This is just as true of photography, as can be seen in those puzzle pictures of everyday objects seen from unusual angles or magnifications, and of all the representational arts. If there are no reference points, there is no recognition. Vision, and the recognition of objects, is a learnt skill rather than an innate ability.

Comic and cartoon illustrators work this system in a very overt and recognisable way. The cartoon symbol for 'bone', for example, is something like a mammalian long bone, but is not pretending to be an accurate representation of any particular item within the skeleton. It does, however, give the most salient points about that kind of object without any extraneous or distracting detail, thus making the image more immediately recognisable, and more effective in that context. This is true for cartoon depictions of all objects, and it explains some oddities of the practice: the universally recognised symbol for 'train' is actually a picture of a steam locomotive, even in places where they have been superseded for forty years. Modern electric or diesel locomotives have far fewer key points, such as funnels and domes, in their profiles, and so do not perform as well in the role of icons. The practice appears simple, but this is deceptive: those who attempt cartoons because they believe that they cannot draw 'properly' find that it actually requires high degrees of observational, compositional and manual skill.

This use of iconography is true for artwork of a less stylised, more naturalistic kind; for example book illustration, film and film graphics. The important point in our present context, i.e. graphic artwork for science fiction, is that the artist has to express a narrative to the viewer using symbols which are familiar *by reference to known objects* – that is, objects from our own present or past (see also Haslam, this volume).

The problems of scale

This process is evident in the ways in which size and the relative scale of objects are represented. By and large the spacecraft of modern science fiction are huge; the *Enterprise* or *Voyager* in *Star Trek*, the *Nostromo* in *Alien* and the many craft in the *Star Wars* film franchise, are only a few of the best-known of these leviathans. In much science fiction, the assumption that progress in development implies progressive enlargement operates full-throttle: probably Gerry Andersons' films and the *Thunderbirds* series are the Platonic ideal of this principle. However, it is difficult to express the scale of these things in space, where there is nothing to compare them with – none of the objects of known size that we normally use for comparative assessment of scale; in fact nothing whatsoever.

However, there are several ways in which it can be done. The icon to which we relate most immediately and completely, in many different contexts, is the human figure. One of these contexts is scale: we know the size of our own bodies probably better than any other unit, and can judge the mass of other objects in relation to it. While the human body is too small a unit to relate directly to these spaceships, it can be done in a series of stages. This is a frequently used device exemplified in the opening credits of the BBC series *Red Dwarf*, where a space-suited figure is shown in relation to a letter-stroke, which is then related to a letter, which is related to a word, which is related to the overall ship. We do not finish the sequence with an accurate assessment of the scale, but that does not matter; what we have is a feeling of monstrosity, the gigantic size of a vessel that – to quote a crew member – is "six miles long and as ugly as Petersen's mother".

Another commonly used indication of scale is the use of windows, which could well be an instance of the way that graphic imperatives outweigh probability. Whether quantities of large picture-windows would really be much in evidence on an actual, functioning space vessel seems open to question. However, we are very used to seeing lighted windows in big structures or images of them: in the cityscapes of office blocks, or ocean liners with their rows of portholes. The image carries the twin messages *big* and *manmade*. It gives a reference to the scale, and is even more effective if, as before, one of the cuts contains a human figure; this ties down the size of the window. These considerations outweigh the actual probabilities, and hence spacecraft always twinkle against the blackness of the Universe with a host of very tiny windows.

Systems of propulsion

To postulate interstellar and intergalactic travel we must also postulate the development of extraordinary means of propulsion, different in kind from anything known at present. The images of spacecraft that are presented may seem to have developed considerably since Dan Dare's jet-fighter equivalents were leaving vapour trails through space, but in fact they still, on the whole, rely on the same basic iconography. The various *U.S. Enterprises* have developed in shape, possibly under the influence of 'flying saucer' stories, but they are still plate metal constructions with engines at the back end (even serviced by Scottish engineers) pushing them through the oceans of space. This points up the importance of convention: the warp drive is an ingenious concept, but it is a means of creating a field of distorted space, not an engine as such. It need not be at the back end. However, the *convention* that vessels move by being pushed along by their engines is so strong that the *Enterprise* needs those glowing blue warp drive coils at the back end to be credible.

Constructional methods and materials

Similar conventions operate in the depiction of constructional methods. It is at least likely that the materials and methods of construction for these vessels would be different as well. Yet there is usually a very clear pattern of metal plating in the outer skin; even the starship *Voyager* (the most recent addition to the *Star Trek* multiverse) has this, though only in a very subtle modulation of colour and shade. There are probably two reasons for this.

Firstly	it is another scale indicator, although not a very precise one. It indicates that the artefact is made up of parts or units, as a fur coat is built up from a number of pelts. There is, perhaps, a suggestion that the more units a thing is made up of, the larger it must be.
Secondly	it is an effect, and a pattern, that is very familiar to us from ship-building, and these are the largest man-made mobile objects that we know. The pattern carries the emotive messages of a liner or a warship: of ponderous weight, colossal size, and tremendous power. These messages outweigh any depiction of postulated material developments – for example a seamless, frictionless surface, or one that (for whatever reason) has an organic appearance – because, for the *dramatic* purposes of the story being illustrated, they are more effective.

Design and appearance

Moving on to the overall design and appearance of these postulated spacecraft, there is evidence of the same depiction techniques: the extrapolation from existing artefacts rather than the envisioning of anything totally strange. In other words, a spaceship has to look like a spaceship – in accordance with certain criteria – in order to work as an illustration. It may be instructive to compare predictions with what actually happened; which we are now in a position to do with the Apollo programme and the moon landings.

In the science fiction of the 1950s, the rocket ship was based very firmly on a selection of elements from real-life working models. Frequently, of course, these were taken from World War 2 aircraft: one item which crops up very frequently is the multi-paned glass nose, a direct copy of that on the Heinkel He 111 bomber. But one of the most used images of this time was the German V2 weapon. This rocket had very clear characteristics: the tail fins, pointed nose, curving line of the fastigiate profile and the chequer pattern of the paintwork. All of these, with modifications, can be seen in the popular art such as magazine and comic illustrations of the period: perhaps the most perfect form being Tintin's rocket in Herge's cartoon book *Destination Moon*. The tail fins, pointed nose, cigar-shaped body – even a modified form of the chequer pattern – are all there.

As a symbol, it works superbly. As a prophecy, it bears very little visual relationship to the Apollo complex which actually achieved the Moon landing. This was a multistage rocket with disposable units, the Saturn rocket had no fins, it was straight-sided with a conical point and the only paintwork was a large United States of America logo (presumably in case it got lost).

The same kind of process can be seen in operation in two 1970s illustrations by Angus McKie. The first represents the *Interstellar Queen*, a proposed 'spaceliner' of the 21st century. Like many other publications of the 60s and 70s, the book presupposes a straight-line progression of space exploration after the Apollo programme: by the year 2000 Mars is not only landed upon but colonised. What the artist has done is to borrow the drop-nose motif from the Concorde airliner, which at the time that the drawing was made carried the appropriate connotations of speed, power, luxury and – above all – modernity. This was grafted on to a more nondescript spaceship structure. The original *function* of the dropped nose (to aid take-off and landing on runways) is redundant here of course; the distinctive shape now has its own iconographic messages.

In the same publication, the same artist has done exactly the same thing with 'Miami Spaceport', only here he has borrowed the roof of the Sydney Opera House. Again, function has been forgotten. The shape of the original roof was dictated by acoustic considerations which would be unlikely to apply to a spaceport. It was the *look* that was important, and in particular the chimerical concept of "modernity" – the up-to-the-minute quality which ensures that your pictures will date very quickly indeed.

Climates of thought

One final area which might be considered is what these images convey about their background; the ethos of thought in which they were conceived. A very noticeable quality about much science fiction of the 60s and 70s is the extreme cleanliness of the shipboard environments. The *Enterprise* does not appear to contain a dustpan and brush, let alone a vacuum cleaner or anything so mundane as a cleaning lady (if one can imagine such a being), yet every deck and console is spotless. This phenomenon is not confined to Starfleet, although it is noticeable that *Star Trek* is almost the only series to carry this squeaky-clean trademark into the 21st century.

Cleanliness is intimately connected with the machine aesthetic; the appreciation of the smooth, flawless, crisp and precise that we associate with man-made materials and environments. The message frequently attached to innovations in the 60s (when 'space-age material' was a frequent claim) was that they were a man-made improvement of imperfect, unreliable and probably grubby Mother Nature. The Conquest of Nature was a part of man's mastery of the planet, which at that time seemed a beneficent and noble process, and the machine aesthetic is part of a visual expression of this idea. Again, Gerry Anderson's productions epitomise this 'Man the Master' mindset, as in his series *Space: 1999*, the Moon has been converted into dump for nuclear waste. After all, what else is it there for?

Changes in ecological awareness during the 80s and 90s are reflected in space décor, which becomes more organic and decidedly more untidy. Even in *Star Trek*, the Klingons have been permitted to not dust *their* spacecraft: it would be extremely unKlingon, and besides it points up the contrast with the highly polished, squeaky clean Starfleet ships. However, this is another instance of how the depiction depends not on likelihood or reasoned extrapolations, but upon the present agenda of the storytellers.

Conclusions

If we look at the pre-launch Space Shuttle sitting on its pad, it is fairly obvious that a designer with aesthetic criteria was never allowed within a mile of the thing, and that such an unwieldy conglomeration of elements could only come about from sheer mechanical necessity. Space hardware is, at the moment, so much on the edge of what is technically possible that feasibility is the only criterion. It will probably be a long time before that changes, which is one reason why artwork, ultimately has little influence on development.

Another reason is that it operates differently from literature, which in many ways is a much freer medium. The apparent function of science fiction, in its more advanced forms, is to stretch the imagination and lead it into unknown territory, but illustration has to work largely with a vocabulary of known items. It seems rather as if, from the written or spoken word, the audience's mind can spin a lattice of images strong enough to embellish the story, without its having to be filled out in every detail. However, if you try to create that picture in "real space", those details have to be there – the picture collapses without them. A picture is a definite statement; by its nature, much more definite than a written description has to be. This is a phenomenon familiar to archaeological reconstruction artists when working on complex scenes: 'everyday life' contains an astonishing amount of factual detail, and every piece depicted must be the result of some kind of reasoned decision.

A conclusion might be that future constructions are of no particular value as a factual guide to future experience, since their material sources are (inescapably) in our past and present. However, they do have other values. They form an archive of how the people of a particular time saw their future (which is, after all, part of their world picture). They are a means of exploring the possible outcomes of present tendencies and trends, and a branch of the representative visual arts in which genuine innovation – if rare in practice – is actually possible.

John Hodgson has worked as a freelance archaeological illustrator and designer since 1985, specialising in reconstructions for the general public. He is chair of the Association of Archaeological Illustrators and Surveyors and a part-time lecturer conducting postgraduate research at Bournemouth University on the theory and practice of archaeological reconstruction.

11

Past Futures or Present Pasts

Rob Haslam

We are used to seeing art as archaeology, from Lascaux to Pompeii, lowly church wall paintings to the Sistine Chapel. The images communicate the artist's impressions of his or her environment at the time and we in turn place our interpretation on the form and style of the images and what they imply, whether they are of prey species, religious figures, rustic Arcadia or the glories of conflict. However, the opposite view, of archaeology as art, is a fairly recent phenomena which owes its popularity to the most potent artistic force in modern society, that of the moving image, be it television or cinema. The merits of small screen versus large screen, Hollywood budgets to BBC cuts, are not within the scope of this paper, and the term 'film' is used as a generic to cover the productions seen on both mediums.

Seminology in the moving image

Whilst fine art has been commonly used to reflect our present and past (leaving aside for a moment short term future visions of eternal damnation and torment for those of a nefarious disposition), film is regularly used to portray and investigate not only the past and present but also the possibilities of the future of humankind. An endeavour which has made a great impact on the public psyche and an even greater impact on the producer's bank balance.

The film director creates images for us by imposing his or her own interpretation upon the script or screen play from which he or she is working. However the technical parameters of cinematography and production time impose limits upon this interpretation, so the director can rely on semiology, a range of codes and symbols, to express or enhance in an instant what would take far too much time in dialogue to explain to the audience.

We all recognise the unspoken meaning of these symbols. The staircase lined with portraits of sour faced ancestors tells us we are in the stately home of the congenitally insane English aristocracy or megalomaniac American industrialist. The moving shadow of the sundial's gnomon conveys the genteel passage of time, whereas the more gritty films use a utilitarian clock to maintain the dramatic tension. Forbidding castles, an unhealthily large wolf population and rapid blood-red sunsets mean that Dracula or some other obscene creature is lurking around the corner. However our faith in the final defeat of evil can always be restored by oblique references to crucifixes, prayers, virginal statues, self-sacrificing priests and such.

Even in a future-scape the same tricks of the trade are used: the inevitable long shot of twinkling stars to tell us that the spaceship has a fair old distance to cover, radio dishes to remind us that home is along way behind. The semiology becomes an integral part of the overall style which the director can impose upon the film for artistic merit, as an aid to narrative and to create the aesthetic richness of which film is capable.

Style as a point of archaeological inference

In archaeology we place great emphasis on style. We attempt to define a period by the style of its pottery, the style of its buildings, the style of artefacts which we recover from the ground. Style gives us a reference frame within which we can work and recognise and use information. Architecture operates within the same parameters, where style points to a period in time when particular social, technological and constructional developments took place or were the norm. The two disciplines can be seen as the opposite ends of the same spectrum of study. After all one individual's architecture will eventually become someone else's archaeology. But how is style applied to archaeology and architecture in film, whether it is fiction, fantasy or just plain fun?

We are familiar with the stylised character portrayal of the archaeologist in film, whether the plot is terrestrially based or located in science fiction or fantasy space. The director is therefore on safe ground. Setting the central characters in an archaeological context gives the audience a frame of reference in which the story can be understood no matter where it is set. The audience know what to expect from an archaeologist, and, as noted above, we all recognise the clichés.

The good (and, from Hollywood's perspective, usually male) archaeologist is clever, resourceful and hunky. He never cries and he always gets the girl, even though he never seems to change his clothes. He is the lantern jawed, square shouldered hero for whom no danger is to great or cipher too confusing. His bespectacled innocence, in front of adoring students, belies eyesight which allows him to blow the balls off a blow fly at a thousand yards with a revolver and an expertise with explosives not normally associated with academia. The new wave archaeologist in film has become a composite of the rugged adventurer and the scientist seen before in so many B movies. The sensible, pipe smoking, type who always seemed to be asked the same question by the heroine in the movie: "You're a scientist Dr. Manly-Smart, surely you don't believe in mummies/curses/vindictive aliens/rubbery looking monsters/or whatever the story is about?"

The bad archaeologist on the other hand (again usually male) is a smooth talking, slick haired, weasely character on really good terms with the local Nazis of whatever planet he is on. He is able to dispatch countless numbers of extras and supporting cast with a selection of high tech weaponry, but always misses the good guy; though he never misses a chance to explain, in detail, exactly what his dastardly plans for our hero are. The villain's Machiavellian cunning knows no bounds and he will stop at nothing to dominate the world, or at the very least ensure that his next excavation is fully funded. We probably all know archaeologists who resemble one of these stereotypes. We of course are all in the first category, our competitors – sorry I mean colleagues – are all in the latter.

Women get a poor deal as archaeologists in film. They only seem to get supporting roles as assistants to one of the male categories. If they are part of the good guys entourage they can either be attractive but dim, beautiful but possessed of a naivety that beggars belief or bright but frumpy and drool over the hero with unrequited passion. If they have fallen in with the bad guy they are sinister nutters with a penchant for uniforms or voluptuous, devious trollops who eventually get their just deserts. Unless of course they are very attractive, well endowed and skimpily clad, in which case they may well be saved from certain damnation by the hero, if he has the time. We expect and enjoy these clichés. We identify easily with the stylised characters because that is what we are: self styled characters with airs and graces with which to soothe shattered egos or bolster reputations. Funny though, you never see hero, heroine or bad guy with a trowel.

Location, location, location

We are all also familiar with the style of artefact recovered by our hero. Squat, ugly statues made of jewel encrusted precious metals, located in labyrinthine, subterranean death traps guarded by unbelievably dedicated hatchet men The statues are inevitably of huge religious significance to a bunch of dirt poor natives who will stop a nothing to protect their treasure from the good guy. Yet for some reason these same natives seem perfectly happy to swap their priceless treasure for a handful of beads with the bad guy.

Then there are the magical artefacts, possession of which enables the forces of good or evil (usually evil) to be called upon by reciting some unlikely verse that would make a budding elementary school poet cringe. Or there is the futuristic style of artefact made of luminous Perspex and possessed of awesome powers. The kind of awesome powers which allows two-pence worth of plastic to create wormholes in space, build Superman a house from ice cubes, move Captains Kirk and Picard from one time to another or at the very least cause Scotty to change the plugs and points on the *U.S.S. Enterprise's* warp drive.

But, more crucially what about the location? How is the architecture or extant archaeology of semi-mythical or futuristic worlds portrayed? How does the director create the setting for another stirring adventure, the kind of setting which will attract a large audience ready to part with hard earned cash? A setting which would allow the advertising hoardings to imply "Lust in the jungle", "Sex in the desert" or imminent invasion by technologically advanced, yet inevitably stupid, extraterrestrials intent on galactic conquest (or at least a season's excavation well away from the tedium of institutional life and with only the local interplanetary field monument warden to ray-gun).

In a terrestrial plot the archaeological style is easy. If the film is set in the Americas we will expect stepped pyramids, big stairs, stake filled traps, snakes, spiders, human sacrifice and bad tempered members of the indigenous population parading about in loin cloths. These locals may live off the jungle using bows, arrows and spears, but could they hit a barn from the inside when it comes to taking pot shots at the hero of the film? Could they buggery!

Should we be transported to the old world, we will again know what kind of dangers will await the hero: tortuous passages through more pyramids (smooth sided ones this time), heavily bandaged villains, mystical amulets, crazed high priests with more make up than clothing, huge blocks of stone which slide effortlessly into place as the treasure of the pharaohs is nicked (or recovered, depending on your ethical view point) and convenient sand storms to provide a cover in which to escape from the clutches of evil.

But what of non-terrestrial based story lines? In science fiction plots, the scope of the director and set designer is limited only by their imagination, but how far does that imagination run? When the director looks to create a setting for his or her film, can they make one up, or do they find that imagining the architectural style of buildings which will not be constructed for centuries or millennia is beyond them? Can they predict the archaeological past of an architectural future, whether alien or human? The answer of course is that they cannot. They have to cheat, either by adopting an archaeo-architectural style, or by interpreting a style, in which to base the plot of the film whilst and pretending it is something else, or by using it as a prop to convey a social or cultural style.

Think of the 'futuristic' buildings in sets from some of your favourite sci-fi films, now with digitally re-mastered extra bits for your anorak (sorry I meant enjoyment) and at only the cost of another copy of a film that you have already bought (at least

Figure 11.1 Tatooine or le Corbusier and Mendelsohn? © Massingheimer Collection

Figure 11.2 Mos Eisley or Trans World Airlines? © Massingheimer Collection

Figure 11.3 Strange alien domain or church designed by Oscar Niemeyer for Brasilia? © Massingheimer Collection

once). Obviously they way to fund space exploration in the future is through fan exploitation. We should perhaps try the same with archaeology.

Could these be farm buildings from Tatooine, Luke Skywalker's home planet, the fantastic imaginings of the creative set designer, his mind freed of the chains of terrestrial confinement? No they are designs by le Corbusier and Mendelsohn. More modernist Spanish Colonial then Obi Wan Kenobi.

Could this image above be Mos Eisley space port where Han Solo's ship is hiding

Figure 11.4 Starfleet Academy or Florida Southern College? © Massingheimer Collection

Figure 11.5 Angel One or Guggenheim? © Massingheimer Collection

from the bad guys in *Star Wars*? It certainly looks futuristic enough. In reality, however, it really is Saarinen's design for the Trans World Airlines wing at Kennedy Airport.

In *Star Trek*, Kirk and Spock seemed to come across some alien construction on an almost weekly basis. Is the image reproduced below, therefore the entrance to some strange alien domain, or just two blokes looking at a church designed by Oscar Niemeyer for Brasilia ?

Picard, Kirk, Spock, McCoy and all our other *Star Trek* favourites went through their essential training at the Starfleet Academy, established (I am informed by those in the know), in AD 2161. Surely the Academy looks more akin to the Florida Southern College designed by Frank Lloyd Wright in 1940?

The class M planet Angel One apparently supports carbon based life forms including an intelligent humanoid matriarchal population (or so the gushing *Star Trek* fanzine blurb assures me). Be that as it may, their architecture still looks like Frank Lloyd Wright to me (above), and is that the Guggenheim Museum, New York City, completed in 1959?

The intergalactic and subaquatic cityscapes created for many a 1930s, 40s, 50s and 60s SciFi flick (the 1969 spectacular *Captain Nemo and the Underwater City* being a good example), often possess incredible, and also largely infeasible, dome constructions. More often than not such domes bear more than a passing resemblance to the ones created by architect Frank Lloyd Wright. He must have a lot of fans in Hollywood.

H. G. Wells wrote of *The Shape of Things to Come*, but when this particular vision of the future was filmed (in 1936 as *Things to Come*), film director William Menzies and producer Alexander Korda (also director of art for the picture), dressed the cast as Romans casually visiting the local Arndale Centre for a spot of advanced consumerism (below). Obviously Well's futuristic society did not possess internet shopping. The sets of course are immensely impressive to see, and you have to congratulate the artists who worked on their production for the clever way in which they are conceived and constructed. But, from a viewpoint in the present, it is still very evident that this is the distant past being polished-up, repackaged and presented as the future. The use of archaeological or architectural style to imply socio-cultural values, also suffers from the same constraint. The semiology behind the archaeo-architectural facade may easily be recognised, even if the truth behind the facade is hugely distorted.

In *Beneath the Planet of the Apes* (1969), the intrepid hero, finds his way through a maze of underground passages to find all that remains of his own world, the higher aspirations of our now destroyed civilisation are represented by disintegrating pieces of classical architecture. Similarly, in the semi-surreal *Atlantis the Lost Continent* (1960), classical architecture is again used to suggest a cultural Arcadia under-pinned by Imperial might and order; a look back at how good things used to be. Unfortunately this particular Atlantis is run by mad scientists and guarded by death rays – just goes to show how wrong you can be. The 1936 chapter spectacular *Flash Gordon*, starring Buster Crabbe, had Romanesque arches and bad guys dressed as Romans. The implication of course is the same: Flash must fight against the dictatorial forces of evil to save the galaxy. Those Romans were obviously a rotten lot.

Industrial (revolution) archaeology, implying all that is bad about the machine age, has never been better portrayed than in Fritz Lang's *Metropolis* (1926): a terrifying vision of the future in which everything is controlled by an elite few and the masses are without hope or prospects. Incidentally, has anyone tried getting money from English Heritage lately?

Figure 11.6 Things to Come (1936): will the future really comprise Romans swarming through hi-tech shopping centres? © The Kobal Collection.

The shape of things to come?

So we can use an archaeological or architectural style to imply a wide variety of backgrounds and conditions, but it is just transporting a perceived quality or style from the past to the future. We can dream up fabulous star drives capable of carrying us to the far reaches of the galaxy, amazing weapons for space ship use and weird creatures to terrify us, or carry indigestion to really quite unnecessary lengths, but the style of future architecture and eventually archaeology has us stumped.

It seems that we cannot boldly go where no architect has gone before, we can only re-interpret what an archaeologist will eventually excavate, someone else's ruins. We are, in other words, doomed to have our past presented as someone else's future. The film makers hands are tied. Architectural style can only move forwards in time at the same pace as the rest of us.

Rob Haslam is a researcher in the Archaeology Group of the School of Conservation Sciences, Bournemouth University. His particular interests include anthropogenic deposition and soils in environmental archaeology and the historical development of landscape and environments. He was previously a MARS (not the planet) project survey co-ordinator.

12

Towards an LSMR and MSMR (Lunar and Martian Sites & Monuments Records): recording planetary spacecraft landing sites as archaeological monuments of the future

Greg Fewer

Imagine the following scenario unfold in the year 2097:

> "The children could hardly wait to jump down onto the Martian surface. They had been cooped up for months aboard the *Sigourney Weaver* on its journey from Earth Orbital Station 5 and now, at last, they could be free of the confines of the ship. After making contact with Martian soil, Ricky and Donna bounded (somewhat shakily, but with much enthusiasm) towards the *Carl Sagan Memorial Station*. They didn't know who Carl Sagan was (and didn't really care), but they had learnt in school that one of the earliest spacecraft sent to Mars had landed at the memorial where it was still to be seen. The children hoped they'd be able to take a piece of the *Mars Pathfinder* spacecraft with them on their way home to earth so that they could prove to their friends that they had been to see the memorial. Their father, however, had warned them that they'd get into serious trouble if he found them tinkering with the old space probe. He was particularly mindful of the recent news coverage of the craft's one hundredth birthday and how scientists visiting the memorial on the occasion had found it to have been damaged by souvenir hunters. He groaned when he saw the kids scramble up *Pathfinder's* ramps and snap its aerial mast in an abortive attempt to climb it..."

One hundred years earlier, as we enter a new millennium, it is a time when we have numerous spacecraft circling our planet, probing various locations of the solar system or lying on the surfaces of other planets. Many of these spacecraft have provided important scientific breakthroughs in the technology of space travel and in astro-nomical research yet there is no international legislative framework that protects these craft or their landing sites from future human interference should astro-tourism ever take off (so to speak). In this chapter, I will outline the extent of human exploration of other planets to date, provide an overview of the international regulations relating to space travel and offer some suggestions on conserving the integrity of spacecraft and their landing or crash sites as places of international historic and scientific interest.

The Sites in question

Although the other planets of our solar system are still beyond the reach of tourists, visitors have offered a constant source of disturbance to remote sites on earth, such as the encampments of nineteenth-century Arctic expeditions including that of the ill-fated Sir John Franklin who sought the Northwest Passage in northern Canada in 1845–48 (Beattie and Geiger 1987, 69–70, 98). The discovery, during excavations carried out in the mid-1980s, of the frozen, and consequently well-preserved, corpses of three members of Franklin's crew made headline news around the world.

The corpses' preservation was due to their burial six feet under the ground in permafrost where they had quite literally been placed into a deep freeze. Even though a century or more has passed since the original deposition of such nineteenth-century explorers' artefacts, the near absence of vegetation and the low density of wild animals and people north of the Arctic Circle has allowed many finds to remain *in situ* on the surface of the soil where they are clearly visible to the visitors of today. Consequently, the Canadian authorities have raised signs at these historic sites with the inscription: 'PLEASE do not remove artefacts' (Beattie and Geiger 1987, plate between p 116 and 117) in a sometimes vain attempt to limit damage.

Interestingly, in the context of this chapter, Franklin expedition archaeologist, Owen Beattie, and his journalist colleague John Geiger found that "Apart from the Antarctic, and perhaps a handful of other places, there is nowhere in the world that a person can face solitude as in the Canadian Arctic. It is perhaps the closest experience on earth to that of the astronauts in space." (Beattie and Geiger 1987, 92–3).

Turning our gaze to outer space, there are a number of spacecraft landing and wreckage sites on Mars and, more particularly, the Moon. The bulk of these date from the late 1950s to the early 1970s during the Space Race between the United States and the Soviet Union. Of unmanned spacecraft on the Moon, the United States had sent *Lunar Orbiters 1–5*, all of which were deliberately crashed onto the Moon's surface once they had successfully carried out their orbital missions (Turnill 1974, 58–9). *Rangers 6–9* were also impacted onto the Moon at the ends of their missions (which were to provide data on the nature of the lunar surface prior to the launching of the *Apollo* series of manually-controlled spacecraft: Turnill 1974, 105–6).

Some remotely-controlled spacecraft were successfully soft-landed by the Ameri-cans onto the Moon and these include *Surveyors 1, 3, 5, 6* and *7, Surveyors 2* and *4* having crashed accidentally (Turnill 1974, 107–8). Meanwhile the Soviet Union successfully soft-landed six spacecraft (*Luna 9, 13, 16, 17, 20* and *21*), crashing seven

Figure 12.1 Surveyor 3 photographed on the lunar surface during the Apollo 12 mission in 1969. ©
NASA and the NSSDC.

others in the *Luna* series. As part of their research programme, two robotic exploratory
vehicles (*Lunokhod 1* and *2*) were deployed onto the Moon by *Luna* spacecraft (Turnill
1974, 134–51). In all, the Moon's surface bears the remains of no less than 29 remotely-
controlled spacecraft and two robotic rovers, to which may be added the lunar modules
and associated equipment of the manually-controlled *Apollo* missions that I will shortly
discuss.

Remote-controlled spacecraft sent to Mars include the Russian *Mars 2* and *3* rovers
(the former having crashed onto the surface), the more well-known American landers
Viking 1 and *2*, and of course the recent success-story of *Mars Pathfinder* and its robotic
rover called *Sojourner* (Turnill 1974, 157–9; Anon 1976; Anon 1998; Begley 1997). The
landing sites of both *Viking 1* and *Pathfinder* have additional historical significance
since both were named after space scientists. That for *Viking 1* is now known as the
Thomas A. Mutch Memorial Station and was named after the NASA Associate
Administrator in charge of the imaging team of that spacecraft. When *Pathfinder*
successfully touched down on Martian soil on 4 July 1997, NASA Administrator Dan
Goldin named it the *Carl Sagan Memorial Station* in honour of the well-known scientist
and science publicist who died in 1996 (Friedman 1997).

It might be added here that Mars and the Moon are not the only planetary bodies
on which space probes have landed or crashed. Venus was studied over many years
by the Russians who sent a series of remotely-controlled spacecraft to explore the

*Figure 12.2 The Thomas A. Mutch Memorial Station, or Viking Lander 1: a self portrait taken in 1976.
© NASA and the NSSDC.*

Figure 12.3 Apollo 15. The lunar landing site photographed in 1971. © NASA and the NSSDC.

planet in the sixties and seventies. Six of these (*Venus 3–8*) penetrated the planet's dense atmosphere either to land or impact onto its surface (Turnill 1974, 172–81). Also, once its orbital mapping mission was completed, NASA's *Magellan* spacecraft was gradually dragged into the Venusian atmosphere in the summer of 1993 to test the theory of aerobraking as a method of slowing down spacecraft in orbit. The experiment proved successful, allowing *Magellan* to add some useful data to that which it had already collected, but it also caused the spacecraft's orbit to decay (as

Figure 12.4 Apollo 15. The Lunar Rover seen in action during the Apollo 15 mission in August 1971.
© *NASA and the NSSDC.*

expected) until it entered the Venusian atmosphere to impact onto the planet's surface on 12 October 1994 (Doody 1994; Magee 1995).

Since the intense pressure, heat and corrosive atmosphere on Venus would make it extremely unlikely for the remains of any of these craft to be found (much less visited), there should be no reason for them to be listed in any inventory of landing and crash sites. The same could be said for the *Galileo* probe that plumbed the upper layers of Jupiter's atmosphere for just over an hour before its signal ended on 7 December 1995 (Young 1996).

Turning to human interplanetary expeditions, the only other planetary body to be visited by people so far is, of course, the Moon. There have been a total of six missions, all of them American, and these took place between 1969 and 1972. *Apollo 11* is probably the best known mission, its lunar module, *Eagle*, having brought human beings to set foot for the first time on the lunar surface on 20 July 1969.

Interestingly, from the point of view of conserving the integrity of spacecraft on other planetary bodies, members of the *Apollo 12* crew removed selected parts of the *Surveyor 3* spacecraft which had landed on the Moon two years previously, its landing site being only 600m from that of the *Intrepid*. These parts were taken back to earth for analysis to learn how conditions on the Moon had affected them over time (Ordway and von Braun 1979, 568b–568c). Thus, the precedent for souvenir-taking has already been set, though at least it was for scientific purposes on this occasion.

The Legislation

Okay, so there are lots of spacecraft, and spaceship debris, scattered across the Moon and Mars (with those on Venus and Jupiter probably being no longer identifiable), but how might they be protected from human interference in the future (should this ever arise)? The most important piece of international legislation in place that may serve as the basis for their protection is what is popularly known as the Outer Space Treaty which was opened for signature at Moscow, London and Washington, on 27 January 1967 (United Nations, 1967). This treaty has been ratified by ninety-one countries (United Nations Office for Outer Space Affairs 1967) and re-affirms an earlier agreement of 1963, by which the General Assembly of the United Nations had declared, "That outer space should be used for the benefit of all people and that no nation could claim any part of it" (Bloomfield 1979, 40e).

The Outer Space Treaty is currently the primary international treaty regarding exploration and use of space and underpins others that have followed it. It states that "the exploration and use of outer space, including the moon and other celestial bodies, shall be carried out for the benefit and in the interests of all countries, [...] and shall be the province of all mankind". It specifies that "there shall be free access to all areas of celestial bodies" and that there will be freedom of scientific research throughout outer space. In addition, no country may claim sovereignty over any part of outer space, such as the moon, on any basis (United Nations 1967b, Articles I and II).

With regard to spacecraft, each of the treaty's signatories retains jurisdiction and control over these and any associated personnel that it launches into space and is internationally liable for damage caused by such craft or its crew to another signatory state or to its citizens (United Nations 1967b, Articles VII, VIII). The liability for damage caused by spacecraft and personnel was spelled out in greater detail in a subsequent international agreement known as the 'Liability Convention' which was opened for signature on 29 March 1972 (United Nations 1972b). Also, according to Article XII of the Outer Space Treaty, all stations, installations, equipment and space vehicles on the moon and other celestial bodies are to be reciprocally open to representatives of the other signatories (United Nations 1967b, XII).

Other treaties that affect the legal status of spacecraft and their component parts include, notably, the 'Registration Convention' of 1975 and the 'Moon Treaty' of 1979. The former, known in full as the 'Convention on Registration of Objects Launched into Outer Space', requires that all space objects "launched into earth orbit or beyond" shall be registered by the launching state (or states in cases of international co-operation) and that the Secretary-General of the United Nations shall keep a register listing standard details of the space objects launched by each country (United Nations 1975).

In fact, two registers are maintained by the Secretary-General. One was begun in 1962, in accordance with a resolution of the General Assembly of the United Nations. This register remains in operation today and records information supplied by states that are not party to the Registration Convention, whilst the other register takes account of launchings made by those UN member states and by intergovernmental organisations that have ratified the convention since 1975 (United Nations Office for Outer Space Affairs, 1975b). These registers would be useful as underlying documents for any future Sites and Monuments Records of Mars and the Moon since every registered item has an identification number which could be used in the classification of each Martian or Lunar site.

The 'Moon Treaty' (United Nations 1979) offers some interesting legislative features. Firstly, Article 11, paragraph 1, of the treaty states that "The moon and its natural resources are the common heritage of mankind", which (I suppose) makes the entire moon a *world* heritage site, not only in the sense that it belongs to everybody on earth, but that this designation happens to encompass an entire *world* in its own right. Paragraphs 2 and 3 of Article 11 also declare that the moon is not subject to national appropriation on any basis and disallows both organisations (whether governmental, inter-governmental or non-governmental) and 'natural persons' from claiming any part of the moon as property. Furthermore, the placing of spacecraft or personnel on the moon cannot be used to create a right of ownership over the surface or even subsurface of the moon.

But what of the spacecraft themselves? Well, Article 12, paragraph 1, declares that all countries that are party to the Moon Treaty "shall retain jurisdiction and control over their personnel, space vehicles, equipment, facilities, stations and installations on the moon". However, Article 15, paragraph 1, states that "all space vehicles, equipment, facilities, stations and installations on the moon shall be open to other States" that are party to the agreement, although advance notice of any projected visits must be given.

There are a number of problems, however, regarding these treaties. Firstly, in no case has *every* country in the world ratified each of the treaties. This means that non-signatory states that gain the capability of space travel might decide to ignore these treaties and do as they please on other planetary bodies. Furthermore, while there is wide international support for the Outer Space Treaty, only eight or nine countries have ratified the Moon Treaty (United Nations 1997). Finally, there is the difficulty of enforcing these treaties. How, in practice, can a country protect its spacecraft, equipment and even its personnel while these are in space or on other planetary bodies? Furthermore, once the crews of any spacecraft have returned home and once remotely-controlled space objects cease to function, the governments of few countries are likely to take much interest in conserving such scientifically redundant equipment.

Another problem of the various UN treaties concerns the extent to which they cover the activities of civilians in outer space. While the *governments* of signatory states of the Outer Space Treaty and – more particularly – the Liability Convention may be held liable for damages caused by the spacecraft they launch, to what extent can the provisions of these treaties be expected to extend to objects independently owned and launched by civilians or non-governmental organisations? How would the activities of civilians on the Moon or Mars be monitored and what kind of legal basis could be used to ensure the prosecution of private individuals or corporate entities for stealing or vandalising parts of planetary spacecraft and their landing sites?

Once the landers, rovers and other equipment on the surfaces of planets have completed their missions, they could become fair game to companies or private individuals interested in salvaging them, especially whenever the government of a

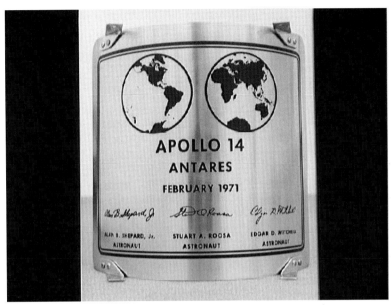

Figure 12.5 View of the commemorative plaque left by the crew of Apollo 14 close to the site of the lunar landing. © NASA and the NSSDC.

country that had launched one of these objects is unconcerned about the object's conservation once it has fallen into disuse. It would, therefore, seem to me that there may be grounds for designating all planetary landing and crash sites to date as historic sites and monuments with international protection in the form of United Nations World Heritage Sites.

The United Nations Educational, Scientific and Cultural Organisation (UNESCO) adopted the World Heritage Convention in 1972 and manages the World Heritage Fund which is used to provide financial assistance in conserving World Heritage Sites (Hickie 1997, 89, 91). If a convention similar to this could be adopted that dealt specifically with the protection of disused planetary spacecraft, their associated equipment and a specified zone around those places where they had landed or roved, perhaps the scenario envisaged at the beginning of this chapter could, for the most part, be avoided. To give it teeth, the governments of each signatory state could be required to enact supporting legislation within their own jurisdictions specifying penalties that would be awarded to those of its citizens who fail to observe the articles of the convention.

To support this convention, I would propose that internationally-funded and publicly-accessible Sites and Monuments Records for both Mars and the Moon could be compiled to raise awareness of this conservation issue and to facilitate any future planning authorities charged with overseeing the commercial exploitation (for example, by mining) of either planetary body. The protected zones would include not only the spacecraft, vehicles and other equipment present on the surfaces of the Moon

Figure 12.6 "Take only photographs, leave only footprints": an imprint left in the lunar dust by an astronaut during the Apollo 12 mission. © NASA and the NSSDC.

or Mars, but also the area around them that has been explored by rovers or by personnel. Crash sites, on the other hand, would include the point of impact of a spacecraft as well as its debris field.

Early in 1996, Charles Thomas remarked in an essay in *British Archaeology* that "It's a great pity that the poor old Moon seems to boast nothing in the way of artefacts beyond the rubbish we've left there ourselves". Thomas made this comment in the context of humans searching for artefactual evidence of sentient life on other worlds. It may be true that, on the Moon, such evidence is restricted to our own explorations, but why dismiss these artefacts as simply 'rubbish'? After all, is it not true that archaeologists spend much of their time searching for and analysing 'rubbish' here on earth? Surely now, twenty-five years after the landing on the Moon of the last spacecraft (*Apollo 17*) to bear human passengers to another planetary body, there is a case for initiating an international agreement to provide legal protection of the remains of our common heritage of early space exploration. We have the time to anticipate and legislate for the conservation issues that will undoubtedly arise once space travel becomes commercially viable. Let us not wait until our space heritage has been pilfered, vandalised or even destroyed before action is taken to preserve what is left of it.

Greg Fewer is a graduate of the National University of Ireland, Cork and is currently a part-time lecturer in communications, Irish social history and local archaeology at Waterford Institute of Technology. He also lectures part-time in Irish medieval history for the National University of Ireland, Maynooth, where he is currently doing a PhD on "Women and property in south-east Ireland, *c*. 1200–1700 AD: an interdisciplinary study". He somehow also finds time to indulge his interest in science fiction and the history of space travel.

13

The Case for Exo-Archaeology

Vicky A. Walsh

Planets outside our solar system have finally been discovered. As we look farther into the universe, the probability of discovering planets or moons capable of supporting life increases. Given the inordinately long period of time necessary to produce intelligent life, and the comparatively short life expectancy of technologically advanced societies, it is much more likely we will discover the *remains* of past civilisations than living cultures we can actually communicate with.

Professional archaeologists must therefore be prepared, not only to respond to unsubstantiated claims of extra-terrestrial remains, but to be actively involved in the search for them. How they define the field of off-world or Exo-Archaeology, how they train themselves in this field to evaluate distant worlds for signs of intelligent life, and how they establish criteria for determining the existence of extra-terrestrial artefacts will be the basis for the future authenticity of archaeological claims on other worlds. In addition to the direct application of archaeological methodology to distant worlds, Exo-Archaeology can be an excellent exercise in space-based methodology for earth-bound archaeologists: attempting to assess remote sensing applications to the planet earth while minimising our human preconceptions. This exercise in objectivity may be a crucial element in training the archaeological students of the future.

What is Exo-archaeology?

Exo-archaeology may be defined as the search for and analysis, interpretation and presentation of, the artefacts and remains of intelligent life beyond the confines of the Earth. There are already in existence a number of professional exo-biologists and exo-palaeontologists (Blake 1995), and it seems likely that an exo-archaeologist cannot be far behind. Exo-archaeology is unlimited in spatial scope as it includes the moon, the planets of our solar system, asteroids and all the space in between, and, more especially, beyond. Such study could certainly include the debris of our own somewhat limited exploration of the universe, and in the future it almost certainly will (see Fewer's chapter in this volume). Some common acronyms currently associated with the search for life beyond earth are ET (extra-terrestrial), ETI (extra-terrestrial intelligence) and SETI (Search for Extra-Terrestrial Intelligence). For our purposes, I will limit discussion within this chapter to the search for remains of ETI, or, to put it another way, an Exo-archaeological Survey.

Why should we assume there are any exo-artefacts or remnants of an ETI to be found? Perhaps first consideration should be given to the Principle of Mediocrity (Casti 1989) in that we are average (there are 23 stars like ours within 13 light years from Earth (Barbree and Caidin 1995) with countless more beyond that), and the likelihood is that there are many more planets with intelligent life somewhere out in deep space. Second, using Drake's Equation (Aczel 1998; Sagan and Shklovskii 1966), an estimate for the number of planets capable of communicating with us ranges from between 104 to 109, and this is calculated only for those civilisations with advanced systems of communication as it does not address less advanced or even extinct cultures.

The current SETI efforts are addressed to detecting cultures capable of deep space communication, that is to say beings more or less like ourselves. Within the SETI programme there is no need for an archaeologist for, if an alien civilisation is encountered, the desired answers to life, the universe and everything could ostensibly be obtained by simply asking them what we want to know. Unfortunately (or fortunately from an archaeological perspective) there are two reasons why we are far more likely to recover the remains of an ETI rather than being able to communicate with an existing one.

Firstly, if the current SETI efforts do detect the existence of intelligent life, the length of time required for the message to be delivered through space and the probability of an even longer time required for us to respond would go beyond the expected life expectancy of "6500 years" given for such a postulated communicating civilisation (Sagan and Shklovskii 1966). So if we, or our probes, do arrive at the location of an ETI, the ETI itself will probably be long gone.

Secondly it is clear that ours is not the oldest star or planetary system. It has taken 4.5 billion years to get where we are now on earth, and there has only been intelligent life on earth for only a fraction of that time. It seems highly unlikely therefore that we will discover another civilisation at exactly the same stage of evolutionary development as we are. Given the extreme age of the universe (and our galaxy), we are far more likely to get there too late, that is to say after they have died out, been destroyed, or moved on. If we are to learn anything from an ETI, we must therefore be prepared to study their remains.

Why should we do it?

So why should a discipline of Exo-archaeology be established now? As has already been noted, the existence of planets beyond our solar system has finally been established (Cohen 1997) and at least one major exploration of another planet, namely Mars, is now in progress. Technological advances in satellites, telescopes, and computing will, over the next few years, allow us to see farther and farther into our own galaxy (Freedman 1998). Eventually these advances may lead to the discovery of planets capable of supporting life. If a programme of proposed investigation commences now, we should, in theory at least, be ready to address the question of whether such planets do contain the remnants of intelligent beings.

Why should trained archaeologists venture into this new domain? Are there not enough 'crack-pots' and 'UFO nuts' out there to continue the search for ETI? Surely NASA scientists would let us know if there are verified remains beyond earth that could be studied? Maybe, maybe not. There have already been claims of archaeological remains on the moon and from Mars (Hoagland 1996) and, as these claimants have not been from a respected discipline such as archaeology, they have been dismissed as fanatics by most serious scientists. On the other end of the spectrum, planetary scientists can be somewhat defensive about the possibility of discovering archaeological remains in space, putting across the view that these are precisely the things that they are *not* looking for.

I believe that archaeologists could enter this argument somewhere within the middle of this clearly polarised debate, applying and expanding their theories and methods to areas beyond the earth. If it is possible to construct an abstract archaeology that can be tested and refined on earth and then applied to areas beyond our planet, then the claims for ETI remains on the moon and Mars may really be evaluated in light of established archaeological theory and analysis, and archaeological expertise could be lent to the continuing search for life beyond earth.

The Search for ETI

Just as early earth archaeologists concentrated on larger, more monumental elements of the human past, such as burial mounds, so too will the first exo-archaeologists be limited to the search for "larger than life" remains on other worlds. Our assumption must be that, as on earth, acts of ETI will produce visible effects on the surface of a given planet and that these effects will be visible from a considerable distance.

The first step will be to identify those planets which are, or which have in the past been, capable of supporting life. We know quite a bit about what conditions are necessary for life (or life at least as we know it) to develop (Gillett 1996; Schmidt 1995). This is a very complicated subject, however, and for our purposes here a summary will have to suffice.

In any solar system, there is an orbital zone around a sun where the radiation levels are optimal for life. This habitable zone is called the eco-sphere or bio-sphere. Any planets that lie outside this zone have either too much or too little solar radiation to support life. Planets that lie within the bio-sphere should therefore be the ones to be evaluated for the other important elements fundamental for life. Water is absolutely essential for the development of the proteins and amino acids that are the building blocks of life. The production of internal heat by volcanic activity is also crucial. Gravity is necessary to retain an atmosphere that also buffers against meteor collisions etc. The planet being investigated should possess a stable orbit and rotation as the length of the day and year, and the existence of seasons are also important developmental factors. A magnetic field will ward off dangerous radiation and the existence of a moon or moons may stabilise the planet and keep the climate relatively constant. Change is good. Extreme change may be dangerous to life.

Evaluating these variables should indicate the likelihood of any planet being capable of supporting the type of life which we would recognise. The existence of these factors for a considerable period in the past should also be determined, regardless of any current planetary conditions. Once a planet is identified as a likely candidate for exploration, we could develop a potential exo-archaeological expedition based upon the current Mars exploration project (Carroll 1997), though with certain obvious modifications.

STAGE I: Global Reconnaissance

Accomplished through the use of orbiting satellites or passing probes which return data to earth for further analysis. Pattern recognition algorithms developed specifically for exo-archaeological survey research (see below for discussion) ought, for our purposes, to be added to current research strategies. In fact, such pattern recognition algorithms could usefully have been put into effect for the most recent Mars missions in order to evaluate the current claims for 'pyramids' and other monumental structures there.

STAGE II: Landed Mission

Planetary landers and explorers could be configured to take, map and accurately record samples within areas of potential archaeological significance. They could also precisely map any regular features encountered during exploration using Global Positioning Station (GPS) technology.

STAGE III: Robots

These could be programmed to return cores and other samples taken within or near to any possible feature of potential archaeological significance, again with a precise location recorded. Such a survey should not be difficult and, given telepresence (virtual reality technology allowing an earth-based observer to see exactly what a robot set on a distant world can) and telemanipulation (allowing an earth-based observer to manipulate objects at a considerable distance within a virtual reality environment connected to a robot mimicking their every move: Stoker 1997), archaeological endeavours are not outside the realm of possibility either.

STAGE IV: Human presence

Though rather unlikely, given the long periods of time involved as well as the extraordinary cost and risk to life, perhaps nothing, with the exception of telepresence and telemanipulation, can replace the human element in detecting patterns of culture within places where others have certainly gone before.

Life signs

With regard to the types of life-signs being looked for during the course of these four proposed stages of investigation, we can consider at least six distinct categories (note – on the table below, the human race lies between categories II and III). The first three of these categories would exhibit some significant modification of their environment that could possibly be detected off-world. Of the three types of advanced civilisation noted (see Table 2), all should exhibit some major evidence of planetary modification. In addition, types II and III should have artefacts and remains beyond the home planet and/or within the immediate area of space (satellites, moon bases, etc.). We must assume that ETIs will seek active control of their environment, as we do, and thereby will make an obvious impact upon it. Any civilisation sufficiently advanced (or primitive?) to be living as one with nature will probably remain largely undetectable from space.

Table 1: Categories of Life

I	Extra-Planetary – space travellers
II	Planetary – world civilisation; high technology
III	Multi-cultural world – some technology, intelligent, organised
IV	Primitive cultures
V	Animal intelligence – not self aware
VI	Non-intelligent, non-self aware life

Table 2: Categories of Advanced Civilisation

I	Control of Planetary energy
II	Control of Solar System energy
III	Control of Galaxy energy

Technology

The crucial technological elements necessary for the discipline of exo-archaeology are Remote Sensing and Automatic Pattern Recognition. The application of remote sensing technology to archaeological projects on earth is well known (e.g. Wiseman 1996), while the detection of surface and sub-surface features has been greatly enhanced by satellite and space shuttle radar imagery as well as through aerial photography. The technical details (Scollar 1990; Vincent 1997) are beyond the scope of this paper except to say that, when available to archaeologists, the ever increasing resolution from satellites will greatly facilitate archaeological research, especially in areas that are inhospitable or largely inaccessible. These same procedures can be applied to the global reconnaissance of other planets, both within and beyond our solar system. However, we do not necessarily know or understand what it is we are actually looking for beyond the confines of earth.

Except for the initial detection of evidence of intelligent life on other worlds, we will need to go beyond remote sensing to Ultra Remote Sensing. Our first images of other planets will come, not from satellites orbiting that world, but from telescopes, long range probes, and other satellites within our solar system focused outward. The technology required for the high degree of resolution that we will need to detect evidence of ETI on other worlds is unfortunately not yet here, nor can we as yet directly view any of the recently discovered planets. In the meantime, we can hone our skills by applying current space technology to earth archaeology, and, in particular, by attempting to answer that age-old question: "Is there intelligent life on earth?" (Sagan 1994).

Is there intelligent life on earth?

Very few human cultural remains are visible from the moon, much less beyond. To discover evidence of our existence from space, an outsider would need to detect evidence of some significant land modification (the major categories of which (e.g. Monastersky 1994) are listed in Table 3). Of these categories, three, housing, mining, and transportation, produce the greatest direct effects on the environment. Agriculture is by far the most common category, though, due to erosion its effect is mainly indirect.

Table 3: Types of land Modification

1	Agriculture (indirect via erosion)
2	Water Systems – irrigation systems, canals – dams and reservoirs
3	Cities – housing – fortifications
4	Transportation Systems – roads, railways

5	Mining
6	Forest Clearance – indirect via erosion
7	Atomic – testing, bombing, radiation disasters

If we are to overcome our anthropocentric biases, we must develop automatic pattern recognition algorithms that can separate out what has been deliberately modified from what has not. This of course is the greatest challenge, for it seems that humans possess a tendency to see distinct patterns even when there are not necessarily any to find. In fact humans have often been known to manipulate or tamper with data until they can see what it was they were hoping to find in the first place. To avoid any potential areas of bias inherent in data reading or recording, a processes must be created that can recognise patterns and evaluate them as being artificial or wholly artificial.

The first stage in investigating another world for evidence of intelligent beings is to establish what is *natural* within each environment. We must obviously assume a feature is natural until proven otherwise (Sagan 1994), so the first search will be for patterns that demonstrate regularity and symmetry. Geometrical shapes, especially straight lines and rectilinear figures, *can* be indicative of artificial construction but must be evaluated in the context of what nature can produce in that area as well. Conversely, a feature that appears to be geometrically irregular might not necessarily be of natural origin either. Both must be compared with what is known of the background environment. On our own world there are many examples of regular figures that are natural and irregular ones that are artificial, for example geological fault lines which can appear very straight and symmetrical.

Matters are further complicated by the observation that humans have often emulated the regular mathematical proportions found in and try to duplicate them buildings and art nature (Huntley 1990; Willis 1995). The problem is how can one tell the difference from a distance? That will be the challenge as we try to establish criteria for evaluation features as natural or artificial both here on earth or elsewhere.

A new sub-discipline of archaeology

Exo-archaeology is going to need new expertise, new sub-disciplines of archaeology, similar to what we have today only with a view towards de-anthropomorphizing theory and methodology. Practitioners will need to create a more abstract, objective discipline of Exo-Archaeology. Archaeology in the future will also need to be the archaeology of current technology, especially space technology. As we see farther into time and space, we will be faced with investigating our own space debris and, perhaps, the debris of others. The satellites, spacecraft, and landers we use today will in turn become the artefacts of tomorrow (Elia 1995; Hamm 1981; Johnson et al. 1995; Fewer, this volume). As we study *our* past and present, we will hopefully become more prepared to study the worlds beyond that await discovery, investigation and interpretation.

Vicky Walsh is the world's first exoarchaeologist and is currently working in the United States of America.

14

Archaeology and the extraterrestrial: Blair Cuspids, Martian monuments and beyond the infinite

Keith J. Matthews

It surprises me that no professional archaeologist has become involved in the debates conducted on the fringes of scientific enquiry concerning supposed evidence for alien activity on other worlds in our solar system. The moon and Mars, especially, have long fascinated the more speculative writers on 'ancient mysteries', while some have cast their net even wider. When archaeologists have ventured opinions on the subject, they have generally been dismissive and sometimes openly hostile, adding fuel to the erroneous claim that there is a 'Scientific Establishment' seeking to stifle debate on these issues. From the other side, engaging in fringe debates can be professional suicide, dragging the archaeologist into areas seen by colleagues as beyond the pale of serious attention (as indeed happened to Tom Lethbridge when he began dowsing with pendula).

However, suppose that our neighbouring worlds did indeed bear the traces of civilisations other than or earlier than our own. This would be a tremendously important discovery, one that would radically change our views of the human past (assuming, as some have done, that such remains were of anthropogenic origin) or provide irrefutable proof of other forms of life in the cosmos (assuming, as others have done, their extraterrestrial origin). There is no 'Establishment' trying to dismiss such claims without examination, merely a reluctance to perform the necessary analysis. I cannot be the only archaeologist to be interested in these matters, though; I have a long-standing interest in astronomy, aliens and ufology, and my disappointment at the obviously hoaxed Roswell "alien autopsy" film (Randles *et al.* 2000, 206) was intense.

As archaeologists, we can make serious and important contributions to what ought to be a proper debate: we are well placed to evaluate the claims for lunar obelisks and Martian pyramids, better at least than the fringe writers making claims about them or the astronomers debunking them. It is often stated by sceptics (usually without any justifying argument) that extraordinary claims require extraordinary evidence. In this instance, they clearly do not require anything extraordinary, just aerial photographs of reasonable quality and resolution. The interpretation of aerial photographs forms an important component of our discipline, and we have extensive experience in distinguishing archaeological from geological or geomorphological phenomena. The same techniques could be deployed in the analysis of not just those objects that have been rightly or wrongly singled out as anomalous by fringe authors, but also of all photographs of other worlds whose resolution is good enough to give us the necessary detail. Those of the Mars Orbital Camera, with resolutions as fine as 1.4 m per pixel, are perfect in this respect.

It is not my intention at the outset either to debunk or support the claims for extraterrestrial civilisations. I suggest that it is a question we must approach with an open mind, otherwise we will simply find evidence to confirm what we already believe, whether in support of the ET hypothesis[1] or against it. By doing this, we can make a real impact on the debate, lending expert opinion on a subject area dominated by non-archaeological speculation and astronomical scepticism. At the same time, we need to examine why it is that we earth-bound humans have such a compelling need to search for life elsewhere. In an age where 'alternative' and 'cult' archaeologies attract possibly larger sections of the public than mainstream archaeology, we owe it to them to present a fuller picture about not just the past but also about the relevance of our discipline to such things as claims for extraterrestrial monuments.

Exobiology in the history of astronomy

The development of astronomy following the invention of the telescope was rapid. Early astronomers seem to have assumed that the planets they now realised were other worlds would be very similar to the earth. To populate them with human beings (or, at least, human-like beings) was a natural assumption. As early as 1698, the astronomer Huygens discussed the features a planet requires to allow it to support life and even speculated about extraterrestrial intelligence in his book *Cosmotheros* (1757).

During the opposition of 1877, Professor Giovanni V Schiaparelli (1835–1910, director of the Brera Observatory in Milan from 1862 to 1900) discovered a network of narrow dark lines running between the larger dark areas on Mars, which he named *canali*, 'channels'. Two years later, he noted that some of the *canali* appeared as double lines, a feature he attributed to vegetation growth due to meltwater from the polar caps flowing along *canali*. Although Schiaparelli nowhere expressed a belief that his *canali* might be of artificial origin, the word was seized upon by certain English-speaking astronomers, who mistranslated it as 'canals' and suggested that Mars was criss-crossed with a network of irrigation channels.

Most notable of these was Percival Lovell, the millionaire philanthropist and amateur astronomer, eventual co-discoverer of Pluto. However, from the outset, both the explanation and existence of Schiaparelli's *canali* were beset with controversy. Many astronomers could not see the features, even under favourable conditions; others thought that they might be cracks in the planetary surface, even cracks in a Mars-wide ice sheet. No convincing photographs of canali were ever obtained. As larger telescopes became available during the first half of the twentieth century, further searches for *canali* failed to reveal them and it became clear that the original observations had been mistaken. It is still unclear what Schiaparelli and other astronomers had observed, although one possibility is that groups of unrelated features on the surface of the planet, at the very limits of visibility through telescopes of the day, were being joined through optical illusions into straight lines.

By the late 1950s, other suggestions were being made about the best way to identify intelligent life on other planets. Most astronomers had concluded that it was unlikely that intelligent life would be found anywhere in the solar system, so techniques were proposed for locating such life elsewhere in our galaxy. In 1959, Giuseppi Cocconi and Philip Morrison of Cornell University published an article in Nature pointing out the potential for using microwave radio to communicate between the stars. At the same time, Frank Drake had reached a similar conclusion, and in 1960, he conducted the first search for signals from outside the solar system. His Project OZMA failed to detect any signals of extraterrestrial origin, but he drew attention to the possibilities of searching for extraterrestrial life in this way.

In the 1960s, the search was led by astronomers from the then Soviet Union, observing large areas of sky, in the assumption that a few very advanced civilisations would be able to radiate enormous amounts of transmitter power. NASA became interested in the search during the early 1970s and a team of consultants drew up Project Cyclops, the foundation on which much of the later work has been based. During the 1970s, many radio astronomers began searches, using existing radio telescopes, and this has continued up to the present day. Important players in the search today include the Planetary Society's Project META, the University of California at Berkeley's SERENDIP Project and a long-standing observing programme at Ohio State University.

By the late 1970s, SETI[2] programmes had been established by NASA at the Ames Research Center and at the Jet Propulsion Laboratory (JPL) in Pasadena. A targeted search was proposed of a thousand sun-like stars that were thought likely to have terrestrial type planets capable of producing civilisations. In 1988, after a decade of study and preliminary design, NASA adopted this strategy and funded the programme. Observations began in October 1992, but within a year, Congress had stopped the funding.

The SETI Institute, established with private funding in 1993, now aims to continue the abandoned programme with funding from the private sector. Project Phoenix (as it is known) continues the targeted search using large radio telescopes. It began observations in February 1995, using the Parkes radio telescope in Australia. From September 1996 to April 1998, the 140 Foot radio telescope at the National Radio Astronomy Observatory in Green Bank, West Virginia, was also used. Observations are currently being made during two three-week sessions each year using the 1000-foot radio telescope at Arecibo, in Puerto Rico. The project examines signals on a single frequency between 1,000 and 3,000 MHz, considered characteristic of an intelligent transmission. The spectrum is broken into narrow 1 Hz-wide channels, which means that two billion channels are examined from each target star.

As home computers became more powerful during the later 1990s, the SETI Institute and Project SERENDIP developed a gigantic distributed computing program (known as SETI@home) to perform the calculations on data sent via the Internet and to return them to the project after completion. It is thought that millions of individuals world-wide now participate in and contribute to the programme. By mid-1999, Phoenix had examined about 500 stars, but no clearly extraterrestrial signals have so far been identified. In the context of scientific research, SETI has been a very small scale and poorly funded programme in view of the potential impact of the discovery of extraterrestrial civilisation.

The search for extraterrestrial life during the second half of the twentieth century was also heavily influenced by the growth of the UFO phenomenon from the late 1940s onwards. While mainstream science continues to dismiss UFOs and anything that might be associated with them by Ufologists, they have continued to fascinate the public. Opinion polls consistently show that a majority of the public in the western world believes that UFOs are structured craft from other worlds. Discussion of supposed extraterrestrial monuments and artefacts cannot ignore this.

The evolution of the 'ET Hypothesis' in Ufology

The UFO age is usually said to have begun when an Idaho businessman, Kenneth Arnold, reported seeing some anomalous objects near Mount Rainier on 24 June 1947 whilst searching for a missing aeroplane (Randles *et al.*. 2000, 18). His description of their motion as being "like a saucer would if you skipped it over water" (quoted in Spencer 1989, 18) led to an inspired newspaper sub-editor dubbing the objects 'flying saucers', despite the fact that Arnold saw them as crescent shaped, with wings but no tails.

Although it is now tolerably certain that what Arnold saw were pelicans or geese (see the detailed analysis by James Easton at http://www.ufoworld.co.uk/saucers. htm), the sighting caught the popular imagination and over the next few months, huge numbers of sightings were reported, many of which conformed precisely to the shape of an upturned saucer, something Arnold had not described. Arnold's claims about the objects, that they were 37 km (23 miles) away, flying at 2100 to 2750 kph (1300 to 1700 mph) and each were two-thirds the length of a nearby DC-4, was based on his mistaken observation that the objects passed behind a peak close to Mt Rainier, whereas the birds had more than likely become invisible against it. Nevertheless, acceptance of his estimates indicated that the objects showed a technology completely unknown on the earth. The ET hypothesis was born.

The immediate impact of Arnold's sighting is shown by the unfolding of events at Roswell, New Mexico, barely two weeks later (Hough and Randles 1991, 161). According to the official press release of 8 July 1947, "The many rumours regarding the flying disc became a reality yesterday when … [the] Air Force … was fortunate enough to gain possession of a disc…" (quoted in Spencer 1989, 26). The matter was soon settled; within hours, the Air Force issued a retraction and showed pictures of Major Jesse Marcel, who had recovered the alleged disc, holding what were clearly

Figure 14.1 Kenneth Arnold and a sketch of one of his flying saucers. © *NASA and the NSSDC.*

the remains of a balloon, said to be the material recovered from the crash site. According to documents released in the 1990s, the original press release was put out in an attempt to divert attention from the fact that the balloon was a classified military test, but it was one that completely misjudged public attitudes to the 'Flying Saucer' phenomenon (Randles *et al.* 2000, 31).

Roswell might have remained a footnote in the history of Ufology had it not been for a series of publications (starting with Berlitz and Moore 1980) that began to suggest a massive government cover-up had taken place. According to these reports, beginning a whole generation after the event, alien bodies had been recovered from the wreckage, including one that was still alive at the time of recovery. Subsequent investigation has merely served to confirm the conspiracy theory for believers in the ET hypothesis, as no evidence for the events alleged to have occurred by Berlitz and Moore has ever been found. The supposed 'alien autopsy' footage, screened world-wide in 1995, and supposed to be secret government film from Roswell, has since been exposed as a poor hoax (Randles *et al.* 2000, 206).

Almost six months after Roswell, on 7 January 1948, residents of Godman, Kentucky, reported to their local Air Force base that a large, glowing and stationary disc was hovering above the town. It took Air Force personnel some time to spot the object, but they agreed to divert a routine flight of P-51 aircraft to investigate. The flight commander, a Captain Thomas Mantell, agreed to fly to it. The aircraft gradually had to back off, as they were not equipped with oxygen masks and despite continued climbing, could not reach it. Only Captain Mantell continued. His last radio message, sent from 4600 m (15,000 feet), reported that the object was still above him. At that point, contact was lost and the remaining aircraft, which had landed to fit oxygen masks, then took off again to search for him. While they were in the air, it was reported that Mantell's aeroplane had crashed nearby. There is little doubt that oxygen starvation had caused him to black out. As for the object he was chasing, it seems that the original observations by local residents were of the planet Venus (in the right position and just about visible in daylight), which explains why the Air Force had difficulty spotting it, whereas Mantell appears to have given tragic chase to a Skyhook balloon. This had been released in Ohio earlier in the day and flying above the 6100 m (20,000 feet) at which oxygen masks were necessary.

By the end of July 1947, a mere forty days after Kenneth Arnold's first report, some 850 stories had appeared in American media about 'flying saucers'. A Gallup poll carried out in August found that while 33% of respondents did not know what the 'flying discs' might be, 15% thought they might be a secret American device, perhaps connected with the atomic bomb, while only 1% thought they might be a Soviet device. At this stage, no-one suggested an extraterrestrial origin.

In the context of global politics, the post-war period was one of growing international tension that would eventually lead to the Cold War and the construction of the Berlin Wall. In the United States, there were fears of Soviet attack and while the government was quick to dismiss any suggestions that the UFOs reported in increasing numbers after mid-1947 were any threat to national security, at the same time, it took an active interest just in case they were secret Soviet aircraft. A Top Secret document *Analysis of Flying Object Incidents in the United States*, Study 203 (Analysis), issued 10 December 1948 by the USAF Directorate of Intelligence and released under the Freedom of Information Act (and now available in transcript at http://www .project1947.com/fig/1948air.htm) assumes that the phenomenon consists either of misidentified domestic aircraft or of foreign (and presumably therefore Soviet) aircraft.

Official explanations usually invoked the planet Venus or weather balloons (often, as seen at Roswell and Goodman, with good reason), and the public saw this as evidence for a cover-up. Many people find it hard to believe that such ordinary objects can be so badly misidentified; experience shows otherwise. By the early 1950s, it was being assumed by the public that as the disks were not part of an imminent Soviet invasion or secret domestic aircraft, they had to be an imminent invasion from another world. The authorities, on the other hand, were genuinely puzzled by an inexplicable but apparently relatively common phenomenon. A general feeling developed that the government knew what was happening and that what it knew was so devastating that it had to be covered up. Nevertheless, reports of actual aliens were rare until the world-wide flap[3] of 1954.

In fact, Arnold's were by no means the first sightings of unidentified objects in the sky. There was a wave of sightings of cigar-shaped objects in 1896–7 across the United States (Randles *et al.* 2000, 15). The objects were propeller-driven cigar shaped dirigibles, whose inhabitants spoke American English, although in one case the alleged witness suggested that the pilots "were inhabitants of Mars, who had been sent to earth for the purpose of securing one of its inhabitants" (quoted in Randles *et al.* 2000, 20). Although the first recorded airship flight was in 1901, it is possible that some of these reports derive from observations of experimental craft, but the sheer numbers of reports cannot be explained solely in these terms. In short, many of the reports are simply not credible as straightforward observations. The charitable view is that they are misinterpretations of other phenomena; a less charitable view is that they are hoaxes. The later history of ufology shows that both interpretations are possible. A third explanation sees it as evidence for an otherwise paranormal phenomenon (Keel 1971, 34).

What is of interest here, though, is that in the 1890s, the occupants of the craft were mostly human and of indigenous, if out-of-state, origin. They were friendly and often either in need of help or offering it. A second wave of airship sightings took place in Europe between 1909 and 1913. Here, the occupants were more sinister and 'foreign', perhaps a reflection of the tensions developing in the years that led up to the outbreak of the European Great War in 1914. Some were reported as having 'oriental' characteristics, while others were said to speak a guttural language.

Between the wars, the major focus of activity was in Sweden, where so-called ghost rockets were observed from 1933; while some of these may have been experimental Soviet or German missiles, viable rocket technology is not known to have existed until the 1940s. During the Second World War, American fighter pilots (particularly in the Pacific) reported small glowing balls, known as foo fighters, which followed their aeroplanes. Overall, nothing in the technology displayed by these early unidentified objects was more than a decade ahead of developments in terrestrial technology, with the exception of the foo fighters, which appear more supernatural than technological. If these early reports are of the same phenomenon, there is little reason for ascribing an extraterrestrial origin to it, as it anticipates and keeps pace with human technology.

The ET hypothesis in ufology, then, developed during the late 1940s as a consequence of politics, particularly the mounting tensions between the Unites States of America and the Union of Soviet Socialist Republics. Indeed, the UFO as a concept did not exist before 1947, and within three years, it became associated with extraterrestrials. The involvement of the US government in the analysis of reports of unidentified flying objects created a climate in which conspiracy theories could flourish and which encouraged the development of an explanation that did not involve terrestrial military powers. Perhaps it is for this reason that the ET hypothesis has had almost universal acceptance for over fifty years among American (and, it now emerges, Russian: Hough and Randles 1991, 190) ufologists, whilst Europeans have tended to resort to a wider variety of explanations. The public perception, nevertheless, is that UFOs are evidence for alien visitations, something that is reinforced by the media, particularly the popular press, Hollywood and American television (notoriously, science fiction series such as The *X-Files* or fundamentally flawed 'documentaries' on the subject such as those produced periodically for cable and satellite television channels).

Table 1: the development of the UFO and alien myth (after Paynter n.d.)

Period	UFOs	Aliens	Government
1947	High-speed, ultra-manoeuvrable craft. May be US secret weapons, Soviet or other.	Not suggested.	Takes a keen interest but is as mystified as the general public.
1948-49	High-speed, ultra-manoeuvrable disk-shaped craft. May be terrestrial weapons or alien space ships.	Here to explore the earth	The Air Force may know more than it is saying.
1950-51	High-speed, ultra- manoeuvrable disk-shaped alien craft have been observed for centuries.	Here to observe human activities such as nuclear testing, which they may consider a threat.	Knows the truth and is covering it up, to prevent panic. May have recovered crashed saucers and alien bodies.
1952	High-speed, ultra- manoeuvrable disk-shaped alien craft have been observed for centuries, and spotted on radar, proving their existence.	Here to observe human activities such as nuclear testing, which they may consider a threat.	Knows the truth and is covering it up, to prevent panic. Has not recovered crashed saucers or alien bodies.
1953-56	High-speed, ultra- manoeuvrable disk-shaped alien craft have been observed for centuries and spotted on radar.	Here to observe human activities such as nuclear testing, which they may consider a threat. Have contacted some humans, expressing concern for the future of the human race.	Knows the truth and is covering it up, to prevent panic. "Men in Black" enforce the cover-up by means of coercion and violence.
1957-63	High-speed, ultra- manoeuvrable disk-shaped alien craft have been observed for centuries, if not millennia, and spotted on radar. Sightings by reliable witnesses prove their extraterrestrial nature. Magnetically stop cars and cause sunburn.	Here to observe human activities such as nuclear testing. May have contacted some humans with messages of peace and brotherhood with the intent of avoiding mankind's self-destruction.	Knows the truth and is covering it up, to prevent panic. The Air Force has smeared reliable witnesses. "Men in Black" enforce the cover-up by means of coercion and violence.
1964-72	High-speed, ultra- manoeuvrable disk-shaped alien craft have been observed for thousands of years, tracked on radar and observed by pilots and astronauts, proving their extraterrestrial nature. Have landed leaving pad prints, radiation and metal samples. Magnetically stop cars and cause sunburn. May be hostile.	Here to observe human activity and to save mankind from nuclear destruction. Have contacted some people, taking some aboard UFOs for medical examination and perhaps breeding experiments. May be mutilating cattle.	The Air Force has fouled up their investigation of UFOs and is covering up their existence, in collusion with the CIA. "Men in Black" enforce the cover-up by means of coercion and violence.
1973-79	High-speed, ultra- manoeuvrable disk-shaped alien craft have been observed by millions of people for thousands of years. Undertaking reconnaissance of military bases and nuclear plants. Hover over power lines and draw energy from them. Land leaving pad prints, burn marks, radiation. Can stop car engines.	Have been seen in or near flying saucers. Mutilate animals. Interested in human activity. Some people taken aboard UFOs for medical examinations.	Knows flying saucers are real, has proof and is covering it up, to prevent panic. Cover-up directed by CIA

1980-86	High-speed, ultra- manoeuvrable disk-shaped alien craft have been observed for thousands of years. Undertaking reconnaissance of Earth. Draw power from electrical lines and stop cars. Have landed, leaving pad prints and other traces.	Grey skin, short and thin with large, bald heads. Physically weak and sickly. Abducting humans, removing sperm and ova to produce human/alien hybrids and save their race. Wipe the memories of their abductees and control them through nasal implants. Mutilate cattle to obtain genetic material.	Has recovered crashed flying saucers and dead crewmen. Has test-flown rebuilt flying saucers and copied their technology. Cover-up, and slandering and intimidation of witnesses, led by CIA.
1987-93	High-speed, ultra- manoeuvrable disk-shaped alien craft have been observed for thousands of years. Have landed, leaving pad prints, caused blackouts and stopped cars. Have crashed, leaving debris and both dead and live aliens.	"Greys" are short and thin with large, bald heads. Weak and sickly, suffering from genetic disorders. Abduct humans and extract sperm and ova to produce hybrids. Erase memories and implant nasal devices. Mutilate cattle for enzymes.	MJ-12 has made a pact with the Greys. Will allow mutes and abductions in exchange for alien technology. Has built huge underground bases for aliens, with money from CIA drug sales and George Bush. Greys and "Ruling Powers" plan to set up a one-world dictatorship and force abductees and others into concentration camps.

Space exploration and the discovery of evidence for extraterrestrial life

When humans first landed on the moon in 1969, there were no signs of extraterrestrial life. This was unsurprising, as earlier satellite missions had confirmed what had appeared to earth-based astronomers to be a completely dead world without an appreciable atmosphere. Similarly, the Voyager missions to Mars and the Venera missions to Venus during the 1970s revealed hostile, barren landscapes. Venus, often regarded in the past as earth's 'sister planet', turned out to be one of the most hostile environments so far discovered, with sulphuric acid rain, temperatures in which lead is liquid and constant high winds. By the mid-1970s, a consensus had developed among astronomers that life in the Solar System was restricted to the Earth.

However, developments in the 1990s saw a number of claims for life on our near neighbours. The most well known of these was the announcement on 16 August 1996 that a fragment of meteorite from Antarctica (known as ALH 84001), shown after its discovery to be of Martian origin, contained fossil traces of bacterium-like structures and telltale formations deriving from the biological activity of bacteria. Critics were quick to point out that some of the tell-tale traces could have formed in a super-heated environment such as that the meteorite would have experienced in passing through the earth's atmosphere, that the structures could be artefacts of the gold coating applied to the surface to prepare for electron micrography and that the bacterium-like structures were too small to accommodate DNA. Nevertheless, the popular media seized on the evidence and the idea that life may once have existed on

Mars is now firmly ingrained in the popular consciousness. Further announcements in early 2001 about discoveries in other meteorite samples (Gibson *et al.* 2001, 30) add weight to the 'pro-life' argument by providing cumulative evidence for the biogenic origin of the features observed in these mineral samples.

Other satellite explorations have suggested possible locations for the development of life in the solar system, most notably the Jovian moon Europa. Although covered in a thick layer of ice, this moon nevertheless appears to possess oceans of liquid water beneath the ice and to have an internal temperature caused by geological activity. This is similar (but not identical) to the conditions under which life is now thought to have developed on earth. No evidence for the presence of life has yet been found, but there are plans for future missions to drop probes through the ice into the oceans beneath in an attempt to identify organic activity.

The 'fringe'

Other developments in the search for extraterrestrial life were taking place, however, in the area of research generally characterised as 'fringe' from the mid 1960s. The works of Erich von Däniken, beginning in 1968 with *Erinnerunger an die Zukunft* ('Memories of the Future', published in English as *Chariots of the Gods?*[4] (von Däniken 1969)), became best sellers within weeks of their publication. His hypothesis that various features of the human past were best explained in terms of extraterrestrial intervention was largely ignored by mainstream archaeology, but found a wide acceptance among the general public (Feder 1995, 46; Williams 1995, 126).

Although he received a great deal of international publicity, his first book drew heavily (and virtually without acknowledgement) on a cult classic, *Le Matin des Magiciens*, by Louis Pauwels and Jacques Bergier (1960), a work that combines philosophical speculation based around the thinking of the mystic Gurdjieff with pseudo-scientific conjecture. During the late 1960s and early 1970s, a whole industry developed around the growing belief of extraterrestrial interference in human history, mostly regurgitating the same pieces of evidence that von Däniken had taken from Pauwels and Bergier (e.g. Kolosimo 1970; Tomas 1971; Berlitz 1972); there was little attempt at originality in most of this work, much of it poorly researched and increasingly derivative. These writers failed to produce a single object of extra-terrestrial origin.

However, by the early 1980s, claims were being made about discoveries of artificial structures on Mars. Unlike the claims of the earlier speculative writers, these claims were based on the physical evidence of satellite photographs from the Viking programme of the mid-1970s and were therefore amenable to testing and (potentially) falsification. However, just as with the claims of von Däniken, mainstream archae-ologists generally chose not to test these claims, simply to ignore or reject them. Given the climate of conspiracy that had developed around the UFO phenomenon and that had gradually infiltrated most areas of the 'fringe', it is unsurprising that denials of artificiality from NASA were seen as deliberate disinformation. It was against this background that the present chapter had its origins.

The Claims

Claims for evidence of extraterrestrial monuments can be divided into three main groups, based on location. First to be considered is the moon, Earth's nearest neighbour and the focus of the earliest attempts at detailed survey by remote sensing. It is the only place other than earth that humans have so far visited (at least, according to conventional wisdom). Second is Mars, which has long been a favoured candidate for being the home of other forms of life. Thirdly are the other planets and their satellites. As human space probes reach further into the solar system (of the major planets, only Pluto, which many not be a true planet, after all, has not so far been visited, although there plans for a 'Pluto Express', to reach the planet in 2013), so we are learning more about other planets and their moons. It is interesting that Venus, which is supposedly better surveyed even than Earth, has not been the subject of speculation about alien life or monuments in recent years (apart from photographs in Childress (1995, 257f) that are captioned to suggest that there may be artificial structures on its surface): even the most enthusiastic believer in extraterrestrials recognises that it is too hostile a place to support any life whatsoever.

1) The moon

Satellite exploration of the moon began in October 1959, when the Soviet probe Luna 3 sent back the first photographs of the 41% that is invisible from earth. Although of very poor quality, they showed a surface more heavily cratered than the side that faces earth, and none of the large, basalt filled 'seas' (or maria) that characterise the near side. Subsequent explorations involved orbiting probes that undertook systematic surveys of the lunar surface. The main rationale seems to have been less for pure selenography (the lunar equivalent of geography) than for identifying potential landing sites for the projected American Apollo missions and manned Soviet missions. The American Lunar Orbiter programme, consisting of five separate probes launched between August 1966 and August 1967, surveyed some 95% of the surface of the satellite. The first two Orbiters concentrated on a band extending 5° north and south of the equator and 45° east and west of the prime meridian. This was considered to provide the best location for the first Apollo mission to land on the moon, Apollo 11 in July 1969.

The Blair Cuspids

On 2 November 1966, NASA published a photograph of a region towards the western edge of the Sea of Tranquillity taken by Lunar Orbiter II (reference number LO2-61H3[5]) at approximately 15.5°E 5.1°N. William Blair of the Boeing Institute of Biotechnology drew attention to a number of apparently anomalous features in the photograph, mainly a series of objects that cast long, clear shadows, contrasting them with the shorter shadows cast by objects that were more obviously boulders.

Figure 14.2 The moon: Lunar Orbiter photograph LO2-61H3. © Malin Space Science Systems/NASA/ JPL.

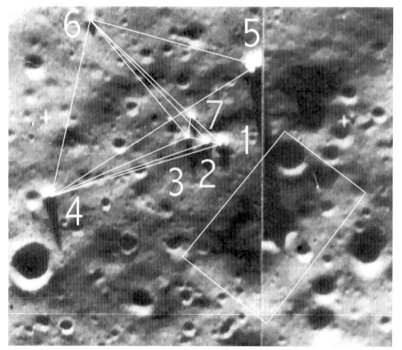

Figure 14.3 The moon: the numbering and geometry of the cuspids. © Malin Space Science Systems/ NASA/JPL.

Blair compared the shadows with those cast by Egyptian obelisks, causing him to suggest that the photograph shows a series of spires. Moreover, the seven objects are arranged in a geometric pattern, with right-angled and isosceles triangles. Close to the 'spires' was a feature that resembled an eroded rectangular trench (Childress 1995, 37). The photograph seems to have attracted little attention at the time, although it has been reproduced (poorly) in a number of publications (including Kolosimo 1970, plates 16 and 17 and Childress 1995, 51). This photograph is reproduced below with a cleaned-up version showing the claimed geometry of the cuspids, together with the supposed 'rectangular trench' next to them. A second photograph of the site was subsequently located by Lan Fleming (reference number LO2-62H3), taken 2.2 seconds after the first. This shows that the largest of the cuspids, number 5, is considerably broader at the base than was originally thought.

It is possible to work out the apparent height of the 'spires' by calculating the length of the shadow and the elevation of the sun above the horizon (which may be expressed mathematically as Height = Length of shadow × the tangent of the sun's elevation). The largest of the objects (Cuspid 5) casts a shadow some 110 m long; given a solar elevation of 10.9°, the tallest object ought to be 21.2 m high (Childress (1995, 37) gives the height as 213 m). This assumes that the lunar surface across which the shadows fall is perfectly flat, but topographical maps for the moon suggest that there is a general trend of between one and two degrees rise to the west, the direction from which the sun was shining at the time of the photograph. This means that the top of the cuspid is 21.2 m above the top of the shadow, but also that the base of the cuspid is itself up to 3.8 m higher than the tip of the shadow. The cuspid's triangulated height should therefore be reduced by this amount, to around 17.4 m. However, that is not the only problem.

These calculations also depend on the sun being a single point of light, whereas it is a disk, causing shadows to have two parts, an umbra (the region in which none of the sun may be seen) and a penumbra (the region of shadow in which a part of the sun's disk may be seen). The angular diameter of the sun, as seen from the earth/moon system, is about half a degree, which means that the tip of the penumbra (which is what is measured as 100 m away from the cuspid) was cast by the lower limb of the sun, 0.25° lower than the 10.9° elevation already considered. Taking this into consideration, the height of the cuspid must be reduced to about 16.9 m. Furthermore, the cuspid stands on the rim of a highly eroded crater, the shadow falling into its interior. A photometric analysis undertaken by Lan Fleming (n.d.) suggests that the height of the cuspid is 12% of the length of its shadow, in other words 13.2 m. This makes it more or less square in profile and not at all anomalous for a lunar boulder. The remaining cuspids, all of which were suspected to be smaller, fare even less well in Fleming's analysis.

The second frame shows a similar feature to the largest of the cuspids inside the rim of a crater, which despite Fleming's analysis (n.d.), raises the question about sloping terrain and the distortion of shadows. Indeed, it is apparent from the photographs that the shadow of Cuspid 5 falls into part of an eroded crater, identified by Blair as a rectangular trench. The trench, in fact, appears to be an optical illusion caused by the overlapping of two extremely eroded craters.

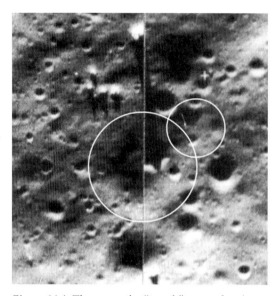

Figure 14.4 The moon: the "trench" as overlapping craters. © Malin Space Science Systems/NASA/JPL.

All in all, the claims made for the Blair Cuspids cannot be substantiated. Whilst their height was originally overestimated, it is evident that they are unusually large boulders, although boulders of comparable size were recorded close up by the Apollo astronauts. However, there is nothing about their recoverable shape that suggests artificiality. Their arrangement is another matter. It is undeniable that Cuspids 4 and 6 form the base of three isosceles triangles with their apices at Cuspids 1, 2 and 3, Cuspids 1, 3 and 7 form a right-angled triangle and Cuspids 4 and 5 form the base of an isosceles triangle with its apex at Cuspid 6. This might be evidence for artificiality if similar arrangements were to be found elsewhere on the moon. One can only suspect that it is a coincidence, as it does not seem to be repeated elsewhere on the lunar surface. Moreover, given the width of some of these boulders relative to their heights, claims of mathematical precision in their arrangement depend on which point on their surface is chosen for analysis. In other words, this arrangement falls well within the mathematical probabilities of occurring by chance rather than design.

Other 'sites'

Numerous other parts of the moon have been the subject of speculations. The VGL organisation maintains a website (http://www.vgl.org/) devoted to locating anomalous features on the lunar surface and the Ukrainian Institute of Anomalous Phenomena, based in Kharkov, has a lunar study programme (Arkhipov 1995, 16). Some of these depend heavily on unsustainable hypotheses about structures on the lunar surface 'revealed' in photographs from the Apollo landings (e.g. Bara and Troy 1997). These photographs, claiming to show glass domes in various states of collapse (and, by implication, extremely ancient) have been over enhanced on computers and show little more than various lens and lighting effects. However, the efforts of Fleming, Arkhipov and their colleagues mean that the surface of the moon is subject to intense scrutiny and potentially interesting features are constantly under analysis. None of those so far proposed has revealed convincing evidence for artificiality, including the supposed 'bridge' in the Mare Crisium, first reported in 1953 (Barclay 1995, 59).

Considerably less easy to evaluate are the claims of David Hatcher Childress, a prolific fringe author whose publications range from monographs on anti-gravity to lost cities of Lemuria, from man-made UFOs to 'free energy'. His claims include not only the ubiquitous pyramids and domes (which are usually the central peaks in impact craters) but also tracks left by automated 'mining drones' (usually the tracks of boulders thrown by meteoric impacts), platforms or terraces, a 'pond', cigar-shaped objects (drawn from UFO mythology) and others. Needless to say, these claims depend on a special way of looking at the photographs: many are so grainy that more than a pinch of faith is needed to see what Childress sees. None would stand scrutiny as aerial photographs of archaeological features. This is not to dismiss them out of hand, merely a recognition that the quality of the data is frequently too poor to draw any meaningful conclusions from them, either in support or in refutation of the hypotheses.

2) Mars

Mars has long been a source of fascination for those who seek life off the Earth. Early astronomers noted seasonal changes: the normally red surface of the planet could be seen to develop darker, greenish patches during the Martian 'summer', as the polar ice caps melt. They darken annually (in Martian terms) and always in the same patterns; in some years, they are more intense than others. This suggested plant growth to many astronomers before satellite exploration. However, the twenty-two close-up photographs sent back by Mariner 4 in July 1965 showed a cratered surface with a thin atmosphere (largely composed of carbon dioxide at a pressure of 5 to 10 mbar). Later missions (especially Mariner 9 in 1971, Vikings 1 and 2 in 1976, Mars Global Surveyor since 1997 and Mars Pathfinder in 1997) have shown a dead planet without liquid water, suffering freezing temperatures and swept by violent winds. Nevertheless, they have also shown that conditions were once very different on the planet, with evidence for plate tectonics (no longer functioning), river channels, ocean shorelines and an atmosphere formerly richer in oxygen. This has led some researchers to suggest that not only life, but also an advanced civilisation may once have existed on Mars.

Cydonia Mensae

The part of Mars that has attracted most attention since satellite exploration of the planet began is the Cydonia Mensae region, located in the planet's northern hemisphere. The region bears traces of former shorelines (it is now accepted by most astronomers that Mars was once home to large bodies of water) and of eroded hills and mountains, corresponding to terrestrial buttes and mesas. A number of features were seen on Viking Orbiter photographs from the mid 1970s that led some researchers to suggest that they were artificial in origin. One of the most impressive parts of this claim was the concentration of anomalies in a single area; these anomalies included what was claimed to be an enormous carved face, three- and five-sided pyramids showing bilateral symmetry and walled compounds. Moreover, some of these features appeared to be in alignment with each other. The so-called 'face' has attracted most attention.

The 'face'

The 'face' has been known as that since NASA engineers dubbed it such as a convenient shorthand.[6] Located at about 40.9°N 9.45°W, it was photographed by the Viking Orbiters 1 on 25 July 1976 whilst obtaining images of a site suitable for Viking

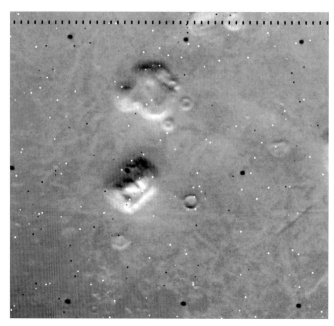

Figure 14.5 Mars: Image 070A13 (detail), north to top (the black dots at regular intervals are registration marks from the camera). © Malin Space Science Systems/NASA/JPL.

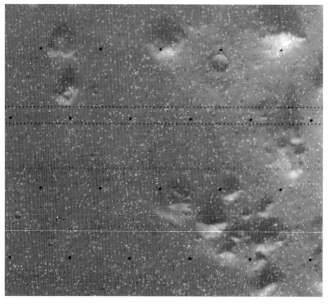

Figure 14.6 Mars: Image 035A72, north to top (the black dots at regular intervals are registration marks from the camera). © Malin Space Science Systems/NASA/JPL.

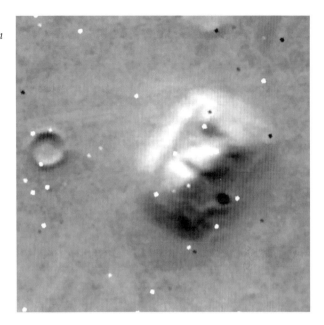

Lander 2. Eighteen images of the region were taken, but of these, eleven have resolutions worse than 550 m per pixel (in other words, no feature less than 550 m across can be seen on these images). Only two of them (frames 070A13, taken on 24 August 1976, and 035A72, taken on 20 July 1976) have resolutions of better than 50 m per pixel.

They show a sub-rectangular elevated feature that displays roughly bilateral symmetry similar to a human face. The length is estimated as 2 km, the width as 1.5 km and the height as about 400 m. The long axis of the face is aligned at a bearing of approximately 329° to the Martian North Pole. In Image 070A13, the sun is 28° above the horizon, while in 035A72, it is 11°; these differences in angle reveal slightly different details in the 'face'.

The 'face' lies close to the boundary between an area of flat-topped mesas and conical hills to its south west, and a much flatter region in which it lies. Claims have been made for the presence of a former shoreline close to the 'face', which may be important in considering its likely origin. Erosion is generally cited as the main factor in the creation of the landforms in this region, but a variety of claims were made during the 1980s and 90s that this was not sufficient to explain a number of features of the 'face' (Carlotto and Stein 1997; Erjavec 1996). The original view of astronomers was that the northern part of Mars had originally been covered with a sediment that subsequently eroded, perhaps as a result of wind action. As evidence for the former presence of surface water on the planet has increased, so it has begun to seem more likely that the erosion in this region may have been exacerbated by former seas.

The initial announcement of the discovery of this feature dismissed it as being 'formed by shadows giving the illusion of eyes, nose and mouth'. The public took little notice of it until DiPietro and Molenaar published an analysis of the formation in

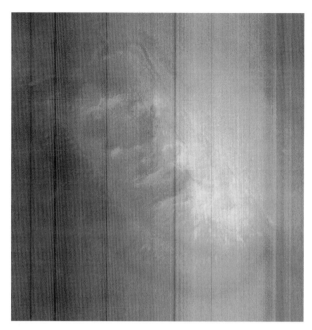

Figure 14.8 Raw image SPO-1-220/03 (5th April 1998), equalised and flipped. © Malin Space Science Systems/NASA/ JPL.

1982, in which they concluded that it was artificial (DiPietro *et al.* 1988). Since then, a number of popular writers have taken up the theme, most notably Richard Hoagland (1987) and Graham Hancock (Hancock *et al.* 1998). The widespread availability of computers for processing digital images from the mid-1980s onwards led to a great deal of amateur work on the Viking Orbiter photographs.

Different techniques for enhancing the photographs have been used, including techniques that attempt to deduce three-dimensional shape from shadows (Carlotto 1996), the interpolation of pixels and so on. These techniques were all used to make the 'face' appear more detailed and more humanoid than on the original satellite images. The 'face' has become an iconic image, familiar to millions; its ghost-like features stare blankly from the covers of numerous books and videos. Demands for photographs of higher quality than those of 1976 (with their resolutions of no better than 43 m per pixel) grew during the 1990s, especially when NASA announced the forthcoming launch of Mars Observer on 22 September 1992 (Hough and Randles 1991, 78). Equipped with a camera that could achieve a best resolution of up to 1.4 m per pixel, the probe was lost on 21 August 1993, three days before entering Martian orbit.

Predictably, the loss of the spacecraft prompted suggestions of conspiracy (Hancock *et al.* 1998, 82). They can be discounted on the grounds of cost alone: had NASA wished to reassure the public that it was interested in finding out more about the face whilst being determined to prove it natural, it could have found a less expensive way of doing it than sabotaging a mission designed to obtain better photographs. Indeed, the less expensive means is what the conspiracy theorists suggested about the results of the next probe, the Mars Global Surveyor: they declared the first photograph of the 'face' obtained by the Mars Orbital Camera (frame SPO-1-220/03) on 5 April 1998 to be fake. The original release of the photograph in an un-enhanced form ought to have reassured the public that NASA was being as fair as possible.

This prompted yet more claims of unfair play when Malin Space Systems (which had designed the camera) released an enhanced version on the following day, removing the more egregious sampling errors from the raw data. The enhanced version shows none of the signs of artificiality alleged for the 1970s images, despite the claims of its supporters. The 1998 image, unlike the Viking Orbiter images, is an oblique, with all the distortion that entails. Even so, the 'face' appears as a highly eroded ridge, with a steep perimeter. A second photograph from the Mars Orbital Camera, taken on 3 June 2000 and released on 31 January 2001, shows only a small part of the 'face', but it confirms the 1998 photograph in every respect. This one, by contrast, is a near-vertical image.

Supporters of artificiality have subsequently focused on the bilateral symmetry of the object, with its central ridge (the nose) and the apparent valley below the nose (the mouth); there is, however, no sign of a depression to the north west of the south western end of the ridge that would provide the missing 'left eye', nor does the ridge appear to be central to the mesa, confirming the lack of symmetry on the unprocessed version of Viking Orbiter image 070A13. To explain the lack of resemblance to the original view of the 'face' as a highly structured and artificial carving, they now have to accept either that it has suffered a great deal of erosion from its pristine form (Fleming 2000) or that NASA has tampered with the photograph taken by the Mars Orbital Camera, as it was the identification of the pristine form that led to the claims for artificiality being made in the first place.

The face therefore emerges as an optical illusion (exactly as its discoverers in 1976 had claimed), known technically as pareidolia. This is the phenomenon that allows believers to see an image of Mother Theresa in a cinnamon bun or the Arabic name of Allah in a sliced aubergine. The basis of the illusion is the human brain's tendency to make understandable and detailed patterns from vague stimuli; the same ability allows us to recognise melodies from short or distorted fragments and to see numbers in patterns of dots used for tests of colour blindness. Faces are one of the first patterns the infant human learns to recognise, so it is unsurprising that a face-like mesa on Mars should be 'read' by so many as an actual representation of a human (or closely humanoid) face.

The 'D&M Pyramid'

Close to the 'face', DiPietro and Molenaar noticed a number of angular peaks. Some of these appeared to be geometrically regular and they dubbed them 'pyramids'. One in particular, to the south west, appeared to possess impressive geometric character-istics. It can be seen on image 035A72, to the right of the 'face' and a better view of it was obtained from image 070A13. From the shadow, it can be calculated that the peak stands some 500 m above the surrounding plain.

Richard Hoagland dubbed it the D&M Pyramid, in honour of DiPietro and Molenaar, and the name has stuck. The better photograph reveals it to be pentagonal

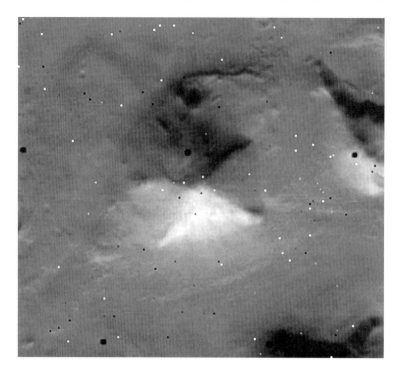

Figure 14.9 Mars: The so-called "D&M Pyramid, north to top. © Malin Space Science Systems/NASA/JPL.

with apparent bilateral symmetry. The supposed main axis points towards the 'face'; the south west angle points towards the 'city' and the north west angle towards a circular feature referred to as the 'tholus', named after its resemblance to the Tholos tombs of the Aegean Early Bronze Age. A variety of mathematical relationships have been claimed for the angles and the ratios between them, involving the square roots of two and three and the relationship e/π (Torun 1996). These relationships are impressive, but they depend on an assumption that one face of the 'pyramid' has been damaged at some stage and that its shadowed face is as apparently smooth as the undamaged faces.

When viewed on a pixel-by-pixel basis, the 'straight' edges can be seen to diverge from their supposed lines by up to two pixels (which, at the resolution of this photograph, is equivalent to 86 m). Moreover, the sides that ought to be of identical length for the ratios to be correct are not. The south western base measures 21.6 pixels (calculated as the hypotenuse of a triangle whose two other sides are 12 and 18 pixels on the image), which calculates to be approximately 930 m; the north western is 23.7 (i.e. $\sqrt{(11^2 + 21^2)}$) pixels or 1020 m. This is a difference of almost 10%. Similarly, the northern and southern faces, which ought to be identical are 27.2 ($\sqrt{(8^2 + 26^2)}$) and 30.8 ($\sqrt{(7^2 + 30^2)}$) pixels respectively (or 1170 m and 1325 m), a difference of more than 13%.

The calculations performed by Erol Torun (1996) are based on Mark Carlotto's enhancement of the image, which interpolates data between pixels; the figures calculated here are based on the original data, lengths of side being calculated by applying Pythagoras's Theorem to a direct count of pixels on Viking Orbiter frame

Figure 14.10 Mars: The north western corner of the D&M Pyramid, image SPO-1-220/03 (5th April 1998). © Malin Space Science Systems/NASA/JPL.

070A13. The margin of error in each calculated length is not greater than one pixel, so even allowing for this (and therefore accommodating Carlotto's enhancements), we cannot state that any two sides are of equal length. The data, poor as they are, will simply not support the assertion. On this basis, we can discount the geometric evidence supporting the contention that the 'D&M Pyramid' is an artificial construction.

Moreover, the same Mars Orbital Camera frame that re-photographed the 'face' in 1998 also clipped the north west corner of the 'D&M Pyramid'. This confirms the analysis of the Viking Orbiter frames, that there is no convincing evidence for artificiality whatsoever in the feature, even though only a small part of it is covered by the image. The sides are not smooth in any sense, the base does not consist of straight lines, nor is there a sharp angle at the corner or between 'faces', at least on this part of the supposed monument. In archaeological terms, the case can be considered closed.

The 'city'

To the north of the face lies an area dubbed 'the city' because of its supposed concentration of monuments. These principally consist of further 'pyramids', generally with three or five faces and therefore quite unlike any human pyramids in Egypt or Mesoamerica. The same general problems that attend the 'D&M Pyramid' apply here. The supposed regularity of these structures vanishes once a careful count is made of pixel numbers on the raw images and allowance is made for the margin of error in pixel size (which is 47 m on this photograph, 035A72). Moreover, the Mars Orbital Camera reveals a mountain very similar to the D&M Pyramid.

At the extreme north western end of the monuments is the so-called 'fort', which, in DiPietro and Molenaar's enhancements, gains a row of cellular structures along its eastern edge. They are too small to be visible on the original Viking Orbiter photograph, which means that no amount of enhancement can bring them out: they can only be artefacts of the enhancement process. The Mars Orbital Camera re-photographed the 'fort' on three separate occasions, each time appearing as a low hill with erosion features that include apparently recent landslips.

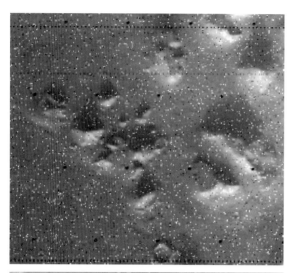

Figure 14.11 Mars: The "City", north to top. © Malin Space Science Systems/ NASA/JPL.

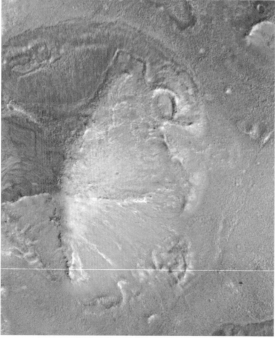

Figure 14.12 Mars: one of the "city centre pyramids" re-photographed by the Mars Orbital Camera. © Malin Space Science Systems/NASA/JPL.

Other 'sites'

Claims for artificiality have been made for several other sites on Mars, mostly in the Cydonia Mensae region. The 'tholus' has already been mentioned, but there is little about its appearance to suggest an artificial origin. Whereas the 1976 Viking Orbiter photographs give it a smooth and near-circular appearance, the Mars Orbital Camera photograph frame m03/00766, taken on 4 July 1999 with a resolution of 3.11 m per pixel, makes it clear that the feature is entirely natural.

There appear to be perhaps three relict shorelines around the feature that suggests it was once an island in the shallow ocean thought to have existed in this area in the remote past. There are also supposed to be further faces, an 'Inca city', runways and other features that cannot be explained in terms of geology (Childress 1995, 192). Again, many of these turn out to be based on enhancements of the Viking Orbiter images that cannot bear the weight of interpretation placed on them.

Claims of this nature are not being made for the Mars Orbital Camera images, except for a few much smaller features that nevertheless also appear to be of geological

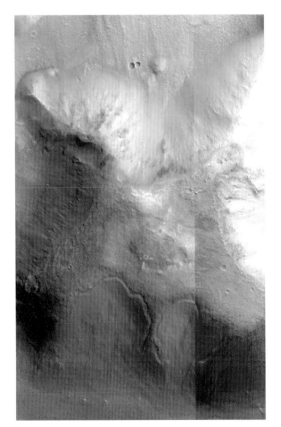

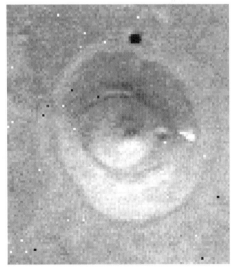

Figure 14.13 Mars: the "fort", combined from Mars Orbital Camera frames 04-01903d and 09-05394d. © Malin Space Science Systems/NASA/JPL.

Figure 14.4 Mars: the "tholus" in 1976, north to top. © Malin Space Science Systems/ NASA/JPL.

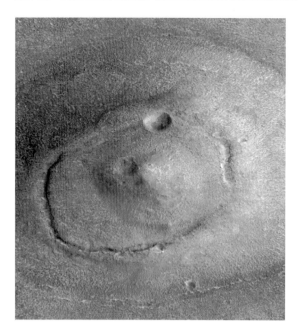

Figure 14.15 Mars: the "tholus" in 1999, north to left. © Malin Space Science Systems/NASA/JPL.

origin. Much of the debate revolves around those features, picked out from the Viking Orbiter photographs, as being anomalous.

There are at least two other claimed faces, in addition to the crater formation dubbed the 'smiley face' by NASA engineers keen to show that the original 'face' was nothing more than an optical illusion. Neither of the two supposedly artificial faces is of a size comparable with the Cydonia Mensae formation, nor is either of them more than vaguely similar to a human face. Both are at very poor resolutions and both resemble pareidolic images of the face of Jesus seen in foliage. Similarly, there have been claims for images of dolphins.

There is no need to examine these claims here, as most investigators outside the 'fringe' have chosen to ignore them, and the claims rarely surface in the fringe literature (other than on websites whose content is often very bizarre). Claims have also been made for the existence of pyramids in Elysium Regio, but they suffer from exactly the same problems as the pyramids of Cydonia Mensae: poor resolution on the Viking Orbiter images and Mars Orbital Camera images that does not support the artificiality hypothesis.

On the other hand, the Mars Orbital Camera is revealing all manner of curious and unexpected formations. The discovery of such features as mottled surfaces apparently deriving from the partial erosion of light sand dunes exposing darker bedrock and so-called 'glass tubes' that seem to be volcanic in origin is important in adding significantly to our understanding of geomorphological (areomorphological?) processes on the planet. The Mars Sojourner roving vehicle also showed much the same sort of surface as the Viking landers had more than twenty years previously, but in greater detail and with the advantage of multiple perspectives. What is significant about recent photographs from the planet is the lack of visible artificial monuments, especially claimed new 'sites'.

3) Other worlds

The moon and Mars have been the focus of most of the speculation about alien monuments and other traces of their activity. This is partly because they are very close neighbours and partly because they are much less hostile than worlds such as Venus (with its surface temperature that would melt lead and sulphuric acid rain) or Jupiter (a giant ball of volatile gases, so massive that its core is composed of metallic hydrogen). Mars, especially, was clearly once more earth-like than it now is (Lammer 1995, 41). However, these problems with more distant worlds have not prevented some authors from detecting all manner of artificial structures on them.

Perhaps the most bizarre of the claims concerns the various planetary satellites or moons, especially of the outer planets. Several of them (the Saturnian satellites Mimas, Rhea and Tethys are the most obvious) have one exceptionally large crater with a central peak. Our own moon has a similar feature, the Mare Orientale on the very eastern edge of the side that faces earth. It has been suggested (Childress 1995, 262) that these features are similar to the umbilical scars resulting from the blowing of glass spheres. The implication is that these satellites are hollow and artificial, claims once made for the Martian moons Phobos and Deimos (von Däniken 1969, 153).

Figure 14.16 Tethys: photographed by Voyager 2 on 25th August 1981. © Malin Space Science Systems/NASA/ JPL.

These are not hypotheses that archaeologists are equipped to evaluate. The opinions of astro-geologists, who are qualified to assess these objects and make deductions about their origins, are that planetary satellites are of much the same age as the planets they orbit and that they display all the characteristics of the same sorts of formation processes as the planets. Large craters of this type are most economically explained as the result of ancient impacts.

Areoarchaeology and Selenoarchaeology: disciplines of the future?

Not one of the sites considered here provides convincing evidence for archaeological remains on other planets and satellites in our solar system (apart, of course, from those remains introduced by humans since the late 1950s: see Fewer, this volume). This does not, of course, mean that such remains cannot exist. They may be there, beyond detection because our recording techniques currently lack the necessary resolution, or beyond detection because they are so alien that we do not recognise them for what they are. The author Arthur C. Clarke (quoted in Klass 1981, 311) once said that a superior alien technology would not be recognisable to us because it would be 'indistinguishable from magic'. This would clearly cause considerable problems for developing a suitable methodology for interpreting satellite and ground-based photographs of other worlds. We need to define criteria for artificiality that go beyond those usually employed by aerial archaeologists.

The method of Carlotto and Stein (1997) uses fractal geometry as a means of characterising natural landscapes. Fractal geometry, in part, describes the phenomenon of self-similarity at different scales or resolutions. Fractals have been used to model coastlines, blood vessel volume and a variety of other phenomena, and on a small scale (< 600 m), can be used to model natural landscapes. Carlotto and Stein therefore propose a technique for recognising non-fractal geometry in a fractal surface as the best means for detecting artificial structures in an alien landscape. They show how it can be used to recognise military vehicles on a terrestrial landscape and then suggest that the Viking Orbiter images of the 'face' also stand out against the fractal background of the Martian plain on which it stands.

There are problems with this technique, however. The assumption that a natural landscape has a fractal dimension of 2.2 to 2.3 at a small scale may be appropriate to earth, with its high rate of weathering and erosion; this may not be the case of Mars. The Viking Lander probes and the Mars Sojourner have both shown that the landscape is covered with numerous small boulders and a very poorly developed soil, conditions that do not match those on earth. The fractal geometry of this type of surface will therefore be very different from that of earth and the criteria for detecting anomalous features will therefore also need to be changed. Secondly, the resolution of the Viking Orbiter photographs does not permit analysis at the small scale (< 600 m) that Carlotto and Stein propose: at the best Viking Orbiter resolution of 43 m, this would mean that analysis would be performed on girds of 14 × 14 pixels. Given that their technique uses a 21 × 21 pixel 'sliding window' for analysis, this invalidates their contention that the 'face' stands out as anomalous on the Viking Orbiter images.

Carlotto's (1996) 'shape from shading' technique appears to offer another method that would allow accurate three-dimensional reconstruction of surface features on a planet from two-dimensional surveys, such as those of the Viking Orbiters or the Mars Orbital Camera. Using a straightforward algorithm, he demonstrates a number of successes and his website offers the chance to submit images for processing. However, stereo pairs are required. In the case of the Mars Orbital Camera, such pairs do not exist. In the case of the Viking Orbiter, pairs do exist, but at different resolutions. Combining the two best images of Cydonia from the Viking Orbiter, the best possible resolution is 47 m per pixel, but this is reduced because of the mismatch between resolutions in the two photographs, as the better is 43 m per pixel; to pretend that they can be matched without appreciable error is to ignore the effect of harmonics (to borrow a metaphor from sonics).

False signals will be created by the overlap of different picture resolutions, which may cause noise in the resultant image that appears to be (and is indistinguishable from) data. Worse still, the 'shape-from-shading' technique is based on the assumption of a uniform surface albedo. This is not the case on Mars, as is amply demonstrated by the visual effect of 'seas', the darker patches observable at a distance (through telescopes or distant satellites), but not close to the planet. The recent Mars Orbital Camera images of mottled surfaces resulting from the weathering of lighter sand away from a darker bedrock provides another instance of strongly contrasting surface albedos. On balance, the technique is too fraught with problems to be usefully applicable to the present data from Mars, and a compensatory factor needs to be added to algorithm for differential albedos.

Resolution of photographs

Indeed, the entire question of identifying monuments on other worlds comes down to a question of image resolution. The 1970s photographs of the Cydonia region do not have the resolution that is achieved for detecting artificiality in human archaeology, let alone something that might have been created by a totally alien life form. The initial claims used evidence that was simply not good enough to support the extraordinary interpretations being made. At a resolution of worse than 40 m per pixel, it is doubtful that any artificial structures could be identified with any certainty on the face of the earth, the one place where we know they exist.

The 1998 Mars Global Surveyor photographs of the Cydonia region were much more detailed than the Viking Orbiter photographs from more than twenty years before: taken at a height of 444 km, with the sun 25° above the horizon, the resolution is 4.3 metres per pixel, ten times better than the best Viking Orbiter photograph. Mars Orbital Camera frame SPO-1-220/03 clearly shows a geological formation (described as a 'mesa'), not an artificial construction. Combining the two images and fitting them to the same Mercator map projection brings out the nature of the formation beyond any doubt: there are no signs that would alert an archaeologist to its artificiality.

The pyramids are superficially more impressive on the Viking Orbiter photographs, although their apparent geometric precision can be shown to be an artefact of

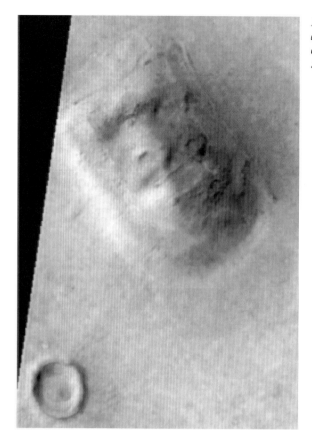

Figure 14.17 Mars: the Viking Orbiter and Mars Orbital Camera images combined on the same projection. © Malin Space Science Systems/NASA/JPL.

enhancement. Even so, they look very unlike many of the geological formations found on Mars, although I am not enough of a geologist (or is the correct term areologist?) to know for certain. Once again, the Mars Orbital camera, with its better resolutions, allows us to state with a high degree of confidence that they do not display signs of artificial construction. The 'city square pyramid', for instance, has a resolution of only 3.42 m per pixel, at which scale it looks entirely natural.

Humanoids or not?

There are numerous other problems, particularly with the identification of Martian 'faces'. Firstly, it is too humanoid. Unless we presuppose that humans are not indigenous to the earth (a view that flies in the face of biological, fossil and genetic data as well as common sense), we have few reasons to suspect that alien intelligences will resemble humans (Spencer 1989, 166).

Whilst bilateral symmetry is a likely feature of most developed life forms, there is nothing about the human form that makes it the best (or most likely) shape to house intelligence; the fossil record demonstrates that not only is our species the result of numerous accidents of evolution, but also that the entire group of Vertebrata with its paired limbs fore and aft is equally accidental. Other groups (such as the Insecta, with three paired limbs, or the Arthropoda, with a pair of limbs for each body segment) could equally have provided the basis from which an advanced intelligence might have developed. Indeed, the human emphasis on eyes as the primary sensory organ (and it is the eyes that dominate in the 'face' on Mars) is a further accident of evolution; other mammals, such as dogs, place a greater reliance on scent and consequently have more developed nasal receptors. The list can be expanded easily, but the basic point remains the same: the view of *Homo sapiens sapiens* as the pinnacle of evolution and therefore as the model for extraterrestrial life forms is a Victorian perspective with roots in the Book of Genesis, not a universal truth.

Alien intelligences ought to posses a number of features that would make them discernible as intelligent to humans. These include the ability to make replicated tools, to follow mathematical principles and to produce functional constructions. All of these are characteristics that their artefacts and monuments ought to possess. One set of obelisks on the moon ought to have similar (but not identical) counterparts elsewhere; mathematical relationships between obelisks ought to be observable between other structures; as well as (presumably) symbolic constructions, there ought also to be (nearby) functional constructions. These are not unreasonable and anthropomorphised considerations, but the logical consequences of intelligent design. The isolation of the claimed lunar monuments is a strong argument in favour of their natural and coincidental origin.

The nature of civilisations

This isolation of most claimed monuments leads us to a consideration of the nature of civilisations. How credible is it that a civilisation leaves traces only a restricted geographical area? Here we run the danger of using human history to justify conclusions about non-human intelligence; however, the human experience of civilisation has been very diverse and is restricted not simply to the Western civilisation that has led to the exploration of space. This is probably something that has not been taken seriously by those who have claimed to detect monuments on other worlds, as so much of the literature proceeds from a basis that these intelligences ought to be 'just like us'. One of the great contributions of post-processual archaeology to our understanding of the past has been the realisation of how different from the present the past really was.

So what generalisations can we make about civilisations? Early civilisations (those of the Neolithic and Bronze Age) were geographically limited. Pyramid Age Egypt was restricted to the Nile Valley (and the monumental pyramids were restricted to a short stretch of the valley to the west and south west of modern Cairo); Aztec Mexico was restricted to the Vale of Mexico; Shang China was restricted to the lower reaches of the Huang He. However, despite the claims of some writers, these civilisations did not develop a technology that allowed them to indulge in space travel. Their monuments – which include enormous constructions – are found only on small parts of the earth's surface.

It is with the development of complex state systems that civilisations become more geographically widespread. The Roman Empire included the entire Mediterranean Basin, large tracts of temperate Europe and parts of the Middle East; the Inka state briefly stretched for 3,500 km along the west coast of South America; the Empire of Mali controlled much of West Africa. These types of civilisations spread their distinctive technologies and monuments well beyond the areas in which they had developed; few fringe writers have ever suggested that civilisations of this type ever travelled into space. The only civilisation that has taken any interest in space travel is precisely that civilisation that set out to explore the world in the fifteenth century and which eventually dominated it economically and politically: European Christendom.

My insistence on space travel as a prerequisite is that the claims for most extraterrestrial monuments (with the exception of those on Mars) locate them on completely dead worlds. There is no possibility that civilisations ever developed on the moon or on any of the satellites of the outer planets, so any monuments identified on these worlds must have been built by beings from other worlds (whether earth or somewhere else). Therefore, we can only make comparisons between our civilisation and extraterrestrial civilisations capable of space travel. This means that we can suggest that they would be the dominant monument-producing civilisation on their home world; that they might set up bases on other worlds in a number of different locations; that these monuments on other worlds would be of primarily technological nature. None of the claims made for monuments on other worlds meets these criteria.

The Martian 'monuments' fall into an entirely different class. The claimed sites are found in a limited area, Cydonia Mensae. This means that, if artificial, the civilisation that produced them would fall into our first class of civilisation: the Neolithic/Bronze Age, geographically restricted type. This is not a type of civilisation with either the capability of or incentive for space travel. It would therefore be indigenous to the planet. However, Mars has not had conditions thought to be suitable for the development of higher forms of intelligence (such as an atmosphere rich in reactive gases necessary for respiration, free-flowing water, climatic variation caused by factors such as plate tectonics and so on) for something like four billion years (Lammer 1995, 41), about 93% of its history. It is virtually impossible that a higher intelligence could have developed on Mars and left monuments that have survived for four billion years. The idea that civilisation on Mars might have been destroyed as a result of the impact of an asteroid on the planet as recently at 20,000 years ago (Hancock *et al.*, 55) are simply preposterous.

Why do people believe irrational and strange things?

It is an enduring problem for archaeologists keen to present their work to the general public that 'alternative' views of the past seem to be more popular than the mainstream. A book claiming that the Indus Valley civilisation was founded by Greys who were lizards from Beta Cygnis will sell more copies than one, no matter how well written, stating that it grew from indigenous farming communities whose social organisation permitted the development of literacy, urban settlement and so on. Even the less bizarre claims (such as those of Graham Hancock, who writes of an older civilisation that he carefully refrains from naming as Atlantis: Hancock 1996, 490) are apt to make a greater impact on the public than those of professional archaeologists. The relative budgets of television programmed devoted to everyday archaeology (such as Channel 4's *Time Team*) and those available to more controversial claims (such as Channel 4's *Heaven's Mirror*) result in the slick presentation of the fringe with the added cachet of expert-bashing and the rather more amateurish appearance of the professional archaeologists' product.

However, it is not simply a matter of presentation. Given a budget twice that of *Heaven's Mirror* for a series of three programmes, it is very unlikely that a conventional archaeological programme would enthuse so many people. Writers of the type of Erich von Däniken or Graham Hancock have built up devoted groups of followers. They promise to lead them on a quest into the unknown with the lure of excitement, discovery and the knowledge that they are aware of more than the experts. They have the 'truth', the 'key'. They are initiates into the true mysteries of the past, something that The Establishment is hiding from us (Steibing 1995, 7).

Archaeologists have a duty to counter this. At a time when academic discourse (especially in the social sciences) is becoming increasingly akin to medieval scholasticism (Kohl 1993, 19; Sokal and Bricmont 1998, 4) and inaccessible to 'non-initiates', we need to be able to convey our complex ideas in simple language. We must not shrink from pointing out the egregious errors of fringe archaeology (Williams 1995, 130). Indeed, a part of the profession involved in education ought to be steeped in the works of the fringe, understanding the evidence used in making the claims, looking at the chains of inference, the bibliographic sources, the writing techniques and the types of illustrative material used. Only then will we be able to get into the mindsets of the fringe writers and their audiences and properly tackle them on their own ground in their own terms.

This chapter began as a specific research question (can we evaluate the claims for monuments on other bodies in the solar system) and has concluded with some more general points. I believe that this is the lesson of all fringe archaeology. By looking at the evidence used by those outside the profession who claim to be able to push it in new directions, we are forced to examine our own assumptions and prejudices. It can only make archaeology richer.

Keith Matthews is currently a Lecturer in Archaeology at the Department of History, Chester College of Higher Education, Bluecoat School, Upper Northgate Street, Chester whilst simultaneously a Senior Archaeologist at Chester Archaeology, 27 Grosvenor Street, Chester, Chester Archaeology, Chester City Council

Notes
1   'ET hypothesis' is the term used by Ufologists to refer to the set of beliefs that characterise UFOs as originating from somewhere other than earth, whether nuts-and-bolts spacecraft or as something else (Randles 1981, 251).

2   Search for ExtraTerrestrial Intelligence.
3   Another ufological term. A 'flap' is a geographically restricted group of sightings occurring
     in a short time. A 'wave' is broader in its geographical span than a 'flap', covering entire
     regions or continents. Flaps are often precipitated by a single media report, leading to
     other reports being made.
4   The question mark was dropped for the paperback and subsequent hardback editions,
     losing a subtlety that gave the original version the feel of a work questioning authority and
     seeking a deeper truth.
5   All satellite imagery is © Malin Space Science Systems/NASA/JPL (various dates) and is
     reproduced with permission.
6   The text of the press release runs: Viking 1–61 P-17384 (35A72) July 31, 1976 This picture is
     one of many taken in the northern latitudes of Mars by the Viking 1 Orbiter in search of a
     landing site for Viking 2. The picture shows eroded mesa-like landforms. The huge rock
     formation in the centre, which resembles a human head, is formed by shadows giving the
     illusion of eyes, nose and mouth. The feature is 1.5 kilometres (one mile) across, with the
     sun angle at approximately 20 degrees. The speckled appearance of the image is due to bit
     errors, emphasised by enlargement of the photo. The picture was taken on July 25 from a
     range of 1873 kilometres (1162 miles). Viking 2 will arrive in Mars orbit next Saturday
     (August 7) with a landing scheduled for early September.

Appendix:
Archaeology in Science Fiction –
A Bibliography

Anita Cohen-Williams

In 1994, I compiled a bibliography of Archaeology in Fiction. In it, there were several sections on science fiction, past peoples, and mythical "lost races", a sub-genre of science fiction that was popular in the late nineteenth and early twentieth centuries. For this appendix, I have updated and expanded some of the references, and combined a few sections. I have not attempted to include all the pseudo-science books that might qualify as science fiction. I have also left out children's literature, and short stories. In compiling this present listing, I have used the following sources: *The Fiction Catalog* (New York: H. W. Wilson); Hoyt, Margaret Archaeology in Literature: A Semi-annotated Bibliography, *Bulletin of the Philadelphia Anthropological Society*, vol.29, 1977 (issued 1980) 1–47; Everett F. Bleiler's *Science-Fiction: The Early Years* (Kent State University Press, 1990); and internet search engines Google.com and iwon.com.

Adams, Douglas 1980, *The Restaurant at the End of the Universe*. New York: Pocket Books. [Among all the other various assorted wonderful material in this book, two of the main characters travel back in time to meet our human ancestors.]

Anderson, Poul 1965, *The Corridors of Time*. Garden City, NY: Doubleday, 1965. [Here the main character is an archaeologist.]

Asimov, Isaac, and Robert Silverberg 1990, *Nightfall*. New York: Doubleday, 1990. [Archaeology on the planet Kalgash shows that civilizations only last for 2,049 years, before being burned to the ground. This was originally a short story by Asimov.]

Asimov, Isaac, and Robert Silverberg 1992, *The Ugly Little Boy*. New York: Doubleday. [Here a Neanderthal boy is kidnapped and sent to the 21st century. This was originally a short story by Asimov.]

Aubrey, Frank 1899, *A Queen of Atlantis. A Romance of the Caribbean Sea*. London: Hutchinson. [Though Atlantis sank in the Sargasso Sea, its mountain peaks remained above the water where the survivors now live.]

Bennet, R. A. (Robert Ames) 1901, *Thyra. A Romance of the Polar Pit*. New York: Henry Holt. [Lost races at the North Pole, comprising a series of Paleolithic groups, and a more advanced group.]

Benoit, (Ferdinand Marie) Pierre 1920, *Atlantida (L'Atlantide)*. New York: Duffield and Cp. Translated from the French by Mary C. Tongue and Mary Ross. Published in London by Hutchinson, 1920 under the title: *The Queen of Atlantis*. [Here the continent of Atlantis is actually in the Sahara.]

Beresford, Leslie 1925, *The Venus Girl*. London: John Long. [A bracelet found on an archaeological dig contains a girl from the planet Venus.]

Bishop, Michael 1982, *No Enemy But Time: A Novel*. New York: Timescape. [Involving time travel to prehistoric Africa.]

Brackett, Leigh 1953, *The Sword of Rhiannon*. New York: Ace. [A defrocked archaeologist arrives on Mars looking for tombs to loot.]

Bradbury, Ray 1950, *The Martian Chronicles*. Garden City, NY: Doubleday. [Archaeologists on Mars appear in the early chapters of the book. This is actually the text that first sparked my interest in archaeology.]

Bradley, Marion Zimmer 1979, *The Ruins of Isis*. New York: Pocket. [Presenting an archaeology of the future.]

Brunner, John 1974, *Total Eclipse*. Garden City, NY: Doubleday. [Archaeologists working on Sigma Draconis III.]

Burroughs, Edgar Rice 1915, *The Return of Tarzan*. Chicago: McClurg. [The ruined city of Opar is in fact a vacation spot for the residents of Atlantis.]

Burroughs, Edgar Rice 1924, *The Land That Time Forgot*. Chicago: McClurg. [Actually three short novels, namely: *The Land That Time Forgot*; *The People That Time Forgot*; and *Out of Time's Abyss*. All three are set on the island of Caspak in the South Pacific.]

Burroughs, Edgar Rice 1924, *Tarzan and the Ant Men*. Chicago: McClurg. [Here lost races of tiny men confront huge Amazons.]

Burroughs, Edgar Rice 1928, *Tarzan, Lord of the Jungle*. Chicago: McClurg. [The Valley of the Sepulcher with descendants of the Crusaders living there much the way their ancestors had.]

Burroughs, Edgar Rice 1929, *Tarzan and the Lost Empire*. New York: Metropolitan. [An area is inhabited by descendants of Roman legionaries who settled there around 100 A.D.]

Carter, Lin 1973, *The Man Who Loved Mars*. Greenwich, CT: Fawcett. [An archaeological expedition is sent to Mars to find the "fabled Treasure City."]

Clock, Herbert, and Eric Boetzel 1929, *The Light in the Sky*. New York: Coward-McCann. [A lost city of immortal Aztecs in Mexico. Very imaginative.]

Converse, Frank 1981, *Van; Or in Search of an Unknown Race*. New York: United States Book Co. [Searching for the lost Inca city of Itambez.]

Crichton, Michael 1976, *Eaters of the Dead: the Manuscript of Ibn Fadlan relating his experiences with the Northmen in A.D. 922*. New York: Knopf, 1976. Reissued as *The 13th Warrior* by Ballantine in 1991 and made into a movie of the same title. [Neanderthals as monsters in a retelling of Beowulf.]

Crichton, Michael 1987, *Sphere*. New York: Knopf. [Underwater archaeological investigation of a spaceship from the future that returned to the past. Made into a motion picture.]

Cussler, Clive 1999, *Atlantis Found*. New York: Putnam. [Mysterious artifacts lead to the discovery of Atlantis in the Antarctic.]

De Camp, L. Sprague 1974 (*c*. 1949), *Lest Darkness Fall*. New York: Ballentine. [Features a time travelling archaeologist.]

De Camp, L. Sprague and P. Schuyler Miller 1950, *Genus Homo*. Reading, PA: Fantasy Press. [Has an archaeologist as the main character.]

d'Esme, Jean (pseudonym of Vicomte Jean d'Esmenard) 1923, *The Red Gods*. New York: Dutton. Translated from the French by Moreby Acklom (*Les Dieux Rogues*, 1923.) [A lost race of Cro-Magnon hunters active in Indochina. Here the archaeology is a bit on the sensational side.]

De Mille, James 1888, *A Strange Manuscript Found in a Copper Cylinder*. New York: Harper. [A lost race at the South Pole called the Kosekin who speak evolved Hebrew. The novel contains some interesting social satire as well.]

De Morgan, John 1887, *King Solomon's Treasures*. New York: Norman L. Munro. [Looking for a treasure and a lost race. Modeled on H. Rider Haggard's novel, *King Solomon's Mines* (see below).]

Doke, Joseph J. 1913, *The Secret City. A Romance of the Karroo*. London: Hodder and Stoughton. [The ancient Egyptian city of Nefert in the Kalahari desert.]

Doyle, Arthur Conan 1912, *The Lost World*. London: Hodder & Stoughton. [The classic tale of a prehistoric area on a plateau in Venezuela.]

Dunn, J. Allan (Joseph Allan Ephinstone Dunn) 1970 (*c*. 1916), *The Treasure of Atlantis*. New York: Centaur Press. [An archaeologist searches for a lost Atlantean city in the Amazon jungle.]

Fletcher, Aaron 1976, *Treasure of the Lost City*. New York: Leisure. [A tale outlining the search for the Cutzulcan, "the oldest civilization in the Americas."]

Gardner, Matt 1972, *The Curse of Quintana Roo*. New York: Popular Library. [A giant alien in a Mayan cenote or well.]

Harrison, Harry *c*. 1969, *Captive Universe*. New York: Putnam.

Haggard, H. Rider 1887, *Allan Quartermain*. London: Longmans. [The lost race novel that began it all (all the clichés, that is). Here Allan and his companions seek a lost race of white men in Africa.]

Haggard, H. Rider 1887, *She: A History of Adventure*. London: Longmans, Green. [The ruins of a huge city and a lost race called the Amahagger, who are ruled by the infamous "She-Who-Must-Be-Obeyed".]

Hume, Fergus 1901, *The Mother of Emeralds*. London: Hurst and Balckett, 1901. [A lost group of Incans live in a series of caves in Peru.]

Hyne, C. J. Cutcliffe (Charles John) 1889, *Beneath Your Very Boots, Being a Few Striking Episodes From the Life of Anthony Merlwood Haltoun, Esq. Transcribed by C. J. Hyne*. London: Digby, Long and Co. [A lost race of Celtic peoples dwelling in caverns under England.]

Hyne, C. J. Cutcliffe (Charles John) 1900, *The Lost Continent*. New York: Harper. [The story of Atlantis. This one suggests that the Yucatan was an Atlantean colony.]

Jackson, James 1928, *A Queen of Amazonia*. London: Henry Walker. [About a lost race of Vikings in the Amazon who rule a group of Aztecs who for some reason speak Quechua.]

Jane, Fred Thomas 1896, *The Incubated Girl*. London: Tower Publishing Co. [An Egyptologist discovers a bronze casket with instructions inside on how to make a human baby with chemicals. Need I say more?]

Janvier, Thomas Allibone 1890, *The Aztec Treasure-House, a Romance of Contemporaneous Antiquity*. Illustrated by Frederic Remington. New York: Harper. [Here the narrator is an archaeologist searching for a lost Aztec city.]

Levinson, Paul 2000, *Silk Code*. Tor Books. [All about Neanderthal DNA and forensics.]

Lisle, Holly 1993, *Bones of the Past*. Baen. [Search for another lost city.]

Long, Frank Belknap 1972, *The Night of the Wolf*. New York: Popular Library. [Archaeologist eaten by artifact!]

Mastin, John 1907, *The Immortal Light*. London: Cassell. [A lost race of Latin speakers in Anarctica. The author unfortunately neglects to explain how they got there.]

Mathews, Cornelius 1839, *Behemoth. A Legend of the Mound-Builders*. New York: J. and H. G. Langley. [The behemoth in question is a raging mammoth who is destroying the towns of the mound-builders, and whatever armies they send out to stop it.]

McCaffrey, Anne 1978, *The White Dragon*. New York: Ballentine. [Concerning the rediscovery of ancient artifacts.]

McCaffrey, Anne 1991, *All the Weyrs of Pern*. New York: Ballentine. [Excavations into the origins of Pern.]

McCaffrey, Anne, and Mercedes Lackey. 1992, *The Ship Who Searched*. Baen. [A young girl becomes ill on her parents' dig on another world.]

McDougall, Walter H. 1891, *The Hidden City*. New York: Cassell. [The lost city of Aztlan, peopled by refugees of Atlantis and the local Indian groups, is apparently located in northwestern Colorado.]

McKillip, Patricia 1985, *The Riddle-Master of Hed*. New York: Ballentine. [An archaeological exploration of an ancient city.]

Merritt, A. 1956 (c. 1919), *The Moon Pool*. New York: Avon. [Archaeologists in Polynesia find a "Nameless Horror."]

Moulder, Victor 1902, *Ophiris, or the Ophir of Solomon. A Story of Adventure and Love in the Land of the Incas*. Smith's Grove, KY: Times Publishing Co. [A lost race of Incas in the Amazon. The Ophir of Solomon becomes Peru.]

Mundy, Talbot (pseudonym of Williams Lancaster Gribbon) 1931, *JimGrim*. New York: Century. [Details the buried cities in the Gobi desert, where the scientific secrets of Atlantis are recorded on golden tablets. A mystic translates them and tries to take over the world. Reads like a lost Indiana Jones movie.]

Mundy, Talbot (pseudonym of Williams Lancaster Gribbon) 1933, *The Mystery of Khufu's Tomb*. London: Hutchinson. [Involves the search for Cheop's tomb which is actually not in the Great Pyramid.]

Norton, Roy 1909, *The Toll of the Sea*. New York: Appleton. [After a series of earthquakes in modern times, the descendants of Atlantis finally settle on a newly formed continent called Azoria.]

Parry, David M. 1906, *The Scarlet Empire*. Indianapolis: Bobbs-Merrill. [Atlantis exists as a social democracy, under the sea in a large crystal dome. Criminals are executed by being eaten by the kraken, a huge sea monster. There is a lot of preaching against socialism in this novel.]

Payne, A. R. Middletoun 1852, *The Geral-Milco: Or the Narrative of a Residence in a Brazilian Valley in the Sierra-Paricis*. New York: Charles B. Norton. [Written as a travel book, and including appendices, this novel features a city-state populated by Incas and Aztecs.]

Rasmussen, Alia A. 1988, *The Labyrinth Gate*. Baen. [Time travel leads to an archaeological excavation in the 19th century.]

Richmond, Walt, and Leigh Richmond 1967, *The Lost Milennium*. New York: Ace. [Features an archaeologist as the main character.]

Rosny aine, J. H. (pseudonym of Joseph-Henri Boex) 1887, *The Xipehuz and the Death of Earth*. Translated by George Edgar Slusser, reprinted by Arno, 1978. [Prehistoric men fight a war of extinction with aliens. Also wrote *Quest for Fireop:*, which was made into a motion picture.]

Savile, Frank 1899, *Beyond the Great South Wall. The Secret of the Antarctic*. London: Sampson, Low, Marston, Searle, and Rivington. [Searching for Mayans in the Antarctic. Truly a lost race.]

Silverberg, Robert 1983, *Valentine Pontifex*. New York: Arbor House. [Discussion surrounding the excavation and reconstruction of the ancient city of the Shape Shifters.]

Simak, Clifford 1978, *Mastodonia*. New York: Ballentine. [Features an archaeologist as a main character.]

Simmons, Dan 1989, *Hyperion*. New York: Doubleday, 1989.

Simmons, Dan 1990, *Fall of Hyperion*. New York: Doubleday. [A father searching for a cure for his archaeologist daughter who caught a disease from her dig.]

Smyth, Clifford 1918, *The Gilded Man. A Romance of the Andes*. New York: Boni and Liveright. [About a lost race of Chibcha Indians living in caves in Colombia.]

Stevens, Francis 1970, *The Citadel of Fear*. New York: Paperback Library. [Archaeologists find ancient Mexican idol which tries a hostile takeover.]

Sullivan, (Edward) Alan 1927, *In the Beginning*. New York: Dutton. [A lost world surrounded by a cactus barrier, in Argentina has a tribe of Neanderthals as well as animals such as saber-tooth cats and giant ground sloths.]

Tucker, Wilson 1974, *Ice and Iron*. Garden City, NY: Doubleday. [An archaeologist in the future has problems with artefacts and bodies popping up out of nowhere.]

Velasquez, Pedro (probably a pseudonym) 1850, *A Memoir of An Eventful Expedition in Central America: Resulting in the Discovery of the Idolatrous City of Iximaya, In an Unexplored Region, And the Possession of Two Remarkable Aztec Children, Descendants and Specimens of the Sacerdotal Caste (Now Nearly Extinct) of the Ancient Aztec Founders of the Ruined Temples of that Country. Described by John L. Stephens, Esq., and other Travellers. Translated From the Spanish of Pedro Velazquez, of San Salvador*. New York: J. W. Bell. [A hoaxed account claiming to have found the lost pre-Conquest city of Iximaya (in the south western corner of Chiapas, Mexico). Domes characterise the architecture, and the author feels that the Aztecs are descendant of the Assyrians.]

Verne, Jules 1916, *Twenty Thousand Leagues Under the Sea*. New York: C. Scribner's Sons. [Features tours of shipwrecks and the ruins of Atlantis.]

Vivian, E. Charles 1922, *City of Wonder*. London: Hutchinson. [Features a lost race on an island in the East Indies.]

Wells, H. G. (Herbert George) 1895, *The Time Machine, An Invention*. New York: H. Holt. [Features the lost races of the Eloi and Morlocks.]

Westall, Williams 1886, *The Phantom City: A Volcanic Romance*. London: Cassell. [Features a lost race of Mayans before the Conquest.]

Westall, Williams 1887, *A Queer Race: The Story of a Strange People*. London: Cassell. [Features a lost race of Elizabethan Englishmen.]

Wilson, Colin 1967, *The Mind Parasites*. Sauk City. WI: Arkham. [An archaeologist finds a huge city under Turkey, but the focus of the story is unfortunately elsewhere.]

Wilson, Colin 1971, *The Philosopher's Stone*. New York: Crown, 1971. [The secret of human prehistory is revealed with the help of archaeologists.]

Anita Cohen Williams is owner of CohWill Consulting, a Search Engine Guru and Listowner of HISTARCH (historical archaeology), SUB-ARCH (underwater archaeology), and SPANBORD (the history and archaeology of the Spanish Borderlands and Northern Mexico).

Bibliography

Aczel, A. D. 1998. *Probability 1: Why there must be intelligent life in the Universe*. New York/London: Harcourt Brace.

Adams, D. 1985. *Hitch Hikers Guide to the Galaxy: the original radio scripts*. London: Pan.

Anon. 1998. Mars Pathfinder mission ends. In *Spaceflight*, 40(1), 8.

Anon. 1976. Mars: the riddle of the Red Planet. In *Time*, 2 August, 16–19.

Arkhipov, A. V. 1995. An Ukrainian moon-study project: the search for alien artefacts on our moon. *Flying Saucer Review*, 40 (2), 16–19.

Arnold, B. and Hassman, H. 1995. Archaeology in Nazi Germany: The Legacy of the Faustian Bargain. In Kohl, P. L. and Fawcett, C. eds. *Nationalism, Politics, and the Practice of Archaeology*. Cambridge: Cambridge University Press, 70–81.

Atkinson, R. J. C. 1978. Silbury Hill. In Sutcliffe, R. ed. *Chronicle: essays from ten years of television archaeology*. London: BBC, 159–173.

Auel, J. M. 1980. *The Clan of the Cave Bear*. London: Hodder and Stoughton.

Bahn, P. 1997. *Journey through the Ice Age*. London: Weidenfeld and Nicolson.

Bacon, 1976. The most sensational Egyptological discovery of the century. *Illustrated London News*.

Banham, R. 1967. *Guide to Modern Architecture*. (3rd ed). London: Architectural Press.

Bara, M. and Troy, S. no date available. *Glass dome(s) in Mare Crisium?* Available from: http://www.lunaranomalies.com/mare.htm. 12th January 1997.

Barbree, J and Caidin, M. 1995. *A Journey through Time*. London: Penguin Studio.

Barclay, D. 1995. *Aliens: the final answer? A UFO cosmology for the 21st century*. London: Blandford.

Barr, M. S. ed. 2000. *Future females, the next generation*. Lanham: Rowman and Littlefield.

Bassett, C. A. 1986. The Culture of Thieves. *Science*, 86, 22–29.

Bear, G. 1998. *Eon*. London: Vista.

Beattie, O. and Geiger, J. 1987. *Frozen in time: unlocking the secrets of the Franklin Expedition*. Saskatoon: Western Producer Prairie Books.

Begley, S. 1997. Greetings from Mars. *Newsweek*, 130 (2), 38–45.

Bender, B. 1993. Stonehenge – Contested Landscapes: Medieval to Present. In Bender, B. *Landscape, Politics and Perspectives*. Oxford: Berg.

Berlitz, C. and Moore, W. 1980. *The Roswell Incident*. London: Granada.

Berlitz, C. 1972. *Mysteries from Forgotten Worlds: Rediscovering lost civilisations*. London: Souvenir.

Bernardi, D. L. 1998. *Star Trek and History: Racing Toward a White Future*. New Brunswick: Rutgers University Press.

Blake, E. 1995. Jack Farmer Exo-paleontologist. *Discover*, 16, 127f.

Bloomfield, L. P. 1979. United Nations (UN). *The World Book Encyclopedia*, vol. 20. Chicago: World Book-Childcraft, Inc, 24–40.

Bond, G. C. and Gilliam, A. 1997. Introduction. In Bond, G. C. and Gilliam, A. eds. *Social Constructions of the Past; Representation as Power*. London: Routledge, 1–22.

Boyes, G. 1993. *The Imagined Village*. Manchester University Press.

Boyd, B. 1996. The power of gender archaeology. In Moore, J. and Scott E. eds. *Invisible people and processes: writing gender and childhood into European archaeology*. London: Leicester University Press, 25–30.

Boyd, K. G. 1996. Cyborgs in Utopia: The Problem of Racial Difference. In Harrison, T. Projansky, S. Ono, K. and Helford, E. R. eds. *Enterprise Zones: Critical Positions on Star Trek*. New York: Westview Press, 95–114.

Brooks, A. M. 1997. Beyond the Fringe: Transfer-Printed Ceramics and the Internationalisation of Celtic Myth. *International Journal of Historical Archaeology*, 1 (1), 39–55.

Brooks, A. M. 1999. Building Jerusalem: Transfer-Printed Finewares and the Creation of British Identity. In Tarlow, S. and West, S. eds. *The Familiar Past?; Archaeologies of Later Historical Britain*. London: Routledge.

Brown M. and Bowen, P. 1999. Last Refuge of the Fairies: Archaeology and Folklore in East Sussex. In Gazin Schwartz, A. and Holtorft, C. *Archaeology and Folklore*. London: Routledge.

Burl, A. 1979. *Prehistoric Avebury*. New Haven: Yale University Press.

Butler, O. E. 1980. *Wild Seed*. London: Sidgewick and Jackson.

Butler, S. 1872. Erewhon (4th ed). London: Trubner and Co.

Carlotto, M. J. 1996. *Shape from shading*. Pacific-Sierra Research, Veridian. Available from: http://www.psrw.com/~markc/Articles/SFS/sfa.html. 8th January 1996.

Carlotto, M. J. and Stein, M. C. no date available. *Method for searching for artificial objects on planetary surfaces*. Available from: http://www.psrw.com/~markc/Pubs/Other/JBIS1990Paper/JBIS1990Paperhtml. 8th January 1997. (Originally published in *J Brit Interplanetary Soc* (1990), 43: pp 209–16).

Carroll, M. no date available. Assault on the Red Planet. *Popular Science*, 01/97, 44f.

Casti, J. L. 1989. *Paradigms Lost*. London: Cardinal.

Cheeryh, C. J. 1989. *The Chronicles of Morgaine*. London: Methuen Mandarin.

Childress, D. H. 1995. *Extra-terrestrial archaeology*. (2nd ed). Stelle, Illinois: Adventures Unlimited Press.

Chippindale, C. 1983 *Stonehenge Complete*. London: Thames and Hudson.

Clarke, D. V. Cowie, T. G. and Foxon, A. 1985 *Symbols of Power at the time of Stonehenge*. Edinburgh: HMSO.

Clark, J. 1952. *Prehistoric Europe: The Economic Basis*. London: Metheun.

Clarke, A. C. 1973. *Rendezvous with Rama*. London: Gollancz.

Cope, J. 1998. The Modern Antiquarian. London: Thorsons.

Cowen, R. 1997. Earth's beyond Earth. *Science News*, 151, 516.

Curwen, E. C. 1954. *The Archaeology of Sussex*, (2nd ed). London: Methuen.

Däniken, E. von. 1969. *Chariots of the gods? Unsolved mysteries of the past*. London: Souvenir.

Darvill, T. C. 1999. Music, muses, and the modern antiquarian: a review article. *The Field Archaeologist*, 34, 28.

Deegan, M. J. 1986. Sexism in Space: The Freudian formula in Star Trek. In Palumbo, D. ed. *Eros in the mind's eye*. Westport: Greenwood, 218–225.

Dick, P. K. 1987. *Galactic Pot-Healer* London: Grafton.

DiPietro, V. Molenaar, G. and Brandenburg, J. 1982. *Unusual Martian surface features*. Glenn Dale: Mars Research.

Doody, D. 1994. Magellan aerobrakes into Venus' atmosphere. *The Planetary Report*, 14(2), 6–13.

Dozois, G. 1994. Untitled, in Dozois, G. ed. *The Mammoth Book of Contemporary SF Masters*. London: Robinson Publishing, 94–5.

Dunne, J. W. 1929. An Experiment with Time (2nd ed). London: A and C Black.

Elia, R. J. 1995. Preserving a Cold War Legacy. *Archaeology*. May/Jun, 48.

Embleton, R. and Graham, F. 1984. *Hadrian's Wall in the Time of the Romans*. Newcastle Upon Tyne: Frank Graham.

Erjavec, J. L. no date available. *Geomorphology at Cydonia*. Available from: http://www.prsw.com/~markc/Other/mars/erjavec.html. 8th January 1997.

Evans, C. 1988. *Writing Science Fiction* London: A and C Black Ltd.

Feder, K. L. 1995. Cult archaeology and creationism: a co-ordinated research project. In Harrold, F. B. and Eve, R. A. eds. *Cult archaeology and creationism: understanding pseudoscientific beliefs about the past* (Expanded edition). Iowa City: University of Iowa Press, 34–48.

Fiske, J. 1983. Dr. Who: ideology and the reading of a popular narrative text. *Australian Journal of Screen Theory*. 13/14.

Fleming, L. 2000. *The MGS Face image in a different light*. VGL. Available from: http://www.vgl.org/webfiles/mars/face/newface/htm. 25th August 2000.

Fleming, L. no date available. *The Cuspids: photometric analysis of slopes*. VGL Available from: http://www.vgl.org/webfiles/lan/cuspids/cuspids5.htm. 8th January 1997

Freedman, D. H. 1998. Beyond Hubble. *Discover*, February, 48.

Friedman, L. D. 1997. Carl Sagan Memorial Station: Pathfinder carried members' names. *The Planetary Report*, 17(5), 18.

Furneaux Jordan, R. 1991. W*estern Architecture* (2nd Ed.). London: Thames and Hudson Ltd.

Gibson, W. 1995. *Neuromancer*. London: Harper Collins.

Gibson, E. K. *et al*. 2001. Life on Mars: evaluation of the evidence within Martian meteorites ALH84001, Nakhla, and Shergotty. *Precambrian Research* 106, 15–34.

Giddens, A. 1993. *Sociology*. Cambridge: Polity Press.

Gillett, S. L. 1996. *World Building*. Cincinnati, Ohio: Writer's Digest Books.

Golding, W. 1955. *The Inheritors*. London: Faber and Faber.

Grinsell , L. V. 1976. Folklore of Prehistoric Sites in Britain. Newton Abbot: David and Charles.

Haggard, H. R. 1998 (originally published 1885). King Solomon's Mines. London: Andre Deutch Classics.

Hamm, M. 1981. *Dead Tech: The Archaeology of Tomorrow*. San Francisco: Sierra Club Books.

Hancock, G. 1996. *Fingerprints of the gods: a quest for the beginning and the end*. London: Mandarin.

Hancock, G. Bauval, R. and Grigsby, J. 1998. *The Mars Mystery: A warning from history that could save life on earth*. Harmondsworth: Penguin.

Haraway, D. 1991. *Simians, Cyborgs, and Women*. London: Free Association.

Hardy, P. 1995. *Science Fiction* (5th. ed.). London: Aurum Press.

Hastie, A. 1996. A Fabricated Space: Assimilating the individual on 'Star Trek': the Next Generation. In Harrison, T. Projansky, S. Ono K. and Helford, E.R. eds. *Enterprise Zones: Critical Positions on Star Trek*. New York: Westview Press, 115–136.

Hayman, R. 1997. *Riddles in Stone: myths, archaeology and the ancient Britons*. London: Hambledon.

Helford, E. R. ed. 2000. *Fantasy girls: gender in the new universe of science fiction and fantasy television*. Lanham: Rowman and Littlefield.

Hickie, D. 1997. *Evaluation of environmental designations in Ireland* . Kilkenny: The Heritage Council of Ireland.

Hoagland, R. C. 1996. *The Monuments of Mars: a city on the edge of forever* (4th ed). Berkeley: North Atlantic Books.

Hoagland, R. 1987. *The Monument's of Mars: a city on the edge of forever*. Berkeley: North Atlantic Books.

Hobsbawm, E. and Ranger, T. 1992. *The Invention of Tradition*. Cambridge: Cambridge University Press.

Hodder, I. 1992. Theory and Practice in Archaeology. London: Routledge.

Holtorf, C. (ed) 1999. *Archaeology and folklore*. London: Routledge.

Honderich, T. 1988. *A Theory of Determinism: The Mind, Neuroscience and Life Hopes*. Oxford: Oxford University Press.

Hough, P. A. and Randles, J. 1991. *Looking for the Aliens: a psychological, scientific and imaginative investigation*. London: Blandford.

Huntley, H. E. 1970. *The Divine Proportion – a study in mathematical beauty*. New York: Dover Publications

Huxley, A. 1932. *Brave New World*. London: Chatto and Windus.

Huygens, C. 1757. Cosmotheros: or conjectures concerning the planetary worlds and their inhabitants. Glasgow.

Irwin, R. 1995. From a science future to a fantasy past. *Antiquity*, 69, 238–9.

Irwin, R., 1994. Fantasy without god. *Times Literary Supplement*, 2 September.

James, E. 1994. *Science Fiction in the 20th Century*. Oxford: Opus.

Johnson, W. Gray and Beck, C. M. 1995. Proving Ground of the Nuclear Age. *Archaeology*, May/Jun, 43f.

Keel, J. A. 1971. *Operation Trojan Horse: an exhaustive study of unidentified flying objects: revealing their source and the forces that control them*. London: Souvenir Press.

Klass, P. J. 1981. UFO's. In Abell, G. O. and Singer, B. eds. *Science and the paranormal: probing the existence of the supernatural*. London: Junction Books.

Kohl, P. L. 1993. Limits to a post-processual archaeology (or, The dangers of a new scholasticism). In Yoffee N. and Sherratt A. eds. *Archaeological Theory: who sets the agenda?* Cambridge: Cambridge University Press, 13–19

Kolosimo, P. 1970. *Not of this World*. (Translated by A D Hills). London: Sphere.

Lammer, H. 1995. Atmospheric mass loss on Mars and the consequences for the Cydonia Hypothesis and early Martian-life-forms. In BUFORA, ed. *Proceedings of the Eighth BUFORA International UFO Congress*. London: BUFORA, 39–42.

Le Guin, U. K. 1993. Always Coming Home. London: Harper Collins.

Le Guin, U. K. 1989. *The Language of the Night*. London: The Women's Press.

Le Guin, U. K. 1969. *The Left Hand of Darkness* London: MacDonald.

Lewis, C. S. 1990. *The Space Trilogy*. London: Bodley Head.

Linebarger, P. M. A. 1948. *Psychological Warfare*. Washington: Infantry Journal Press.

Loewen, J. W. 1995. *Lies My Teacher Told Me*. New York: The New Press.

Lower, M. A. 1861. Old Speech and Manners in Sussex. *Sussex Archaeological Collections*, 13, 209–220.

McIntyre, V. N. and Anderson, S. J. eds. 1976. *Aurora: Beyond Equality*. Conneticut: Fawcett Publications.

Magee, K. 1995. The mystery of Maxwell. *The Planetary Report*, 15 (1), 12–14.

Malone, C. 1989. *Avebury*. London: Batsford.

Merrick, H. and Williams, T.(eds.) 1999. *Women of other worlds: excursions through science fiction and feminism*. Melbourne: University of Western Australia Press.

Merrifield, R. 1987. *The Archaeology of Ritual and Magic*. London: Batsford.

Meskell, L. 1999. Feminism, paganism and pluralism. In Gazin-Schwartz, A. and Holtorf, C. *Archaeology and Folklore*. London: Routledge.

Mitchison, N. 1987. *Early in Orcadia*. Glasgow: Drew.

Monastersky, R. 1994. Earth Movers. *Science News*, 146, 432.

Moser, S. 1998. *The Cultural Dimensions of Archaeological Practice: The role of fieldwork and its gendered associations*. Paper for School of American research Conference "Doing Feminist Archaeology" April 1998.

Moser, S. 1996. Science, stratigraphy and the deep sequence: excavation *vs* survey and the question of gendered practice in archaeology. *Antiquity*, 70 (270), 813–820.

Ono, K. 1996. Domesticating Terrorism: A Neo-colonial Economy of Difference. In Harrison, T. Projansky, S. Ono K. and Helford E. R. eds. *Enterprise Zones: Critical Positions on Star Trek*. New York: Westview Press, 157–188.

Ordway, F. I. and von Braun, W. 1979. Space travel. *The World Book Encyclopedia*, vol. 18. Chicago: World Book-Childcraft International, Inc, 560–73.

Orwell, G. 1949. *Nineteen Eighty-Four*. London: Secker and Warburg.

Pauwets, L. and Bergier, J. 1960. *Le matin des magiciens*. Paris: Gallimard.

Paynter, R. no date available. *Scientific skepticism, UFOs and the flying saucer myth*. Available from: http://www.geocities.com/Area51/Corridor/8148. 1st September 1999.

Pierce, J. J. 1993. Introduction. In Smith, C. [psuedonym of P. M. A. Linebarger], *The Rediscovery of Man; The Complete Short Science Fiction of Cordwainer Smith*. Framingham, Massachusetts: The New England Science Fiction Association Press, vii–xiv.

Pierce, J. J. 1988. Cordwainer Smith – The Shaper of Myths. In Smith, C. [psuedonym of P. M. A. Linebarger], *The Rediscovery of Man*. London: Victor Gollancz Ltd, xi–xix.

Pitts, M. and Roberts, M. 1997. *Fairweather Eden*. London: Century.

Pratchett, T. 1998. *Carpe Jugulum*. London: Gollancz.

Pratchett, T. and Briggs, S. 1995. *The Discworld Mapp.* London: Corgi.

Pratchett, T. 1992. *Lords and Ladies.* London: Gollancz.

Pratchett, T. 1988. *Strata.* London: Corgi.

Pratchett, T. 1988. *Wyrd Sisters.* London: Gollancz.

Pratchett, T. 1986. *The Light Fantastic.* London: Gollancz.

Project 1947. 1948. *Analysis of Flying Object Incidents in the United States, Study 203, 10th December 1948.* (Issued by) USAF Directorate of Intelligence, Washington D.C. Available from: http://www.project1947.com/fog/1948air.htm. 12th September 2000.

Randles, J. 1981. *UFO study: a handbook for enthusiasts.* London: Robert Hale.

Randles, J. Roberts, A. and Clarke, D. 2000. *The UFOs that never were.* London: London House.

Rao, N. 1997. Interpreting Silences: Symbol and History in the case of Ram Janmabhoomi/Babri Masjid. In Bond, G. C. and Gilliam, A. eds. *Social Constructions of the Past; Representation as Power.* London: Routledge, 154–164.

Ricoeur, P. 1984. *The Reality of the Historical Past.* Milwaukee: Marquette University Press.

Richards, J. M. 1961. *An Introduction to Modern Architecture.* London: Cassell.

Russell, B. 1961. History of Western Philosphy and its Connection with Political and Social Circumstances from the Earliest Times to the Present Day (reprint of 2nd ed). London: Routledge.

Russell, L. and Wolski N. (forthcoming) Beyond the Final Frontier: 'Star Trek', the Borg and the Post-colonial. In Ivison D. ed. *Postcolonial Readings of Science Fiction.*

Sagan, C. and Shklovskii, I. S. 1966. *Intelligent Life in the Universe.* New York: Holden-Day.

Sagan, C. 1994. The Search for Terrestrial Life. *Scientific American,* October, 93ff.

Schmidt, S. 1995. *Aliens and Alien Societies.* Cincinnati. Ohio: Writer's Digest Books.

Scollar, I. *et al* 1990. *Archaeological Prospecting and remote Sensing.* Cambridge: Cambridge University Press.

Shanks, M. and Tilley, C. 1987. *Social theory and archaeology.* Oxford: Polity Press.

Somerville, E. M. 1996 Piltdown reflections: a mirror for prehistory. *Sussex Archaeological Collections,* 134, 7–20.

Smith, C. 1993. [psuedonym of P. M. A. Linebarger]. *The Rediscovery of Man: The Complete Short Science Fiction of Cordwainer Smith.* Framingham, Massachusetts: The New England Science Fiction Association Press.

Smith, C. 1988. [psuedonym of P. M. A. Linebarger] *Norstrilia.* London: Victor Gollancz Science Fiction, Victor Gollancz.

Sokal, A. and Bricmont, J. 1998. *Intellectual impostures: postmodern philosophers' abuse of science.* London: Profile.

Spencer, J. 1989. *Perspectives: a radical examination of the alien abduction phenomenon.* London: Futura.

Sprigge, T. L. S. 1995. Tender and Tough-Minded. In Honderich, T. ed. *The Oxford Companion to Philosophy.* Oxford: Oxford University Press, 869.

Stapledon, O. 1979. *Starmaker.* London: Magnum Books.

Stapledon, O. 1978. *Last and First Men.* London: Magnum Books.

Stoker, C. 1997. *Telepresence for Planetary Exploration*. NASA Ames Space Science.

Steibing, W. H. 1995. The nature and dangers of cult archaeology. In Harrold, F. B. and Eve, R. A. eds. *Cult archaeology and creationism: understanding pseudoscientific beliefs about the past* (Expanded edition). Iowa City: University of Iowa Press, 1–10.

Summers, A. 1994. *Damned Whores and God's Police*. South Yarra: Penguin Books.

Tomas, A. 1971. *We are not the First: Riddles of Ancient Science*. London: Souvenir.

Thomas, C. 1996. Diggers at the final frontier. *British Archaeology*, 11, 14.

Torrens, H. S. 1998. Geology and the Natural Sciences: Some Contributions to Archaeology in Britain 1780–1850. In Brand, V. ed. *The Study of the Past in the Victorian Age*. Oxford: Oxbow.

Tulloch, J. and Alvarado, M. 1983. *Doctor Who: the unfolding text*. London: MacMillan.

Tulloch, J. and Jenkins, H. 1995. *Science fiction audiences: watching Doctor Who and Star Trek*. London: Routledge.

Turnill, R. 1974. *The Observer's Book of Unmanned Spaceflight*. London and New York: Frederick Warne and Co.

United Nations. 1997. OS/1727: Legal Subcommittee of Committee on Peaceful Uses of Outer Space, Vienna, 1–8 April 1997. Press release dated 9 April 1997.

United Nations- Office for Outer Space Affairs. 1979A. *Agreement Governing the Activities of States on the Moon and Other Celestial Bodies*. United Nations, Vienna. Available from: http://www.oosa.unvienna.org/SpaceLaw/moon.htm. 12th February 2001.

United Nations- Office for Outer Space Affairs. 1979B. *Agreement Governing the Activities of States on the Moon and Other Celestial Bodies*. United Nations, Vienna. Available from: http://www.oosa.unvienna.org/SpaceLaw/moontxt.htm. 11th September 2000.

United Nations- Office for Outer Space Affairs. 1975A. *Convention on Registration of Objects Launched into Outer Space*. United Nations, Vienna. Available from: http://www.oosa.unvienna.org/SORegister/regist.htm. 12th February 2001.

United Nations- Office for Outer Space Affairs. 1975B. *Convention on Registration of Objects Launched into Outer Space*. United Nations, Vienna. Available from: http://www.oosa.unvienna.org/SORegister/registxt.htm. 11th September 2000.

United Nations- Office for Outer Space Affairs. 1972A. *Convention on the International Liability for Damage Caused by Space Objects*. United Nations, Vienna. Available from: http://www.oosa.unvienna.org/SpaceLaw/liability.htm. 12th February 2001.

United Nations- Office for Outer Space Affairs. 1972B. *Convention on the International Liability for Damage Caused by Space Objects*. United Nations, Vienna. Available from: http://www.oosa.unvienna.org/SpaceLaw/liabilitytxt.html. 3rd August 2000.

United Nations- Office for Outer Space Affairs. 1967A. *Treaty on principles governing the activities of states in the exploration and use of outer space, including the moon and other celestial bodies*. United Nations, Vienna. Available from: http://www.oosa.unvienna.org/SpaceLaw/outerspt.htm. 11th September 2000.

United Nations- Office for Outer Space Affairs. 1967B. *Treaty on principles governing the activities of states in the exploration and use of outer space, including the moon and other celestial bodies*. United Nations, Vienna. Available from: http://www.oosa.unvienna.org/SpaceLaw/outersptxt.htm. 27th October 2000.

Van Vogt, A. E. 1951. *The Voyage of the Space Beagle*. London: Grayson and Grayson.

Vincent, R. 1997. *Fundamentals of Geological and Environmental Remote Sensing*. London: Prentice Hall.

Wailes, B. and Zoll, A. L. 1995. Civilization, Barbarism, and Nationalism in European Archaeology. In Kohl, P. L. and Fawcett, C. eds. *Nationalism, Politics, and the Practice of Archaeology*. Cambridge: Cambridge University Press, 21–38.

Williams, S. 1995. Fantastic archaeology: what should we do about it? In Harrold, F. B. and Eve, R. A. eds. *Cult archaeology and creationism: understanding pseudoscientific beliefs about the past* (Expanded edition). Iowa City: University of Iowa Press, 124–33.

Willis, D. 1995. *The Sand Dollar and the Slide Rule*. Reading, Mass: Addison Wesley.

Wiseman, J. 1996. Wonders of Radar Imagery. *Archaeology*, Sep/Oct, 14.

Wiseman, J. 1996. Space Mission and Ground Truth. *Archaeology*, Jul/Aug, 11.

Whitfield, S. and Roddenbery, G. 1968. *The Making of Star Trek*. New York: Ballantine Books.

Wolmark, J. 1994. *Science Fiction, Feminism and Postmodernism*. Hertfordshire: Harvester Wheatsheaf.

Young, R. E. 1996. The wild ride of the Galileo probe: sampling Jupiter's atmosphere. *The Planetary Report*, 16 (6), 4–9.